THE UPSKIRT EXHIBITIONIST

'You're so hot,' he breathed shakily as he pushed his finger deeper into my tightening sheath.

'Am I?' I said, concealing a grin as I clutched the ten pound note in my hand.

'God, yes. And so incredibly tight. It's been a long time since I've slipped my finger into a virgin girl.'

A virgin girl? I mused in my wickedness. That's what I wanted him to believe, I thought, as he massaged the wet inner flesh of my tight vagina. I wanted him to think me an innocent little virgin girl who was desperate to pass her exams with excellent results. I should have come across as shy when I'd stripped naked, I reflected. I should have looked anxious and . . . I'd been far too quick to strip naked in front of him. But it was too late to change things now. I wasn't yet practised in the fine art of deception. But I was learning fast.

THE UPSKIRT EXHIBITIONIST

Ray Gordon

The LAST
WORD *in*
FETISH

nexus

enthusiast

This book is a work of fiction.
In real life, make sure you practise safe, sane and consensual sex.

7

First published in 2007 by Nexus Enthusiast

Reprinted 2009

Copyright © Ray Gordon 2007

The right of Ray Gordon to be identified as the Author of the Work has been asserted in accordance with the Copyright, Designs and Patents Act 1988.

A catalogue record for this book is available from the British Library.

www.nexus-books.com

Typeset by TW Typesetting, Plymouth, Devon

Penguin Random House is committed to a sustainable future for our business, our readers and our planet. This book is made from Forest Stewardship Council® certified paper.

Printed and bound in Great Britain by Clays Ltd, St Ives plc

ISBN 978 0 352 34122 8

Little Miss Innocent

Two years ago, I received an email from a young lady called Annette. She wanted to know whether I'd help her to write what she called her 'confession'. I was rather busy but I replied suggesting she give me an outline of her idea. Hearing nothing for two weeks, I thought she'd had a change of mind – until an email arrived one morning. Skipping through the text, I began to take notice.

. . . I was sitting in the park and this man kept looking up my skirt. I knew that he could see my knickers and I knew that he was thinking about my pussy crack, so I opened my legs wider to give him a better view. He smiled at me and I felt really sexy and I knew that he wanted to see more . . .

Annette then sent me several emails describing her naughty antics in the park. Reading her disjointed episodes of panty flashing, I knew that this would be a major job. But there was something about her story that intrigued me. Annette mentioned flashing her knickers to her father's boss and her college teacher, and my interest grew. Several more emails arrived, and I spent two days copying and pasting. The result was the beginning of Annette's book.

When I met Annette in a wine bar, two months and fifty-odd emails later, I found her bubbly and chatty

1

and easy to get on with. But, above all, she radiated an air of angelic innocence. I couldn't believe that this was the girl who had unashamedly revealed her sexual exploits to me. In her early twenties, she was attractive with long blonde hair, slim and yet curvaceous, and delightful company. She was wearing a high-necked blouse and a long skirt, and was far from the sort of girl I'd imagined her to be. She'd had no problem with emailing the graphic details of her sexual encounters. But would she have the courage to tell me, face to face, of her most intimate sexual relationship?

We talked about the book and, showing no signs of embarrassment, she opened up and told me, in graphic detail, of her darker side. Sipping red wine, she talked about her encounters with older men, and where those relationships had taken her. She revealed her masturbatory habits and her innermost thoughts, and talked openly about orgasms and sex. We chinked our glasses together and toasted the book. We were in business.

At the end of our first meeting, she grinned. 'I'm innocent,' she said impishly with a sparkle in her blue eyes. 'It's not my fault if I inadvertently open my legs and men look up my skirt.' Innocence was what Annette called her trade secret. 'I'm Little Miss Innocent, aren't I?' She then told me about her first knicker-flashing experience . . .

Ray Gordon

My Sexual Awakening

I was reading a magazine, relaxing on the sofa after a boring day at college. I looked up as my mother walked into the lounge and passed a cup of coffee to my dad's boss. As she turned to leave the room, she stared at me and froze. Gasping, making strange facial expressions, she nodded towards my legs. She looked angry as she mouthed something and frowned at me, but I didn't know what I was supposed to have done wrong. She glared at me, but I had no idea what she was getting at. I'd cleared up my bedroom, done my college work . . . what was her problem?

Dad came into the room and passed some papers to his boss. They talked about some project or other they were working on and seemed oblivious to me. Mum again glared at me and nodded her head towards the magazine covering my thighs. Didn't she want me to read it? I wondered. It was only a TV magazine, so what was the problem? She then asked me to help her with something and indicated for me to follow her.

'What is it?' I asked her as she ushered me through the hall to the kitchen.

Closing the kitchen door, she frowned at me. 'For God's sake, Annette,' she whispered through gritted teeth. 'Why were you sitting like that?'

'Like what?'

'With one leg over the arm of the sofa and your knickers showing. What will Mr Johnson think?'

'My knickers showing?' I gasped. 'But . . . I didn't realise.'

'He's your father's boss, Annette. He's come here to talk to your father about promotion, and you show him your knickers. For God's sake, have you no decency?'

'All right, all right,' I sighed. 'I didn't realise. I was relaxing and I didn't realise. I'm sorry, OK?'

'You're old enough to know better,' she persisted. 'If you didn't wear such ridiculously short skirts . . .'

'It's not that short, mum. All my friends take the hems up on their skirts and –'

'If you're going to wear short skirts, at least learn how to sit properly.'

After the lecture, I went up to my bedroom and gazed at my reflection in the full-length mirror. Something strange happened to me as I lifted my skirt and focused on the tight material of my white knickers. My stomach somersaulting, I felt sexy, horny. I was young and had never experienced such powerful and amazing emotions before. I suppose I was a slow starter, a late developer. Focusing on the crack of my pussy, clearly defined by my tight knickers, I felt a pang of excitement run through my womb. My nipples were erect and incredibly sensitive. I wondered what was happening to me.

Recalling mum's words, I lowered my skirt and held my hand to my mouth. What must Mr Johnson have thought of me? I reflected. I felt embarrassed and ashamed as I imagined him looking at my knickers. But, strangely, he'd woken something within me. My shame melting as my arousal heightened, I knew that he'd woken something which would never sleep again.

4

Had he imagined my pussy crack as he'd gazed at my tight knickers? I wondered excitedly. Had he pictured my naked body? Butterflies fluttered in my stomach as I slipped my hand up my skirt and pressed my fingertips into the soft bulge of my knickers. My pussy lips felt swollen and puffy, and there was a damp patch on the crotch of the white material. My libido had been fired. Like a monster surfacing from the deep, sex had, at long last, reared its beautiful head. Thanks to my dad's boss and my mum's lecture, I was now sexually aware of my young body.

After dinner, I went to the park and sat on a bench by the pond. I needed my own space, time to think, to contemplate my amazing discovery. I'd never given a thought to my body or the way I sat. I'd never given a thought to my knickers. Some of the girls at college regularly talked about sex and went into fits of giggles, but I'd never taken an interest. Although I had friends, I'd always been shy and a bit of a loner. I'd not joined in with the dirty talk. Sex had never concerned me, until now.

Whatever had surfaced from the deep would not only never sleep again, but would change my life. I call it a monster because monsters are frightening. My sudden and powerful arousal was frightening. My hormones had been let loose and were coursing through my veins to take control not only of my body, but my mind. Some of the girls at college used filthy words. Fuck, cunt, wank . . . they were words that I'd been brought up to believe were dirty and vulgar. But they were to take on a new meaning. They would become words of sex.

Sitting on the bench, I realised that my knickers were soaked. The dam had burst, and my juices of arousal were flowing freely. My clitoris swelling, emerging from its hiding place for the first time, I was gripped by an overwhelming desire to do something sexy. Twisting my long blonde hair around my fingers, I bit my lip. What had happened to me? I wondered anxiously. I was acutely aware of my erect clitoris, my flowing juices. What was this monster that had risen from the deep?

Watching a middle-aged couple walking by the pond, I began to tremble. My breathing fast and shallow, my stomach churning, my heart racing, I parted my thighs as the woman knelt down and fed the ducks and the man turned and looked at me. As he stared at my knickers, I felt a pang of excitement course through my virgin womb. His eyes darting between the woman and me, he seemed to be mesmerised by the triangular patch of material bulging between my slender thighs. I felt naughty and parted my legs further, making out that I was watching the ducks as he gazed between my naked thighs. His eyes widened and he licked his lips. What were his thoughts? I wondered as he half-smiled at me. What images were looming in his mind?

I'd not worn my short denim skirt with knicker-flashing in mind. But, as the man gazed longingly at the tight crotch of my knickers, I knew that I'd never wear jeans again. He couldn't take his eyes off me, and I again wondered what he was thinking. Did he fancy me? Was he picturing my tight pussy crack? The woman threw the last of the bread to the ducks and grabbed his hand and led him away. My first deliberate flashing episode was over in seconds, but it had left me on a high. After years of dormancy, I felt sexually alive, acutely aware of the curves and mounds of my young body.

That night in bed, I kicked the quilt off and lay with my legs open wide. I could feel my outer lips swelling, the petals of my inner lips opening like a flower as my clitoris emerged. My fingers toying between my thighs, running up and down the open valley of my pussy, I realised how incredibly wet I was. I'd been creaming my knickers for some time, but I'd never known such a deluge of hot sex milk to flow from my yearning vagina. Instinctively massaging the solid head of my clitoris, I reached beneath my thigh with my free hand and slipped two fingers deep into the wet sheath of my virgin pussy.

I'd never touched myself before, never explored the hot depths of my vagina. Some of my college friends went into town on Saturdays and hung around with boys. I'd heard that they strutted around in their short skirts and skimpy tops and flirted with boys. I preferred to stay at home during the weekends and get on with my college work or have Diana round for a sleep-over. Diana was my best friend, my only real friend. We'd listen to music and chat, only emerging from my bedroom for food and drink. As I massaged my erect clitoris, I couldn't imagine Diana playing with herself. She wasn't like that.

My pioneering orgasm came with an explosion which rocked my young body. Shockwaves of sex crashed though me and shook me to the core as I lay whimpering and writhing on my bed. Never had I known anything like it, never had I known such fantastic sensations. Increasing my fingering rhythm and my clitoral massaging, I pictured the man in the park gazing at my knickers as my orgasm again peaked. The thought of him staring at the crotch of my knickers driving me wild, I drifted into a crazy fantasy as I sustained my new-found pleasure.

The man was there, in my room, watching as I fingered my vagina and massaged my clitoris. He stood by my bed and gazed at the swollen lips of my pussy gripping my thrusting fingers. He reached out and squeezed the firm mounds of my petite breasts and pinched my sensitive nipples. My orgasm seemingly never-ending, I listened to the squelching of my sex milk as I fingered my vagina and rubbed my pulsating clitoris vigorously. The fantasy melted as my orgasm receded. The man faded, leaving me alone in my room. I was still trembling as sleep engulfed me. Trembling uncontrollably in the aftermath of my first orgasm.

My dad got his promotion and his boss regularly came round to discuss business. Whenever the opportunity arose, whenever mum wasn't around and dad wasn't looking, I'd sit on the sofa with my thighs apart and show my knickers to his boss. His eyes would widen and my clitoris would swell and my sex milk would flow into the crotch of my knickers. I had no idea what I was doing to the man, what was stirring within his trousers. To me, it was just an exciting game. Showing my knickers to a middle-aged man made me feel sexy, dirty, naughty. It was just innocent fun.

I overheard my parents talking one evening. Mum was asking why Mr Johnson came round so often. Dad reckoned that there was no need for his visits, but he got on well with his boss and they were becoming good friends. And there was another promotion in the offing. Dad reckoned that, whatever the reasons for the visits, whatever the attraction, it was helping him climb the promotional ladder.

The formalities finally dropped and Mr Johnson became Derek. He wasn't married and didn't live far away so he never turned down the offer of an evening meal. He was in his forties and Mum got on well with him. But I knew that I was the attraction. He'd gaze

8

at me across the dining room table, flash me a quick smile when my parents weren't looking. I often noticed him staring at my blouse or T-shirt. My breasts were small, but firm and nicely pointed. Many times, as he gazed at my breasts, I wondered what his thoughts were. Did he fancy me?

After the meal one evening, mum and dad were clearing the dining-room table and I sat in the lounge with Derek. Wearing my short denim skirt, my thighs slightly parted, I displayed the triangular patch of white cotton bulging to contain my full sex lips. He appeared to be watching the news on television but, out of the corner of my eye, I could see him looking at my knickers. Moving about on the sofa, I opened my legs to the extreme as I made myself comfortable. He adjusted the crotch of his trousers and fidgeted in the armchair. In those early days of sexual discovery, I had no idea what I was doing to my voyeur. I had no idea that the sight of my knickers was stiffening his cock.

'You're a very pretty girl, Annette,' he said, smiling at me.

'Thank you,' I breathed. Returning his smile, I felt my clitoris stir between my swelling pussy lips.

'You look like Hayley Mills did when she was younger.'

'Oh, right,' I murmured, wondering who Hayley Mills was. 'How's my dad doing at work?' I asked him.

'Very well indeed,' he replied, unable to drag his gaze away from the bulge of my knickers. 'I haven't told him yet, but there's a vacancy coming up on the top floor. It's a good position with an excellent salary.'

'Will he get it?' I asked him hopefully.

'There's a good chance, yes.' He fiddled with the crotch of his trousers again. 'As I was saying, you're a very pretty girl. I'll bet you have all the boys chasing you.'

'Not really,' I said with a giggle. 'Well, I suppose some of them do.'

'You don't have a boyfriend, then?'

'No, not yet.'

'So, what do you do in your spare time?'

'I go to the park, mostly. I like sitting by the pond in the evenings.'

'I often walk in the park in the evenings.' He raised one eyebrow and grinned at me. 'I might bump into you some time.'

As mum brought the coffee in, I closed my thighs and concealed the wet crotch of my knickers. I'd never seen Derek in the park, and I knew that he was lying about walking there in the evenings. I also knew that he'd make a point of going there to meet me. But what would he say if he met me? What would he do? Perhaps he'd want to sit with me by the pond and chat about this and that. Perhaps he'd ask me to show him my knickers. Was I playing a dangerous game? I wondered. Dangerous or not, it was extremely exciting.

I was right: Derek turned up at the park the following evening. But, keeping his distance, he didn't approach me. I watched him hovering behind some bushes about twenty yards from where I was sitting. He was too far away to see my knickers so I kept my thighs pressed together. I felt wet, aroused, sexy. But, after ten minutes, I became bored. I was sitting on the bench, he was watching me . . . what was the point? I then did something stupid.

Walking into the wooded area behind the bench, I followed the narrow path through the trees to the railway cutting. I knew that he'd follow me, but I didn't know what my plan was. I had no plan. I was playing a silly game, a dangerous game. But Derek was my dad's friend, a family friend, and I knew that I was safe enough. Hearing twigs cracking as he approached, I leant on the ivy-covered fence and watched a train snaking its way through the cutting far below. As the train disappeared into the tunnel, I smiled. Did Derek fancy me? I again wondered in my naivety. Turning, I expected to see him there. But I was alone in the clearing.

Hearing a rustling sound, I realised that he was hiding behind the bushes. I could just make out his face through the foliage. He was lurking, watching me. Why didn't he want to chat to me? I wondered. Perhaps he didn't know what to say. Perhaps he just wanted to look at me, my short skirt and naked thighs. As I lifted my skirt and looked down at my white knickers, I had no idea that I was moulding my future. Had I known then what I know now . . . But it was exciting, and completely innocent.

Leaning against the fence with my skirt up around my waist, my knickers blatantly displayed to a middle-aged man hiding in the bushes, I felt incredibly aroused. Dare I go further and pull the front of my knickers down? I wondered. Dare I allow Derek to see my sex crack? I was learning, discovering. But how far should I go in my quest for carnal knowledge? I instinctively knew that what I was doing was wrong. But my libido was rising fast, blurring my mind and taking control.

Another train clattered through the cutting as I slipped my hand down the front of my knickers and felt the wetness of my crack. My outer lips were puffy and swollen, my clitoris painfully solid. The sound of the train fading, I became oblivious to my surroundings as I massaged my clitoris. Standing with my feet wide apart, I leaned back against the fence and closed my eyes. I thought that I'd found heaven as I rubbed and caressed the sensitive tip of my clitoris and neared my desperately needed orgasm. Dizzy in my arousal, I felt that I was flying through purple clouds of sexual bliss. Orgasms, my drug, my fix ... Was I addicted?

The explosion came quickly. My legs sagging beneath me, I tossed my head back and let out whimpers of pleasure as my climax shook my young body to the very core. Crying out in the grip of the most powerful orgasm I'd ever experienced, I wondered whether my pleasure had been heightened because I was being watched by a man. Exposing my knickers had sent my libido soaring. Masturbating before a man was propelling my arousal to frightening heights.

My orgasm finally beginning to wane, my head lolling forward, I slowed my massaging rhythm and teased the last ripples of pleasure from my clitoris. Trembling uncontrollably, I was brought back to earth by the sound of another train rumbling through the cutting. The birds were singing in the trees high above me. I opened my eyes and gazed at the bushes. Derek was still there, the bushes rustling as he moved about. The stark reality of what I'd done suddenly hitting me, I pulled my hand out of my knickers and tugged my skirt down.

Guilt and embarrassment swamped me. I couldn't believe how I'd behaved. What must Derek have thought of me? He must have thought me a common tart, a filthy slut. I knew that I'd never be able to face him again. Having slipped my hand down my knickers and masturbated myself to a massive orgasm, I could never look him in the eye again. At least he'd not seen my pussy crack, I tried to console myself. But he'd watched me come and ...

Hearing him slip away, making his escape and leaving me alone with my shame, I realised that he'd not known that I'd known that he'd watched me masturbate. I was innocent, I thought. As far as I was concerned, I'd been alone in the woods. I was innocent. What would my mother think? What would my father say? My fingers were wet with my juices of arousal, my knickers were soaked. I was as guilty as hell.

After that fateful evening in the woods, I didn't flash my knickers for over a week. I kept away from the park and did my best not to masturbate in bed at night. Whenever Derek called at the house, I stayed in my room. But, when he came to dinner, I had to sit opposite him at the table. I knew that he was gazing at me, recalling my masturbating in the woods, my illicit coming. Not once did I raise my head and lock my eyes with his. My stomach churned as he looked at me, my hands trembled and my heart raced. But this time it wasn't arousal. It was guilt and shame. I'd made a stupid mistake, and tried to forget the horrendous incident. Never again, I decided.

My erect clitoris calling for my intimate attention as I lay in bed one night, I tried to ignore my needs and go to sleep. I was trying to get back to normal, trying to forget about sex and flashing my knickers. I didn't want to masturbate. After my shameful act in the woods, I wanted to forget the whole thing. A battle raging in my mind, my juices of arousal trickling from my vaginal entrance and running down to the tight hole of my bottom, I finally slipped my hand between my thighs and stroked the fleshy cushions of my outer sex lips. I couldn't stop myself as I ran my fingertip up and down my drenched crack. My arousal was stronger than I.

My legs wide apart, I closed my eyes and massaged the solid bulb of my clitoris with a frightening urgency. After over a week of abstinence, I was desperate to come, desperate for the relief of orgasm. Was Derek lying in his bed with his quilt pushed back? I wondered excitedly. Was he wanking his hard cock? Was he picturing my tight knickers as he wanked? In my naivety, I wondered whether he'd like to go out with me. Boyfriend and girlfriend.

My orgasm erupting within my pulsating clitoris, I stifled my whimpers of ecstasy. Arching my back, I stretched my outer labia wide apart and vibrated the sensitive tip of my pleasure bud with my fingertips. My tightening vagina was neglected, yearning for my thrusting fingers – I needed more hands. Derek's hands? My climax peaked as I imagined him fingering me. Should I meet him in the woods by the railway cutting and allow him to pleasure me? Should I take my game a step further?

Whimpering and writhing in my bed, I finally drifted down from my orgasm and lay panting for breath. I could never give up masturbating, I knew as I slipped two fingers into the wet sheath of my pussy. Squeezing the firm mounds of my breasts with my free hand, I pinched and pulled on my sensitive nipples. My body was alive with sex, glowing in the aftermath of a heavenly orgasm. I felt beautiful, sexy, warm inside. The monster had risen.

I went to the park the following evening. Half-hoping that Derek would be there, half-hoping that he'd not come looking for me, I sat on my bench by the pond. All day at college, my clitoris had been stirring beneath its pink hood and my knickers had filled with my hot cream. I'd had a shower when I'd got home and had changed into my denim skirt and a tight T-shirt. I'd brushed my long blonde hair and applied a little makeup and I was ready. Ready for what? I had no idea.

Noticing a shadow fall across the grass in front of me, I turned and looked up at the figure silhouetted by the evening sun. Derek was wearing an open-necked shirt and jeans. Moving around the bench and sitting beside me, he smiled. Had he been to the park every evening in the hope that I'd be there? I wondered as he looked down at my naked legs. I felt nervous, imagining that this was what it must be like on a first date. He spoke first, asked me how I was.

'I'm fine,' I replied. 'I was just about to go home.'

'I've just been into the woods,' he said. 'There's a fence at the end of the path. You can look down at the trains.'

'I've never been in there,' I breathed. 'I like sitting by the pond.'

'Do you want to come and take a look?'

I forced a giggle. 'I'm not really into trains,' I said.

'No, I mean . . . walk through the pine trees with me. I like the woods, have done since I was a boy. Come and take a look, then I'll walk you home.'

'OK,' I said, rising to my feet. 'But I can't stay long.'

Following him across the grass to the trees, I looked up at the sunlight sparkling through the leaves high above me. The smell of pine was filling my nostrils, the birds were singing . . . I loved the woods. Derek knew that I did, and he knew why. Secluded, private, an ideal place for a teenage girl to masturbate. This was an amazing game, I thought, following him along the narrow path. He knew that I'd been there before, he knew that I was lying . . . And he knew that I'd leant against the fence and slipped my hand down my knickers and masturbated myself to a massive orgasm.

'This is it,' he said as we approached the fence. 'It's a lovely spot. I come here most evenings and watch the trains. I find it relaxing after a day at the office.'

'Yes, it is nice,' I murmured.

'You've never been here before, then?'

'Once or twice, maybe,' I confessed.

'How do you relax after a day at college?'

'By sitting by the pond and watching the ducks.'

'Have you ever come to this spot to unwind and relax?' he persisted.

'I don't think so,' I replied. 'Well, I'd better go now.'

'You remember I told you about the vacancy on the top floor?'

'Er . . . yes, yes I do.'

'I might be putting your dad up for the job.'

'Really? Wow, that's good.'

'The thing is . . . it rather depends on you, Annette.'

'On me? I don't understand. What have I got to do with it?'

'We've become friends, haven't we?'

'Well, I suppose so.'

'I'm always round at your house, discussing business with your dad or staying to dinner. I thought we might get to know each other a little better.'

'Oh, right.' I instinctively knew that I was treading on dangerous ground.

'I thought we might meet regularly, here in the woods.'

'Meet in the woods? What for?'

'To relax and chat. As I said, it's a nice spot.' He looked down at my nipples pressing through the tight material of my T-shirt and sighed. 'I'll be honest with you, Annette,' he said softly. 'I don't think your dad is quite ready for promotion.'

'Why not?'

'Don't get me wrong, he's a good man, a valuable asset to the company. It's just that I think it's a little

16

too early to have him on the top floor. Maybe later, when he's more experienced. What do you think?'

'I don't know anything about his work. You said that it depends on me. What did you mean?'

'You might be able to help me to decide.'

'How? What's my dad's job got to do with me? I don't understand.'

'You want to help your dad, right?'

'Yes, if I can.'

'Sit down on the grass for a minute,' he said, dropping to his knees. 'Join me on the grass and I'll explain.'

He didn't have to explain. I knew exactly what he was getting at. This was my fault, I knew, as I sat on the grass and did my best to conceal my knickers. I'd led him on, allowed him to see my knickers on many occasions, masturbated knowing that he'd been watching me . . . and now he wanted to see more. I couldn't just walk away. My dad's promotion depended on me. Even worse, if I didn't do what Derek wanted, would my dad get the sack? Blackmail. What did Derek want? To look, to touch, to . . . I'd have done anything for my dad. Would I do anything for Derek for my dad?

As Derek grinned at me, I wished that I'd been more like the other girls at college. They were always on about boys and sex. They knew things, they were experienced. Jenny Collins was forever talking about wanking her boyfriend and watching his spunk shoot out. Had she been in my situation, in the woods with Derek . . . would she have wanked him? Was that what he wanted me to do to him? I recalled one of my dad's expressions as Derek gazed at my naked thighs. I'd dug myself into a hole, and couldn't get out.

'I've become very fond of you, Annette,' Derek breathed, again focusing on my naked thighs. 'You

17

have beautiful long blonde hair, a pretty face, a wonderful body –'

'I think I'd better go home,' I cut in. 'Mum wants me to help her with –'

'Surely you can spare a few minutes to help me decide about your dad's promotion?'

'Well, yes, I suppose so.'

'When I've been to your house, I've often seen your knickers,' he said unashamedly.

'What?' I gasped, holding my hand to my mouth. I tried to pull the hem of my denim skirt down further to cover my thighs. 'What . . . what do you mean?' I managed to ask him.

'When you sit on the sofa, you're obviously not aware that your legs are apart and your knickers are showing.'

'I had no idea,' I said shakily.

'Don't be embarrassed, Annette. You have a beautiful young body, and lovely slender legs.'

'I feel awful,' I said, rising to my feet. 'I honestly had no idea.'

'Lift your skirt up and show me your knickers,' he ordered me, looking up at me.

'Lift my . . . No, I . . . I can't,' I stammered. 'I . . . I have to go home.'

'Don't you want to help your dad?'

'What? Yes, of course I do.'

'You allow me to see your knickers when we meet here in the woods, and I'll make sure that your dad gets the job on the top floor.'

Blackmail. The dreadful word careered around my mind, hurting me. I'd gone too far with my silly game, my dangerous game, I knew, as Derek reached out and stroked my lower thigh. This was all my fault, I reflected anxiously. I'd led Derek on, shown him my knickers, gone into the woods knowing that

18

he'd follow me, masturbated knowing that he was watching and . . . But I'd not expected this. I'd not expected him to ask me to lift my skirt up and show him my knickers. I hated my denim skirt. I should have worn jeans or . . .

'So, what's it to be?' he asked me.

'What do you mean?'

'I only want to look at your knickers, Annette. You allow me to look, and I'll make sure that your dad gets promoted.'

'But . . .'

'If you don't, then I can't say what the future holds for your dad. The company is in the process of downsizing. That means that we're laying off some of the staff. I wouldn't want to see your dad lose his job.'

'If I don't show you my knickers, you'll sack him?' I breathed incredulously.

'I'm not going to sack him,' he returned with a chuckle. 'All I'm saying is, when this comes up at the next board meeting, I can put a good word in for your dad. Not only that, but I can put him up for promotion. I only want to look at your knickers, Annette.'

Stepping back, I lifted my skirt up over my stomach and allowed him to gaze at my knickers. They were pink, the ones I'd bought in town with mum a week before. When I'd got them, I'd known that I'd be parting my thighs and showing them to Derek. But I'd never dreamed that he'd demand that I lift my skirt and show him. Never dreamed that he'd blackmail me. As he stared at the tight crotch, I instinctively knew that this was only the beginning. He'd want to meet me in the woods again. He'd demand that I lift my skirt and . . . Would he demand that I pull my knickers down?

19

'Very nice,' he murmured, licking his lips. 'You have beautiful thighs, Annette. Wonderfully smooth, unblemished skin and . . . What do you do when you come here in the evenings?'

'I don't do anything,' I replied. 'I don't come here.'

'Really? I thought that you often came here. I've seen you walking into the woods before. Do you pull your knickers down when you come here?'

'No, I . . .'

'Come on, you can tell me what you get up to when you're alone in the woods.'

Hearing voices, I lowered my skirt as Derek leapt to his feet and brushed the grass from his trousers. Kids were playing in the woods, their laughter and squeals echoing through the trees. Had they not turned up, I dread to think what would have happened. Following Derek along the narrow path to the park, I knew that I'd had a lucky escape. But what would tomorrow bring? He wanted to meet me again, he wanted to see my knickers again . . . My dad's job was on the line.

'Same time tomorrow?' he said as we emerged from the trees and crossed the park.

'I . . . I can't,' I replied shakily. 'I'm busy tomorrow.'

'Busy doing what?'

'I have to help mum.'

'You wouldn't want me to be too busy to attend the next board meeting, would you?'

'Well, no.'

'In that case, I'll meet you in the woods at the same time tomorrow evening.'

As we went our separate ways, I felt dreadful. The pit of my stomach was churning and my chest felt tight with anxiety. My dilemma was a nightmare. I had no idea what to do. I imagined my dad losing his job, and it would be my fault. If I gave Derek what

20

he wanted, I'd drown in my own guilt. If I allowed dad to lose his job, I'd never be able to forgive myself.

Wandering home, I decided to keep out of Derek's way. I'd stay in my room when he came round to the house, go out if he was due to stay to dinner. I'd been stupid, I reflected anxiously. I'd made a big mistake. My dangerous games had led me along a path to an impossible situation. I was young and had never experienced worry. My parents had had problems over the years, complained of worry and sleepless nights, but I'd never understood. I'd always been happy, carefree. Until now.

Annette and I met in a park in Brighton and sat on a bench, of all places, beneath the July sun. She was wearing a short denim skirt and for a moment I imagined myself to be one of the characters in the book. Pushing such thoughts out of my mind, I switched my tape recorder on and asked her about her feelings of guilt and shame. She looked down at the ground and then threw her head back and gazed at the cloudless sky. She was obviously feeling uneasy, so I suggested that we leave it for the time being. Sighing, she twisted her blonde hair around her fingers and then offered me a smile.

'No, it's OK,' she said. 'Yes, I did feel guilty and I was ashamed. But it wasn't that I had a problem about the things I'd done. It was the future that worried me. I honestly thought that my dad would lose his job unless I met Derek again.'

'Didn't it occur to you that Derek was bluffing?' I asked her.

'No. Well, I suppose it crossed my mind. It seemed that, whichever option I chose, I'd end up in trouble. If I met Derek in the woods, he'd want to go further. If I didn't meet him, my dad would lose his job. And, if my dad got the sack, it would be my fault. I honestly didn't know what to do.'

'You talked about a monster surfacing from the deep. You then said that sex had reared its beautiful head.'

'Masturbating was beautiful. My libido had been fired and I'd discovered masturbation and orgasms. The monster was beautiful.'

'So, was there a side of you that wanted to go further with Derek?'

'Yes, I think so. I wanted to learn about sex but ... What you have to understand is that I was young and confused. I hate the term, "sheltered life", but that's what I'd had. An only child, I didn't mix easily and found it difficult to make friends. I developed late, physically, and had never given sex a thought. I mean, I knew about sex and stuff, but I'd never bothered about it. Did I want to go further with Derek? The thought of being blackmailed terrified me. At the same time, the thought of showing my pussy to an old man excited me. Well, I suppose he wasn't that old. But I had loads of stuff coming into my head. My mum and dad, Derek, morals, right and wrong and all that stuff. My mind hurt with worry.'

'What do you think Derek's thoughts were at that time?'

'Looking back, it's obvious that he had one thing on his mind, and there's only one way to put it. He wanted to fuck me. I mean, what man wouldn't? I was fresh-faced and young and innocent. I was quite attractive and ... I was a virgin. If I'd known then what I know now ... Think about it, a pretty little virgin girl with a man as old as my dad. Of course he wanted to fuck me.'

'How did you cope with college the following day?'

'I told mum that I wasn't feeling well and I took the day off ....'

The Journey Begins

My fear had melted my new and exciting feelings of sex. Although I was in bed with my naked pussy only inches from my fingers, I had no inclination to masturbate. I didn't want to go to the park and flash my knickers. I didn't want to masturbate and experience a massive orgasm. I had no thoughts of sex or orgasms. My libido had been killed.

Dad phoned at lunch time and told mum the good news. He'd been offered the job on the top floor. Apparently, Derek had called a meeting and dad had been brought in to be told of the decision. Mum was ecstatic, over the moon. She went on about dad's increase in salary, how he'd worked hard for the company and had been rewarded for his efforts . . . I tried to come across as pleased, but it wasn't easy. Dad's promotion had nothing to do with how hard he'd worked for the company. He'd been rewarded for my efforts. Derek had kept his side of the bargain, and now I had to keep mine.

Dragging myself out of bed at five o'clock, I dressed in my denim skirt and T-shirt and made my way to the park. I didn't want to go there, but I had no choice. I was two hours early, but I needed to sit by the pond and think. The ducks seemed happy. They had no worries, unlike me. A thousand thoughts battered my tormented mind as I gazed at the ducks. I had to keep my side of the bargain, I had to lift my skirt up and allow Derek to look at my knickers and . . . he'd want me to pull my knickers down, I knew. And then he'd want to touch me.

Feeling easier as I evaluated the situation, I found that I was able to think clearly. If Derek wanted me to pull my knickers down and show him my crack . . . The fog that had blurred my mind was clearing. In my musings, I realised that I could turn the situation round. I had what Derek wanted, and he'd tried to blackmail me to get his own way. If I turned things round and told him what I wanted in exchange for showing him my crack . . . it might just work, I thought. Dad had got his promotion, so what did I want from Derek?

Wishing I'd not arrived so early, I left the bench and wandered over to the swings. Recalling my early days as I swung back and forth, I thought how uncomplicated life was then. No worries, no problems . . . I couldn't deny that I'd brought all this on myself, but it had started out as fun. Showing the tight crotch of my knickers had turned me on. I didn't want to give up my new-found game, but . . .

Noticing a man approaching, I stretched out my legs and parted my feet wide. I looked up at the sky and swung higher as he stopped and gazed at my white knickers. The thrill of the game sending my arousal almost out of control, I knew that I could never stop showing off my knickers. Why should I? It wasn't as if I was exposing my pussy to men. Showing my knickers was harmless enough.

The man settled on the grass and didn't attempt to avert his gaze and make out that he wasn't looking up my short skirt. I reckoned that he was in his thirties, and I realised that men of all ages would appreciate a glimpse of the triangular patch of material between my thighs. My stomach somersaulting, my clitoris swelling, I wondered whether his cock was hard as he stared at me. Would he pay me to pull my knickers down and show him my crack? I wondered in rising wickedness. Would he think about me the next time he wanked his cock? As a couple approached the swings, he leapt to his feet and made off. I'd wanted him to stay and gaze at me, but it was over. Leaving the swing, I wondered where my bad thoughts were coming from as I headed back towards the bench. I was thinking like a common slut. But my excitement far outweighed my guilt.

Derek turned up at seven o'clock with a huge grin across his face. Saying nothing, he sat next to me and gazed longingly at my thighs. Was his cock stiff? Had he been wanking and thinking of my pussy as his sperm had jetted from his knob? Brushing his dark hair away from his forehead, he looked up and locked his eyes to mine. There was expectation reflected in the dark pools of his eyes. He obviously thought that he had me where he wanted me, but he was very wrong. I had to make a stand, or forever be a slave to Derek.

'You heard the good news?' he asked me.

'About dad? Yes, yes, I have.'

'It worked out well, Annette.'

'Yes, it did. I showed you my knickers, and dad got his promotion. Look, I've been here for two hours so I'd better get back.'

'But . . . Annette, I got your dad promoted to the top floor.' He was obviously flustered. 'And now you must keep your side of our deal.'

'I did,' I returned, grinning at him. 'Last night, I showed you my knickers. That was the deal, wasn't it?'

25

'No, no. We arranged to meet here this evening so that I could take a proper look at you.'

'A proper look?' I echoed, cocking my head to one side. 'You want to see my knickers again?'

'I thought you might show me more than your knickers, Annette,' he breathed softly. 'I thought you might pull them down and show me your –'

'What do I get in return?' I cut in.

'Your dad was promoted. That was the deal.'

'You're getting confused,' I said with a giggle. I did my best to conceal my trembling hands. 'You're getting mixed up. Dad's promotion was in exchange for my showing you my knickers last night.'

'No, Annette,' he said firmly. He was becoming agitated, there was anger reflected in his dark eyes now. 'You're the one who's confused.'

I began to feel unsure of myself as he stared at me. I'd done well, so far. But now I wasn't sure what to say. I had to be strong, I thought as he stood before me and asked me to go into the woods with him. He wanted to see more of my young body, but what did I want in return? Dad had got his promotion, so what else was there I wanted? Money?

'I might be here tomorrow evening,' I said, leaving the bench.

'Annette, I want you to come into the woods with me now,' he persisted.

'As I said, I've been here for two hours. If I meet you here tomorrow, what do I get out of it? What will I gain?'

'I've already told you that –'

'I could do with a new stereo system. The one in my room doesn't work properly.'

'A new stereo?' He frowned and shook his head. 'Look, you've got all this back to front. I got your dad promoted and now I want –'

'We both want things,' I cut in. I felt strong, in control. 'Anyway, I must go now.'

Walking away, I couldn't believe that I'd taken control of the situation. Feeling elated, I looked back over my shoulder a couple of times. Derek was sitting on the bench, staring at the ground. I'd not only taken control, but turned the situation back to front. I'd worried myself silly, I'd not slept properly, I'd taken a day off college ... A realisation hit me as I walked home. I was beginning to understand the power of my young body, and the gains it could bring me.

When I got home from college the following afternoon, there was a new stereo system waiting for me. Mum said that Derek had won it in a competition, but had no use for it. She said that he was a nice man. How kind of him. Little did she know that I was to pay for the present. Now the ball was back in my court. He'd given me the stereo, and I had to give him what he wanted. What did he want? I wondered naively as I changed into my denim skirt. He could look at my knickers again, I decided. No, he'd want to see more. Maybe I'd pull the front of my knickers down and show him my crack.

Although I felt in control, I didn't like the predicament I was in. To make matters worse, a boy from college had asked me out and I'd accepted. He was nice, and I thought that I'd like to get to know him. I'd said that I'd meet him in the park on Saturday morning. Things were moving too fast, I knew, as I finished my makeup and gazed at my reflection in the full-length mirror. Would the boy want to see my knickers? Would he want to fuck me? I had to remain in control. A boyfriend of my own age, and my illicit relationship with Derek ... I had to keep my two lives apart.

Sitting on the bench by the pond, I realised that my libido was rising. My knickers felt damp, my nipples were hard and acutely sensitive. Was I ready to be touched? Did I want Derek to touch me? Dripping in confusion, I didn't know what I wanted. I wasn't even sure that I wanted the new stereo system. Hearing a noise behind me, I turned. Derek was hiding behind the bushes edging the woods. Peering at me, he scanned the park before beckoning me to join him. His black hair was dishevelled and he looked worried. Why was he hiding?

'I don't want people to see us together,' he said as I joined him.

'Why not?' I asked him.

'Because . . . Did you like the stereo?'

'Yes, thanks. I haven't tried it yet. I'll have to get dad to help me set it up.'

'Well, here we are,' he said as we reached the fence. 'So, let's have a look at you.' Dropping to his knees, he yanked my skirt up over my stomach. 'Very nice,' he breathed.

'Derek, I thought that you . . .' I began as he stroked the smooth flesh of my inner thighs.

'You've got your stereo, and now I want to take a proper look at you.'

'But . . .'

'You've messed me about too much as it is, Annette. You've got your stereo, and now I want to look at you.'

As he tugged my knickers down to my knees and gazed at my sex crack, I felt numb. This wasn't what I'd expected. I was stunned, unable to move. I'd imagined him standing back and looking at me as I'd lifted my skirt up. I'd thought that he might ask me to pull the front of my knickers down and . . . I was losing control, I knew, as he gazed at the most private part of my young body. I'd not even dreamed that he'd kneel before me and pull my knickers down. The fragrance of the pine trees had once excited me, but now?

'You're beautiful,' he breathed, huskily. His voice was deep, sexual. 'Never have I seen such beauty.'

'You've looked, so . . .' I began, stepping back and pulling my knickers up.

'Is that it?' he asked me with a chuckle. 'A two-second glimpse in exchange for a brand-new stereo system?'

'Yes,' I returned firmly. 'The deal was that I show you my knickers, not my pussy.'

'No, Annette. That wasn't the deal at all. I said that I wanted to see more of you. As I said, you've messed me about too much as it is. That stereo system wasn't cheap. If you think that a quick glimpse of your pussy is enough, then you're very wrong.'

'I'm not cheap,' I returned, wondering how I'd thought up such a good line.

'What do you think you've got in your knickers? Gold? You've not got anything that every other girl in the world hasn't got. There are plenty of other girls, Annette.'

'Yes, there are. But how many of them would come to the woods with you and allow you to pull their knickers down?'

'In return for a new stereo system? Quite a few, I would imagine. You seem to be forgetting something.'

'Oh?'

'Your father and his job. I'm his boss, Annette.'

'In the office, you're his boss. Here, in the woods, I'm your boss.'

'OK, boss. Let's lighten up a bit. Will you allow me to look at you again?'

'No, I . . .'

'Come on, Annette. This is only a bit of fun. Where's the harm in showing me your pussy crack?'

'All right,' I finally conceded. 'You can look, but not touch.'

Stepping forward, I lifted my skirt and pulled my knickers down to my knees. Derek gazed longingly at my crack, but he didn't attempt to touch me. Not only was I in control again, but my libido was rising fast. I could feel the wetness oozing between my swollen pussy lips, my clitoris inflating, emerging from beneath its pink hood. The birds singing, the smell of pine filling my nostrils, I felt completely relaxed.

'I'd love to stroke you,' Derek breathed.

'All right,' I said. 'Stroke me, but nothing more.'

'You feel so soft and smooth,' he said, running his fingertip over the fleshy swell of my outer lips. 'You're absolutely beautiful.'

'I'm also the boss,' I murmured shakily as my clitoris called for attention. 'OK, that's enough.'

'But . . . for God's sake, Annette. I've given you a new stereo system. Please, be fair.'

'Fair? What do you mean?'

'You know what I mean. Look, I want us to be friends. I don't want to have to get nasty.'

'Nasty?' I murmured, wondering what he intended to do.

'I could tell your dad things, tell him things about you. I could say that you come here with boys and strip naked. I could tell him that I've seen you wanking boys in the woods. So, what's it to be? Do you want us to be friends? Or would you rather I talk to your dad?'

'Maybe I should talk to him about you,' I countered futilely.

'Yes, maybe you should. You might like to tell him that he only got his promotion because you pulled your knickers down. Would you like me to tell him?'

'Yes,' I returned. 'You tell him all about it. He'll never believe you.'

'Won't he? If I say that you asked me to come into the woods with you, if I say that you pulled your knickers down and I was shocked . . . Shall we put it to the test? Let's tell him and see what his reaction is.'

'I have to go now.'

'I'll walk with you,' he said, turning to leave. 'Come on, let's go and tell your dad all about it.'

'Wait,' I said softly.

'I thought you were in a hurry to get home?'

'No, I . . . I have some time.'

Lifting my skirt, I pulled the front of my knickers down and displayed my sex crack to his wide eyes. My heart racing, my legs trembling, I was floundering in unimaginable confusion. My arousal was rising, my stomach somersaulting, and I felt sexy and horny as never before. But I knew that this was wrong. Derek was the same age as my father. To allow him to see the most private part of my body was very wrong. But what else could I do?

'I knew you'd see sense,' he said, smiling at me. 'We're friends, Annette. And I want us to stay that way. I might buy you presents now and then, if we get on all right.' Stroking my long blonde hair, he grinned at me. 'Why don't you lift your T-shirt up and show me your little titties?'

'I need a new television for my bedroom,' I stated. 'Mine's an old black and white one. I want a colour TV.'

'I'm sure that I can arrange that. You show me your tits and I'll –'

'I'll meet you here tomorrow evening,' I cut in, pulling my knickers up and lowering my skirt.

31

'You want the TV first?'

'Yes, of course.'

'You drive a hard bargain,' he sighed. 'But I'll agree to your terms if you strip naked for me tomorrow.'

'Yes, all right,' I said, immediately wishing I hadn't.

'Good. That's settled, then. I know that we're going to get on really well, Annette. We'll become good friends. You'd like that, wouldn't you?'

'Maybe.'

'Have you ever seen a cock?' he asked me unashamedly.

'I . . . yes, I have,' I lied.

'Have you ever touched a cock?'

'Yes. Look, I have to go now.'

'Have you wanked a boy?' he persisted, following me along the path to the park. 'Have you watched the spunk shoot out?'

'I'll see you tomorrow evening.'

'All right, Annette. Same time tomorrow, OK?'

'OK.'

Walking across the grass, I knew that I was digging myself deeper into a hole that I'd never get out of. Turning, I noticed Derek slip back into the woods. He was probably going to wank, I thought, recalling the girls at college talking about boys wanking their cocks and shooting out their spunk. A new television? I mused. Mum and dad would think it odd if Derek kept buying me expensive presents. How deep would the hole become?

In bed that night, I wondered why I'd lied to Derek about touching a cock. He'd think that I'd had experience, and would undoubtedly ask me to touch his cock. He'd want me to wank him, I knew. He'd want me to hold his cock, wank him and make his spunk shoot out. All this had started as a silly game, I reflected. Showing my knickers as I'd sat on the sofa, masturbating in the woods when I knew that he was spying at me from the bushes . . . I'd made one stupid mistake after another. But there was nothing I could do about it now.

A new television was waiting for me when I got home from college. Mum said that Derek had dropped it round earlier in the day. She also said that she thought it odd that Derek had won yet another competition. I didn't know what to say to her. I made out that I was surprised, and very pleased, but I averted my gaze as she stared at me and asked me what I did in the park every evening.

'You're always going there,' she said. 'What on earth do you get up to?'

'Nothing,' I murmured. 'I just sit by the pond and watch the ducks.'

'Do you meet anyone there?'

'No,' I returned, rather too quickly.

'Annette, is everything all right?'

'Yes, of course.'

'It's just that . . . Oh, I don't know. You always wear your short skirt. Why don't you wear jeans anymore?'

'It's summer, mum. It's too hot for jeans.'

'Are you sure that you don't meet anyone in the park?'

'Of course I'm sure,' I snapped.

'All right, I only asked. You seem to have changed recently. If there's anything you want to talk about, you will come to me, won't you?'

'There's nothing I want to talk about.'

'I worry about you, Annette.'

'There's nothing to worry about, mum. I'm fine, OK?'

* * *

Derek wasn't there when I got to the park. I sat on the bench, hoping that he'd been held up and couldn't make it. Biting my lip, twisting my hair nervously around my fingers, I couldn't imagine taking all my clothes off. No one had seen me naked for years, not even my mum. To stand before Derek with nothing on . . . But I knew that I had to do it. If not today, then tomorrow, I'd have to strip naked before Derek.

My breasts were small and hard, and I wondered whether Derek would want to touch them. Would he squeeze them? Would he feel the firmness of my teenage breasts? I felt as if I was alone in the world as I gazed at the sunlight sparkling on the water. I looked around the park. It was deserted, apart from a figure in the distance. It was Derek. Why couldn't it have been someone else, anyone else? As he approached me, I felt my stomach churn. This was it, I thought. I had a new stereo system, a new television . . . and now I was to pay.

'You look good enough to eat,' he said, standing before me. 'Shall we go into the woods?'

'Yes,' I breathed, leaving the bench and following him across the grass to the trees. 'I . . . I don't have much time.'

'It's a lovely evening,' he said as we approached the fence by the railway cutting. 'Are you pleased with the television?'

'Yes. It's nice, thanks.'

'It cost me a lot of money. As you said, you're not cheap.'

'No, I'm not.'

'Worth every penny, though.' Leaning against the fence, he grinned at me. 'OK, now you can strip for me.'

'There might be people around,' I murmured. 'I mean, if someone comes into the woods . . .'

34

'There's no one around, Annette. The park was empty, and there's no one here. It's just you and me.' He looked me up and down and grinned again. 'Start by taking your T-shirt off.'

Tugging the garment over my head, I felt embarrassed as he gazed at my small bra. Beaming, he licked his lips and instructed me to continue. I was supposed to be in control, I reflected. I was in control, wasn't I? My stomach churning, my hands trembling, I reached behind my back and unhooked my bra as he stared at me. The cups falling away from my firm breasts, my nipples rising in the relatively cool air of the woods, I hung my head and gazed at the ground as embarrassment engulfed me. I'd watched my tits develop and grow over the years. They were my secret, my prized possession. But now they were on show to a middle-aged man.

'Very nice,' Derek said. 'You're an attractive girl, Annette. I'm glad we've become good friends. You want us to be good friends. don't you?'

'Yes, yes I do.'

'That's good. You may take your skirt off now. I want to see your tight little knickers.'

Lowering my skirt, I allowed it to fall down my legs and crumple around my ankles. Derek said that I had a cameltoe, but I didn't know what he meant. He looked me up and down, breathing heavily and licking his lips again as he admired my near-naked body. A train rumbled through the cutting, and I wondered where the passengers were going. Were they looking out of the windows? They were hiding in their little worlds. They had no idea what was going on in the woods at the top of the steep embankment.

Following Derek's instructions, I tugged my knickers down and kicked them aside along with my skirt. Standing upright, I felt goose pimples rising on my skin as he cast his eyes over my nakedness. The woods seemed cooler than usual. There again, I'd never stripped naked beneath the pine trees. A realisation hit me as I brushed my blonde hair away from my face. I was young and not unattractive. And I had what men wanted. Derek had given me a stereo system and a television. He obviously liked my body, thought my body was worth the money. I could have any man I wanted, I mused happily. My embarrassment fading, I felt good, sexy. I was in control.

'May I touch?' Derek asked me, reaching out and stroking the firm mounds of my breasts with the back of his hand.

'Yes,' I murmured, my sensitive nipples becoming erect and hard.

'You're a lucky girl to have me here to look after you,' he said.

'You're the lucky one,' I returned as he squeezed each firm breast.

'How do you work that out?'

'How many girls of my age would strip naked and allow you to touch them?'

'In return for a TV and hi-fi, most girls would.'

'No, Derek. I doubt that any girl of my age would strip in the woods for you.'

'So, what makes you different?'

'I know how men think,' I lied. 'I know what men want. I also know what I want, and how to get it.'

'You've done well out of me, Annette. Your dad's promotion, a TV and hi-fi system . . .'

'And I intend to do far better.'

'What do you mean by that?'

'You'll find out. I'd better get dressed and go home now.'

'No, not yet.'

36

'I stripped for you, Derek. That was the deal, wasn't it?'

'Yes, but ... I've spent a lot of money on you, Annette.'

'So you keep saying. And I've kept my side of the bargain.'

'Just let me kiss you. Down there, I mean.'

'All right, you may kiss me,' I conceded. 'But nothing more.'

My stomach somersaulting as he knelt before me, I felt powerful. A man kneeling at my feet like a servant. I felt good inside. He'd had to ask my permission to touch my breasts and kiss my pussy. I'd successfully turned the situation round, I reflected happily, as he pressed his mouth to my pussy lips and kissed me there. The feel of his wet tongue delving into my sex crack sent quivers through my pelvis. I realised that I was desperate for an orgasm. But, stepping back, I knew that I had to remain in control.

'No,' I said firmly. 'That wasn't part of the deal.'

'Please, Annette,' he whined, rising to his feet. 'Just let me taste you.'

'Tomorrow, maybe. I have to go now.'

Again looking my young body up and down, he adjusted the crotch of his trousers. I could have sex with him, I knew, as I felt my young womb contract. But I didn't want that. What did I want? I needed to come, but didn't want things to go too far. His saliva cooled my tight crack as a gentle breeze wafted through the clearing. I was acutely aware of my nakedness, my yearning for the relief of orgasm.

'Annette, I've spent a lot of money and –'

'Tomorrow,' I interrupted him. 'Don't push me, or you'll not see me here again.'

'Don't push me,' he snapped angrily. 'I've had just about enough of your bloody games. You've been leading me on, and you know it. I got your dad promoted, I've spent money on you . . . and all you keep saying is, tomorrow, tomorrow. I've waited long enough. Today, Annette. Do you understand?'

'I won't come here again if you . . .'

'You're right, you won't come here again. Shall I tell you why?'

'I know why. Because I won't come here to meet you.'

'No, no, no. You won't be allowed to come here, Annette.'

'What do you mean?'

'You'll be grounded. Once your parents discover what you get up to in the woods, you'll be grounded for months on end. The time has come to stop playing games, Annette.'

'But . . . what do you want me to do?'

'Nothing. Just stand there and allow me to stroke and kiss you.'

'Is that all?'

'Yes, that's all.'

I closed my eyes and tried to imagine that I wasn't there as he again knelt before me. I tried to convince myself that I was dreaming. This was a dream, a nightmare. But with the feel of his wet tongue running up and down my crack, how could I imagine that I wasn't there? Standing naked in the woods with a middle-aged man licking my pussy, I knew only too well that this wasn't a dream. His tongue pushing further into my crack, he reached behind me and clutched my firm buttocks. Pulling me closer, his mouth hard against my pussy lips, he slipped his tongue into my virginal sex hole and tasted me.

His slurping and sucking sounds drowned by a train rumbling noisily through the cutting, his saliva streaming down my inner thighs, he moved up my open sex valley and sucked my erect clitoris into his mouth. I was going to come, I knew, as he slipped a finger deep into my tightening vagina. I'd never been licked and sucked before. I'd never been fingered. I'd always imagined that my first sexual encounter would be with a boy of my own age, not a middle-aged man. But did it matter? Young or old, a male was pleasuring me. At least Derek had experience and knew exactly what to do.

I felt his finger massaging deep within my vagina, and my clitoris began to pulsate within his hot mouth. I quivered as my trembling legs began to sag beneath me. The sensations were truly amazing, and I was beginning to forget that this was a middle-aged man pleasuring my young body. In a dream-like state, I imagined that the boy I fancied was kneeling at my feet. I was to meet him on Saturday. Would he finger my tight vagina and suck my erect clitoris? Would he fuck me? The girls at college were always talking about getting fucked. Was that what I wanted?

I didn't know what I wanted as my orgasm stirred and my breathing became fast and shallow. I could feel my juices of desire flowing from my vagina as my young womb contracted. I was desperate to come, desperate for the relief of orgasm. But the reality of the situation again loomed. This was my first time with a boy, with a man. Etched forever in my memory would be my first orgasm with a middle-aged man. I was drifting helplessly in my worrying thoughts. Derek was as old as my father, and yet . . .

'Come for me,' he breathed, his tongue repeatedly sweeping over the sensitive bulb of my erect clitoris.

'I can't,' I gasped.

'Relax, Annette. Relax and come for me.'

Although I loved the incredible sensations, there was no way I could relax. My mind in turmoil, I tried desperately to imagine that a boy of my own age was sucking my sensitive clitoris. I wanted to come, I needed to come. I began to think that it would have been different if I'd already been with a boy. Then, this wouldn't be my first time and I'd feel better. Or would I? First time or hundredth time, I couldn't get away from the fact that Derek was an old man.

'That's enough,' I finally managed to breathe.

'Annette,' he murmured, looking up and frowning at me as I stepped back. 'Why didn't you come?'

'I can't come with you,' I replied, grabbing my clothes from the ground. 'It's not right.'

'Of course it's right,' he said with a chuckle. 'You're female and I'm male. Of course it's right.'

'You're old and I'm young,' I countered, hurriedly dressing. 'This is wrong.'

'You've a lot to learn,' he sighed.

'Maybe I . . .'

My words tailed off as he pulled out his erect cock. I stared at his purple knob as he retracted his fleshy foreskin. My heart racing, I watched as he ran his hand up and down his shaft. I'd never seen a cock, I'd never seen a man wanking or spunk shooting out of a purple knob. Clutching my T-shirt to my young breasts, I watched his knob appear and disappear as his foreskin rolled back and forth. His balls bouncing as he wanked, he was breathing heavily, moaning softly. Frozen to the spot, I watched and waited in anticipation for his spunk to jet.

'Wank me,' he gasped. 'Please, wank me.'

'No, I . . . I can't,' I stammered.

'For God's sake, just do it.'

His spunk jetting from his knob as his legs crumpled, he let out a long low moan of pleasure. I was amazed by the sheer size of his solid cock and swinging balls. No way would his shaft fit into the tight sheath of my pussy. Wondering how much sperm a man produced, I watched the white liquid splattering over the short grass. I was tempted to grab his cock and bring out the last of his sperm, but it was all over too quickly. I'd lost the chance to wank my first cock. With a long thread of creamy liquid hanging from his deflating knob and finally dropping to the ground, he leant against the fence to steady himself as I finished dressing.

'I needed that,' he murmured, raising his head and gazing at me. 'Why the hell didn't you wank me?'

'Because you haven't given me a new computer yet,' I returned.

'What? If you think I'm buying you a bloody computer, then . . .'

'I have to go now,' I cut in, leaving the clearing and following the narrow path through the trees.

I could hear him calling me as I walked briskly across the park. Reaching the road without looking back, I reckoned that I'd finally established my position as boss. Derek now had to play it my way, or he'd not see me again. The chances of him running to my father with his tales were pretty slim, I mused. What were the chances of him buying me a new computer? Whether I got a computer or not didn't really bother me. I didn't want to have to wank him and bring out his spunk. As far as I was concerned, the game had come to an end.

As I lay in my bed that night, I reflected on the day's events. I'd been fingered, had my clitoris sucked almost to orgasm, and I'd watched a man wank. I was learning, gaining experience. But I decided that any further sexual encounters would be with a boy of my own age. I was sure that Derek wouldn't pay for a new computer. If he did . . . I'd cross that bridge when I came to it. Pulling my quilt over my naked body and closing my eyes, I was sure that my sexual relationship with my father's boss had come to an end.

I met Annette for lunch in a small bistro in Brighton. Rather than her denim skirt, she was wearing a pink summer dress. Tall and slim, she looked incredibly feminine with her long blonde hair cascading over the mounds of her breasts. Breaking my reverie, she talked about the book and pointed out that I'd embroidered her story in one or two places. Acting as editor and proofreader, she was determined to ensure that I got it right. I countered her allegation by suggesting that parts of her story were already verging on the realms of fantasy rather than fact, to which she took umbrage.

'Not only is every word true,' she stated firmly, 'but there are things that I haven't told you.'

'Such as?' I said, waiting expectantly for her reply.

'Such as ... I'll tell you another time. I haven't finished telling you about Derek yet.'

I backed off. 'Did you believe that Derek would buy you a computer?' I asked her.

'There was a power struggle going on between Derek and me. I felt that I'd won the battle when he gave me the stereo system. He then said that he'd give me a television if I stripped naked for him. I suppose I got carried away and pushed my luck too far by asking for a new computer.'

'You knew what he'd want in return. Didn't you think about the consequences?'

'Yes and no. I mean, I thought that I was winning the game. I thought that I was in control but ... I suppose it's like gambling. You put money into a fruit machine and win. So you put more money in and then more, and then you lose the lot. I realised that I'd gone too far with Derek when he talked about my parents grounding me. I was rather old to be grounded but my parents were fairly strict and old-fashioned. I was deliberately taunting him with my young body, but I didn't expect him to threaten to tell my parents about me.'

'You said that, when he pulled your knickers down, you were stunned and unable to move. At that point, you must have realised that he'd want to go all the way with you. You must have also realised that you were losing the power struggle?'

'Yes, I was stunned when he pulled my knickers down. When he licked me . . . I still believed that I was in control at that point. I suppose I hadn't thought about the consequences. To me, it was a game.'

'A game that you wished you'd never started?'

'At first, I loved the game. Showing my knickers really turned me on, and the men loved it. But the game got out of hand when Derek pulled my knickers down and licked me. At that moment, I did wish that I'd never started it.'

'How did you think you'd put an end to it?'

'I suppose that I thought I'd put an end to the game when I asked him for a new computer. He couldn't keep spending money on me, and I was sure that the game was over. I just wanted to forget about Derek and move on.'

'How did you plan to move on?'

'To be honest, I didn't have a plan. I'd heard nothing from Derek for several days, there was no sign of him or a new computer, and I thought it was over. I felt a mixture of relief and disappointment, but decided that it was for the best.'

'Disappointment? Are you saying that you would have liked to have gone further with him?'

'I didn't know what I wanted. I'd discovered masturbation and I'd been licked and I'd watched a man wank. I felt sexually alive but, in the battle between right and wrong, the right side was winning. Derek was as old as my dad, and I knew that what I'd done with him was wrong. As I said, I didn't have a plan for moving on. I went to the park and ...'

My Deflowering

I met the boy in the park on Saturday morning. His name was David and he was fun to be with. More to the point, he was my age. We sat on the bench by the pond and chatted about the ducks. He joked about this and that and made me laugh and I felt at ease with him, relaxed. But, lurking in the depths of my mind, thoughts of his cock wouldn't leave me. Did he wank? Had he been with a girl?

I was wearing my denim skirt, and I parted my thighs just enough to allow him to see the triangular patch of my white knickers hugging my swelling pussy lips. I could feel my womb contracting, my clitoris stirring, as he lowered his eyes and gazed between my legs. I imagined wanking David, running my hand up and down his hard cock and feeling his spunk running over my fingers. Did he know what to do with a girl? I mused as he raised his head and locked his eyes to mine. Did he know about pussy fingering and licking and sucking?

'I like you a lot,' he breathed softly. 'I think you're very pretty.'

'Thank you,' I replied, realising the immense difference between David and a middle-aged man. 'I like you, too. Would you like to walk through the woods with me? There's a fence where we can look down at the trains.'

'OK,' he agreed readily, his face beaming.

Reaching the fence, I looked at the ground where Derek had splattered his spunk. There was no sign of the white liquid, nothing to reveal my dark secret. David leant on the fence, watching a train. He knew nothing of my visit to the woods with an older man. Recalling Derek wanking, his spunk jetting from his purple knob slit, I felt my arousal rising fast. My hormones were gushing and sex was rearing its beautiful head again. I needed to come, I knew, as I felt my juices of desire seeping between the engorged lips of my pussy. Would David make me come? Would he finger my vagina and suck my yearning clitoris to orgasm?

Standing behind David, I slipped my hand up my skirt and felt the wetness of my knickers. As he talked about the train and the tunnel, I knew that he wasn't going to make a move towards me. He was more interested in the trains than in my young body, my wet pussy. Sitting on the grass with my chin resting on my knees, the bulge of my knickers clearly displayed between my thighs, I wondered how to make the first move. I wanted to wank David's cock and watch his spunk flow. I didn't feel that I was ready for full-blown sex. I just wanted to feel the hardness of his cock in my hand, the creamy wetness of his spunk on my skin.

As David turned and stared at my knickers, I realised how different the situation was from my last visit to the woods. Derek had been upfront, he'd unashamedly asked me to strip naked and show him my pussy slit. David stared at my knickers, but he didn't make a move. Perhaps he was unsure of me, I mused. Parting my legs, allowing him a better view of the tight material covering my full sex lips, I began to wonder whether my game only worked with Derek.

There again, the man by the pond had been interested in my knickers. Until his wife had dragged him away, he'd been unable to take his eyes off me. So why wasn't David interested?

David came across as shy, and probably unsure of himself. I knew that, if I suggested I wank him, he'd think me a slut. Word would get round and I'd soon have a name for myself, a reputation. Now, I was beginning to feel unsure of myself. Perhaps my young body wasn't so attractive after all. I'd thought that my new game, my knicker flashing, would bring me what I wanted from any man of any age. David and I were alone in the woods, and his cock was so near. I knew that this was an opportunity not to be missed. I needed the experience, and this was the time and place.

'Do you wank?' I asked him, hoping that I wasn't making a huge mistake.

'What?' he gasped, his eyes widening.

'Do you wank?'

'Well, I . . . No, I don't.'

'Why not?'

'Because . . . I just don't.'

'I was hoping that you'd show me,' I persisted, tilting my head to one side and grinning at him. 'I've never seen a cock.'

He lay on the grass beside me with his hands behind his head, and I wondered whether that was his way of offering me his cock. There was a slight bulge in his jeans, but I didn't think it big enough to denote an erection. Had the sight of my knickers aroused him? Was he picturing my swollen pussy lips, my tight sex crack? Another train rumbled through the cutting, and he started talking about the tunnel again. I was going to have to make the first move.

Reaching out, I tentatively squeezed the crotch of his jeans. His only reaction was to close his eyes, and

I knew that that was the cue for me to go ahead. He was young and shy and probably naive, but I had experience. I was in control. Fumbling with his jeans, I felt stupid as his zip stuck. This was all I needed, I thought angrily. This was to be my first cock, and I couldn't undo his zip. Releasing the metal button of his jeans, I finally managed to pull his zip down. I was almost there, my prize veiled only by his boxer shorts.

I tugged his shorts down and grabbed his penis, feeling its softness and warmth. My first cock, I reflected happily, as his shaft began to inflate in my hand. Cupping his balls in the palm of my free hand, I watched them roll. The black curls covering his scrotum moved as his balls stirred and heaved. I felt his balls, kneaded them gently, stroked them through the thin sac of his scrotum. His penis was beautiful. Long, hard, thick . . . Did he wank? Desperate for his sperm, I gripped his erect shaft. I'd watched Derek wank and bring out his spunk, so I knew exactly what to do. I was gaining experience, learning fast.

Slipping my fingertip through the small hole in his foreskin, I probed his moist knob. He gasped and arched his back, and I knew that he was enjoying my intimate attention. Although I was desperate for his fresh spunk, before I wanked him I wanted to examine his cock. Pulling his foreskin back, I eyed his knob slit and imagined his creamy spunk jetting. My mouth watered as I gazed at the silky-smooth surface of his glistening sex globe, studied his slit, the rim of his knob, the tight piece of skin joined to his foreskin. His shaft twitched and swelled as I ran my fingertip over his purple cock-head, and I knew that he wanted me to bring out his spunk.

Moving my hand up and down the hard shaft of his penis, I grinned as he gasped and trembled. I couldn't stop thinking that this was my first cock, my first wank. This was a new and exciting experience, and I knew that I'd become hooked on wanking boys. How many boys would I bring to my secret spot in the woods? How many cocks would I wank? I was sure to get a bad name for myself, a reputation at college, but I didn't care. My hormones had been released, my libido fired. And the monster would never sleep again.

Wanking David slowly, moving his foreskin back and forth over the globe of his knob, I didn't want his spunk to shoot too soon. I was enjoying myself, and didn't want my pleasure to end. Watching his knob slit appear and disappear, I recalled the days before Derek had triggered my libido. I'd enjoyed listening to music, watching television and doing my home-work. Things had changed dramatically. Rather than homework, I had boys on my mind. Diana hadn't been to my house for over a week. She was my best friend, and I'd neglected her. But I'd discovered a new and stimulating way of spending my spare time.

I knew that Diana wouldn't understand if I told her about Derek. Allowing a man as old as my father to finger my pussy and suck my clitoris ... she'd think me a slut. Maybe I was a slut, I reflected, as David's young body became rigid. Slut. I didn't like the word. In my mind, it conjured up a common, scruffy girl. I wasn't common or scruffy. So, what was I? A tart? A slag? I needed to talk to someone about my exploits in the woods. I needed someone's opin-ion, and I decided to phone Diana. She wouldn't understand, but I needed to talk to her.

'Don't come yet,' I breathed as David gasped and shook uncontrollably. Releasing his cock, I tickled his rolling balls with my fingernails. 'You're a naughty boy,' I said, delighting in my new-found game. 'You mustn't come until I say so.'

49

Leaning over, I kissed the hairy sac of his scrotum and breathed in his male scent. My arousal reaching frightening heights, I felt my clitoris swell as I licked his balls. Desperate for his intimate touch, I was sure that he'd attend my feminine needs once I'd wanked him. Derek had fingered my vagina and sucked and licked my clitoris, but I'd not been able to come. I hadn't felt at ease with Derek. But I was perfectly relaxed with David and I knew that I'd reach an orgasm quickly.

Savouring the heady taste of his scrotum, again breathing in his scent, I moved up and licked the solid shaft of his young cock. I'd heard the girls at college talking about sucking cocks and swallowing spunk, but I'd never been interested in their sex talk. I'd thought their giggled stories about boys' cocks were stupid, until now. Things had changed, the monster had surfaced from the depths of my mind. This was an opportunity not to be missed, I thought, as I eyed the purple globe of David's swollen knob. I'd had a chance to wank Derek's cock, and had let it slip by. If I didn't suck David's knob, I'd lie in bed that night riddled with regret.

Retracting his foreskin fully, I parted my red lips and sucked his ripe plum into my thirsty mouth. The taste was amazing, salty and sexy, and I knew that this was the first of many knobs I'd suck. The monster had gripped me, and I was hooked on cock sucking. Wondering what spunk tasted like, I kneaded his heaving balls and wanked his shaft. Should I swallow his male cream? Would it do me any harm? In my naivety, my inexperience, I wasn't sure whether I should drink his spunk.

David gasped and writhed as I snaked my tongue over the silky-smooth surface of his knob. Propping himself up on his elbows, he stared in disbelief as I took his ripe plum to the back of my throat and sank my teeth gently into his veined shaft. Locking my eyes his as I sucked and gobbled, I knew that he was about to come and fill my mouth with his spunk. Had he been with a girl? I again wondered. Had he come in a girl's mouth? Sure that we were both enjoying our first time together, I wanked his shaft faster and sucked on his knob as he began panting for breath.

His spunk jetted from his throbbing knob and bathed my tongue. I closed my eyes and savoured the aphrodisiacal taste of his male seed. I'd done it, I thought happily, as his cock twitched with its sperm pumping. I'd wanked a cock, sucked a knob, taken spunk into my mouth. But my cheeks were filling, because I still hadn't swallowed. I had to decide quickly, I knew, as my mouth began to overflow. His cream was running down his shaft, bathing my hand as I wanked him. I was wasting spunk.

Gulping down his sperm, repeatedly swallowing hard, I drank from his fountainhead as he let out low moans of pleasure. This was what Derek had wanted me to do, I reflected guiltily. My dad's promotion, a television and stereo system ... Derek had done a hell of a lot for me, and I'd given him next to nothing in return. Sucking out the last of David's creamy spunk, I wondered what he'd give me in return for the pleasure of my mouth. I doubted that he had enough money to buy me presents, but I wanted something in exchange for sucking his cock and drinking his spunk. But this was our first time, I reflected. I liked David, and I hoped to see him again. My body wasn't something to be sold.

'That was amazing,' he gasped as I slipped his deflating cock out of my sperm-flooded mouth. 'How many cocks have you sucked? Is this your secret cock-sucking place in the woods? How many boys have you brought here?'

Why all the questions? I wondered. 'Yes, this is my secret spot,' I replied. 'But I don't . . .'

'You're almost as good as Jenny Taylor. She's a brilliant cock-sucker.'

My stomach churning, I couldn't believe what he'd said. I'd thought that we were boyfriend and girl-friend, I'd thought that we would be seeing each other again and . . . Jenny Taylor? She was older than me, and she was a slut. She was one of the girls who strutted around town in a miniskirt and flirted with boys. Had David fucked her? I wondered angrily as he zipped his jeans and climbed to his feet. Standing, I licked my sperm-glossed lips and decided to conceal my jealousy, my anger.

'You're not as big as the other boys,' I sighed. 'But I suppose a small cock is better than no cock.'

'Not as big?' he said with a chuckle. 'I'm bigger than most. Anyway, when do you want to meet me again? We could come here after college and . . .'

'I don't think I want to meet you again, David. I was wrong about you.'

'What do you mean?'

'It's not just your cock. I thought that we . . . Never mind.'

'OK,' he said, walking away. 'There are plenty of other girls.'

That's exactly what Derek had said, I reflected as David left the clearing. *There are plenty of other girls.* Maybe they were both right and most girls would go to the woods and strip naked and suck and fuck and . . . Diana wouldn't strip naked in the woods and allow men to finger her vagina and suck her clitoris. Confused, I didn't know what to think. Was I a slut? Or was I a normal teenage girl? Did men want to look up my short skirt and gaze at my knickers? Or was it all in my mind?

The taste of sperm lingering on my tongue, my knickers soaking up my juices of desire, I felt neglected. David had enjoyed his orgasm, and then deserted me. Derek would have loved me, I reflected. He would have pushed his fingers deep into my pussy and sucked my clitoris to orgasm. Why hadn't David wanted my young body? I again wondered. Perhaps I shouldn't have said that his cock was small. Perhaps I should have been nice to him.

Tugging my T-shirt over my head, I dropped it to the ground and gazed at the erect teats of my firm breasts. My arousal was running high. I felt wicked, sexy, naughty. I also felt very angry as I cupped my breasts in my hands and squeezed them. My nipples protruding from the dark discs of my areolae, I again wondered why David hadn't wanted me. What was wrong with my breasts? Were they too small? I'd not worn a bra in the hope that David would feel my tits through my T-shirt. Hadn't he noticed my nipples outlined by the tight material?

Hearing a train, I leant on the fence and looked down the embankment. I was half hoping that the passengers would see me, gaze at my young breasts, but the train disappeared into the tunnel. As I leant further over the fence to watch a rabbit, the rough wooden rail bit into my sensitive nipples. I stepped back, grimacing as I massaged my breasts. My teats were marked, but the pain wasn't unpleasant. David should have massaged my firm mounds, sucked my nipples and . . . He'd obviously thought my breasts too small to bother with.

Moving away from the fence, I walked over to a bush and pressed my tits against the rough leaves. The sensations were heavenly, a mixture of mild pain and pleasure. Taking a step forward, the leaves and branches biting into the firm mounds of my breasts,

I let out a rush of breath. A mixture of anger and arousal firing me, I felt that I was punishing my young body. David hadn't wanted my body, he'd ignored my breasts, so I had to punish them.

Rocking from side to side, the leaves and branches scraping my breasts, I began to wonder what was wrong with me. This wasn't normal, I knew, as my nipples became inflamed and puffed up. I had no idea what had got into me, why I was doing this to my young body. But I couldn't help myself, I couldn't stop. My clitoris swelling, my pussy milk flowing into the tight crotch of my knickers, I was desperate for an orgasm. But I couldn't understand my state of mind, why I was behaving like this. I wanted to feel the rough leaves against my pussy lips, scraping against my . . .

Hearing voices somewhere in the woods, I grabbed my T-shirt and tugged it over my head to conceal my weal-lined breasts. Had I not been disturbed, I don't know how far I would have gone. Would I have slipped all my clothes off and allowed the leaves to scratch my naked body? Feeling guilty, confused, I brushed my long blonde hair back with my fingers and waited until the voices faded before leaving the clearing and returning to the park.

Sitting on the bench by the pond, my breasts stinging like hell, I reckoned that I was going crazy. To treat my young body like that, to deliberately scratch the smooth skin of my unblemished breasts . . . Did I need help? Did I need to see a psychiatrist? As I gazed at the ducks, I realised that I was desperate for the relief of orgasm. Sucking David's cock and drinking his spunk, stimulating my breasts with the rough leaves . . . my arousal was reaching frightening heights and I needed to come.

Wondering whether to go back into the woods and appease my yearning clitoris, I slipped my hand between my thighs and felt the wetness of my knickers. My sex milk was flowing, my outer lips were sensitive and puffy, my clitoris was painfully solid . . . Watching a group of kids run into the woods, I was about to go home and masturbate in the privacy of my room when I noticed a man approaching. Realising that it was my next-door neighbour, I hoped that he'd pass by without recognising me. I lowered my head and stared at the ground, but he called out.

'Hi, Annette,' he said, beaming as he neared the bench.

'Hi, John,' I breathed, forcing a smile.

'You waiting for someone?' he asked me, standing before me.

'No, no. I was about to go home.'

He frowned and moved closer. 'You've got scratches all over your neck. Are you OK?'

'Yes, I . . . I fell over in the woods.'

'You look like you've been dragged backwards through the bushes,' he quipped. 'Are you sure you're all right?'

'Yes, I'm fine. I tripped and fell head first into a bush.'

'I used to play in the woods when I was a kid,' he began. 'I used to climb the trees and . . .'

As he rambled on about his childhood, my arousal got the better of me and I parted my thighs. He looked down, his words tailing off and his eyes widening as he focused on the tight crotch of my wet knickers. He was in his forties, and I knew that I was playing a dangerous game. Flashing my knickers to my next-door neighbour was not a good idea. But it was as if I had no control over my actions. My libido was driving me on, and I imagined the middle-aged man slipping his fingers into my knickers and rubbing my hard clitoris to orgasm.

'You're a pretty little thing,' he said, his gaze locked on the tight material bulging with my sex lips. 'You've turned out to be a very attractive young lady.'

'Thanks,' I murmured. My flashing was working. 'You're very kind.'

'As you probably know, I'm moving to a new house next week.'

'Yes, mum told me that you were moving.'

'It's a shame we didn't get to know each other a little better.'

'What do you mean?' I asked him, cocking my head to one side.

'We've never got to know each other properly, have we? Had I realised that you'd grown into a beautiful young lady –'

'What would you have done?' I cut in, the thrill of the game sending quivers through my womb. 'If you'd realised earlier, what would you have done?'

'What would I have done? Or what would I have liked to have done?'

I looked up and frowned. 'I don't understand,' I lied.

'I would have got to know you, brought you little presents. I would have invited you round to my place. As you know, I live alone and . . .'

'I wish I'd known,' I sighed. 'I would have liked that. You're moving away, so it's too late now.'

'I'm not moving until next week. We have a little time to get to know each other.'

'What sort of presents?' I asked him, parting my legs further.

'Well . . . what sort of presents would you like?'

'I need a new computer.'

He laughed and shook his head. 'I meant little presents,' he said.

'But that is a little present.'

'Yes, well . . . I was thinking more along the lines of flowers or . . .'

'We have flowers in our garden.'

'Or chocolates.'

'Oh, I see,' I sighed, closing my thighs.

'I wasn't thinking of buying your friendship, Annette.'

'No, I suppose not.'

Leaving the bench, I walked towards the woods. I knew that he'd follow me, and I was right. He'd seen my knickers, and he was obviously hoping to see a lot more of me. The game had started, and I felt my wetness seeping into my knickers as my excitement heightened. He talked about the pine trees and said how nice it was to be walking through the woods with such a beautiful young girl. My stomach somersaulting, my clitoris calling for attention, I felt powerful. I had what he wanted and, unlike David, he was taking an interest in me. Reaching the fence, I turned and smiled at him.

'I often come here,' I said. 'I like watching the trains.'

'It's a nice spot. Do you come here alone?'

'Yes, I do.'

He brushed his dark hair away from his lined forehead and locked his eyes with mine. 'I'm in my forties, Annette,' he began. 'I'm a hell of a lot older than you, but . . . I find you incredibly attractive.'

'Thanks,' I breathed, sitting on the soft grass and resting my chin on my knees.

He gazed at the bulge of my knickers between my thighs and smiled. 'You say you want a new computer?'

'Yes, my old one has gone wrong.'

'Can't your parents buy you one?'

'Maybe. It's just that you mentioned presents, and I thought . . .'

'They're very expensive, Annette. I'm moving house and I've had to pay out a hell of a lot of money recently.'

'You don't have to buy me a present.'

'If I did buy you one . . . What I'm trying to say is . . . would you let me get to know you properly?'

'Yes, of course.'

'I mean, properly.'

'I know what you mean.'

'Do you?'

'Yes, I do. You buy me a new computer, and I'll meet you here this evening. Bring it round to my house this afternoon, OK?'

'If I do . . . I don't want to spend all that money just to find that you don't turn up.'

'I'll be here,' I assured him.

'We are talking about the same thing, aren't we? I mean, we're not going to meet here this evening to watch the trains or have a chat. And, if I do spend all that money, we will meet here more than once.'

'We can meet here several times, if you want.'

'OK.' He rubbed his chin and stood before me. 'Prove to me that you're serious,' he said, towering above me. 'Prove to me that you're serious, and I'll buy you a new computer.'

Parting my knees, I pulled my wet knickers to one side and exposed the swollen lips of my pussy. He looked flustered, agitated and nervous, as he brushed his hair back. Dragging his eyes away from my milky-wet sex crack, he looked around the clearing as if making sure that we were alone. I knew that I'd have to go all the way with him that evening. There was no way he was going to buy me a new computer in return for fingering my tight vagina. He'd want all

58

that my young body had to offer. Was that what I wanted? Did I want sex in return for a new computer?

'It's a deal,' he breathed as I covered my pussy lips with my knickers and stood up. 'I'll go into town and get you a computer.'

'OK,' I said, tossing my long blonde hair over my shoulder. 'Bring it to my house this afternoon, and I'll meet you here at seven o'clock this evening.'

'Your parents . . .,' he began. 'How will we explain about the computer?'

'Leave that to me,' I replied, wondering what on earth I was going to say to my mum.

'I'm not sure about this,' he mumbled.

'Why not?'

'Because . . . to be honest, I don't trust you. OK, you've shown me what you have to offer. But how do I know that you'll give it to me? Do you do this sort of thing with other men?'

'No, I don't,' I snapped. 'I'm not too sure about this, either. I think we'd better forget it.'

'Hang on, hang on. I wasn't turning down your offer. I'm a little worried, that's all. I mean, you're the girl next door. I know your parents and –'

'You're right,' I cut in. 'I think it's too risky.'

'Tell me one thing, Annette. Have you done this with other men? I mean, taking expensive presents in return for sex.'

'No, never,' I lied. 'I desperately need a new computer and . . . I've always liked you, John. I've never had a boyfriend and I was hoping that we could get to know each other.'

'It seems that we both want to get to know each other properly,' he breathed softly.

Squeezing my breast through my T-shirt, he leaned forward and pressed his lips to mine. I knew that I shouldn't be doing this, I knew that it was wrong. But

59

with my stomach somersaulting and my clitoris swelling, I lost myself in his passionate kiss as he slipped his tongue into my mouth. I thought that I was dreaming as he ran his hands over the firm mounds of my breasts and tweaked my erect nipples. My knickers wet with my juices of desire, my clitoris demanding attention, I relaxed completely as he laid me on the ground. Again kissing my full lips, slipping his tongue into my mouth, he pulled my T-shirt up and kneaded my young breasts.

He said nothing about the scratches adorning the tight skin of my breasts. I doubted that he believed I'd fallen into a bush. Perhaps he thought it best not to ask me what had happened. Perhaps he thought that I went with several men, sold my body for crude sex. Sucking one sensitive nipple into his hot mouth, he pinched and pulled on the other. The sensations were amazing and I knew that, at long last, I was about to take another step along the path towards my inevitable deflowering. All thoughts of right and wrong faded as his hand slipped up my skirt and he pressed his fingertips into the soft swell of my wet knickers. Taking presents in return for sex, the fact that he was my next-door neighbour, his age ... nothing mattered as he eased his fingers beneath my knickers and massaged my swollen vaginal lips.

A train rumbling through the cutting, the sun sparkling though the leaves high above me, the birds singing ... I was in my sexual heaven. As he tugged my knickers down, I brought my knees up and allowed him to pull the garment off my feet. My legs again outstretched, spread wide, I arched my back as he slipped two fingers deep into my tight and very wet vagina.

Sucking hard on each nipple in turn, biting gently on my teats, he massaged the wet inner flesh of my convulsing sheath. I could feel my pussy milk flowing down between my naked buttocks as his thrusting fingers caressed the sensitive tip of my erect clitoris. My half-naked body trembling uncontrollably, I let out a gasp as my nipple left his mouth and he moved down to my navel. Licking, nibbling, kissing, he ran his wet tongue over my lower stomach and then down further to the waistband of my skirt.

Would he lick and suck my clitoris? I wondered dreamily as he pulled my skirt high up over my stomach and kissed the gentle rise of my mons. I'd felt Derek's tongue between my pussy lips, his hot mouth sucking on my clitoris. But I'd been too tense to allow my orgasm to come. Although John was in his forties, and he was my next-door neighbour, I felt relaxed enough to reach the pinnacle of my sexual pleasure.

His fingers sliding out of my tight sex sheath and parting my swollen labia to the extreme, he repeatedly ran his tongue over the intricate folds of my inner lips. My breathing fast and shallow, my petite breasts heaving, I closed my eyes and dug my fingernails into the soft grass as he sucked my solid clitoris into his wet mouth. I was almost there. I was about to enjoy my first orgasm induced by a partner. Teetering on the verge of my climax, I thought that my clitoris was about to explode when images of my mother loomed in my mind. She was watching me, shaking her head and mouthing something. Trying to let myself go and allow my pleasure to come, I clutched John's head and ground my flesh hard against his mouth.

'I'm coming,' I gasped as images of my mother melted and I gave my body to John. My mind blowing away on clouds of lust, my head lolling from side to side, I cried out as the explosion came and rocked my young body to the core. The birds fluttered from the trees as I again cried out in the grip of a beautiful orgasm. I knew that sex was my destiny. Flashing my knickers had brought me so much. A stereo system, a television, and now I was to be given a new computer. And I was also enjoying immense pleasure.

My orgasm heightening, waves of sexual ecstasy crashing through my young body, I shook uncontrollably as John forced several fingers deep into my contracting vagina and sucked hard on my pulsating clitoris. His free hand groped my petite breasts, pinching and pulling my erect nipples. I thought that I'd never come down from my sexual heaven as orgasmic milk gushed from my vagina.

John sustained my incredible pleasure until I began to drift down slowly from my orgasm. I didn't think of his pleasure or satisfaction as he slipped his fingers out of my milk-drenched vagina. In my dream-like state, it didn't occur to me that a middle-aged man's dream was to get his hands on a young girl's naked body. I'd discovered that flashing my knickers to men brought me attention and gifts, but I had no idea just how men craved what I had to offer.

Half-opening my eyes, I propped myself up on my elbows and was about to thank John when he pulled out his erect penis. Moving between my splayed legs, he was about to impale me on his solid cock. My heart racing, my stomach churning, I didn't know what to do as his purple plum neared the gaping valley of my pussy. I didn't want sex with a man as old as my father, I didn't want to lose my virginity to my next-door neighbour or . . .

'What's the matter?' he asked me as I moved back and closed my legs. 'Annette? What's wrong?'

'I . . . I don't know,' I stammered as I gazed in awe at the sheer size of his erect cock. 'I thought you were going to buy me a computer?'

'I will,' he returned. 'I'll buy one this afternoon.'

'OK, I'll ... I'll meet you here this evening,' I breathed anxiously.

'For God's sake, Annette. You can't stop me now. I want you now, I need you now.'

Parting my legs, he breathed heavily as he pressed his huge knob hard against the open entrance to my hot vagina. My mind swimming in turmoil, I didn't know what I wanted, as his knob slipped into the tight sheath of my pussy. He was going to buy me a computer, he'd given me pleasure, and now ... His solid shaft entered me, my hymen gave way, his knob journeyed along the tight tube of my vagina to my cervix and he let out a rush of breath as his huge balls pressed against my naked buttocks. I gazed at the illicit coupling, my outer lips stretched tautly around the root of his cock, and realised that I'd lost my virginity.

I'd always known that the day of my deflowering would inevitably come, but I'd thought that I'd be ready for it. I felt as though I'd been swept along, I'd had no control or say. As John withdrew his hard shaft and slowly drove into me again, I began to relax. This was what I'd wanted. I was sure he'd found his rhythm. I'd wanted to lose my virginity and gain sexual experience. But my mind was still torn, the battle between right and wrong was raging again. This was a middle-aged man, he was my next-door neighbour ...

'All right?' he asked, his smiling face above me as he rocked back and forth.

'Yes,' I murmured. 'I ... I think so.'

'Like it?'

'Yes.'

I closed my eyes and let myself go as he increased his shafting rhythm. I was no longer a virgin, I

63

thought happily. The monster had risen and led me down the path to my deflowering. I was being fucked. Listening to the squelching sound of my vaginal milk, I felt my outer sex lips rolling back and forth along his penis. The sensations were heavenly and I discovered that if I swivelled my hips, John's rock-hard shaft massaged the sensitive nub of my clitoris. I was going to come, I knew, as my young body rocked with my pioneering fucking.

John gasped, his cock swelling within my tight vaginal sheath as his sperm filled me. I could feel his cream bubbling inside me as he tossed his head back and let out a low moan of pleasure. My clitoris exploding in orgasm, I instinctively lifted my feet off the ground and wrapped my legs around his back. Penetrating deeper, he fucked me harder as his spunk gushed and overflowed from my convulsing vagina. I could feel his orgasmic liquid running down between my buttocks, bathing my anus, as my climax peaked. I was being fucked, I again thought happily. I was being fucked for the first time. I was a woman at last.

'God, you're tight,' he gasped as he finally slowed his shafting rhythm. 'You're an angel.'

'Don't stop,' I breathed in my sexual delirium as my orgasm again rocked my young body. 'Please, don't stop fucking me.'

'I'll never stop fucking you, Annette. You're beautiful, and I'll never stop fucking your beautiful cunt.'

The words that had once seemed so crude were now words of beauty. Fuck, fucking my cunt . . . My life had changed, I mused, as my climax began to wane and John's sperm-flow stemmed. I'd been fucked, and I'd discovered womanhood. Resting my legs on the ground as John slipped his deflating penis out of my sperm-flooded vagina, I lay twitching and convulsing beneath the trees in the aftermath of our fucking. What would the evening bring? I wondered as he zipped his trousers. Another fucking?

'I'll see you later,' he said, clambering to his feet.

'Yes, later,' I murmured, stretching my arms out and relaxing on the soft grass. 'Come round to my house this afternoon. I'll meet you here this evening and . . .'

Sitting up as John slipped away, I wondered why he'd not stayed a while longer. He'd scurried off into the bushes like a frightened rabbit and left me alone with my thoughts. Looking down at the creamy spunk dribbling from my sex slit, I wondered what I'd done. I'd lost my virginity to a middle-aged man, to the man who lived next-door, a man as old as my father . . . It was no good looking back. What was done was done.

I got dressed, left the woods and sat on the bench by the pond and gazed at the ducks. They were oblivious to the events in the woods. Nothing had changed for them. They swam and quacked and . . . Everything had changed for me. My virginity stripped, sperm oozing into the crotch of my knickers, everything had changed. Would my mum guess what had happened? Would she realise that her little girl had been fucked? If she found out that the man from next-door had fucked her daughter . . . She'd never discover the truth, I was sure of that.

Meeting Annette, I showed her the chapter on her deflowering. We'd worked together on the chapter, so I was confident that she'd give it her approval. She read it twice, and then slipped the sheets of A4 back into the envelope. My confidence waned as she frowned and shook her head negatively.

'What do you think?' I finally asked her.

'It's OK,' she replied.

65

'Only OK?'

'No, no, it's perfect. I was just thinking about meeting David in the park. Had he shown more interest in me ... who knows where I'd have been now?'

'Your feelings for David haven't come across, have they? Should we add how you felt about him?'

'I had no feelings for David,' she returned firmly. 'He used me and I used him.'

'But, when you scratched yourself in the bushes ...'

'You think that was a form of self-harming because David didn't want me?'

'You said that you felt that you were punishing your young body because David didn't want you.'

'It wasn't David, it was ... I'd been turned down, rejected, and I couldn't understand why. It could have been anyone, it wasn't just David. I'd been neglected, my feminine needs ignored. After the pleasure I'd given him, I'd thought that he'd bring me pleasure. When he said that I was almost as good as Jenny Taylor ... that was the turning point. It was then that I realised that men wanted what I had, but they didn't want me. Then, John, my neighbour, turned up.'

'Did you go with John because you were on the rebound from David?'

'I wasn't on the rebound. Oh, I don't know. Maybe I was. But it wasn't love or anything like that. I suppose I went with David to keep my mum happy. The thing is that I was learning about men and what they wanted from me. In the woods with John ... that was my first orgasm with a man. I'd not planned to go all the way with him. At that stage, I'd not planned to get fucked by anyone. It was just a game to me and, when he mentioned buying me presents, I played the game by asking him for a computer.'

'Do you think that, behind the game and the television, the stereo and computer, you were looking for love?'

'I didn't know what love was. In fact, I still don't. I was looking for several things. Sexual gratification, someone to take an interest in me and buy me things . . . Showing my knickers to men had given me power, but I had no idea how to use that power. I was like an unguided missile, going off in all directions. John came along and made me feel wanted. He made love to me and . . . it was amazing.'

'So, you wanted to meet John again?'

'Yes, very much. The trouble was that my mother became suspicious. Later that day, I was at home and . . .'

Mother Knows Best

I was in my bedroom when my mother opened the front door to John and invited him in. I could hear them talking in the hall, and I felt my stomach churn as John mentioned a computer. I'd not planned what I was going to say to my mother, how I was going to explain why John had bought me a new computer. I should have planned something, but I'd not been able to dream up a convincing lie. Creeping on to the landing, I bit my lip and twisted my long blonde hair nervously around my fingers as I listened to their conversation. If John said the wrong thing, if he mentioned the park or . . .

'It's a long story,' John said. 'My parents got me a new computer only a week after I'd already bought one. I'd told them that I'd bought one but they're getting old and had forgotten. So I now have two new computers.'

'Well, if you're sure you want to give it to Annette . . .' my mother began.

'Of course I'm sure. I don't want to ask my parents for the receipt so that I can take it back to the shop. They like to think that they've helped me out and I don't want to spoil it for them. Apart from that, I'm moving house and I really don't have the time.'

'That's very nice of you, John. I'll call Annette and she can thank you.'

'No, don't worry. I'll see her later or whenever. Well, I'd better go and get on with the packing. I've a hell of a lot to do.'

'Thanks very much, Annette will be delighted.'

'It's my pleasure,' John said as he left.

Closing the front door, my mother looked up as I bounded down the stairs. 'You're doing well, young lady,' she said. 'John's given you a brand-new computer.'

'Wow,' I gasped, trying to show surprise as I gazed at the box on the hall floor. 'That's fantastic.'

'A stereo, a TV, and now a computer . . . you're doing very well. It might be an idea to do something for John in return.'

'Do something for him?' I breathed. 'What do you mean?'

'Well, you could help him with his packing. He's moving soon and –'

'Yes, I . . . I might do that,' I cut in, wondering whether it would be a good idea to go to his house.

'You could go round this evening and offer to help him.'

'I'm going to the park this evening.'

'Again?'

'Yes, I like it there.'

'Annette, I know I've asked you this before . . . Do you meet someone there?'

'No, of course not.'

'Why do you say, of course not? There'd be nothing wrong with meeting a friend or . . .'

'I like to sit alone by the pond or walk through the woods.'

'If you walk through the woods, why don't you wear your jeans? I mean, a short skirt is hardly suitable for walking in the woods.'

'I've told you before, mum. It's summer, it's too hot to wear jeans.'

She looked down at my short denim skirt and frowned. 'Annette, I want you to tell me the truth,' she said concernedly.

'The truth? About what?'

'Derek gave you a new stereo system and then he turned up with a new television. Now, John's come round and given you a brand-new computer.'

'So? What are you getting at?'

'They're both middle-aged men, Annette. And they're both single.'

'I don't see what that has to do with . . .'

'Have either of them made a pass at you?'

'No, of course not.'

'You're young and very attractive, Annette. As I said the other day, middle-aged men . . . Some middle-aged men like young girls, teenage girls. All I'm saying is . . .'

'I know what you're saying, mum.'

'Do you?'

'Yes, I do. For God's sake, I'm not interested in old men. Anyway, why suggest that I go round to John's house if you think that he's going to . . .'

'I don't know,' she sighed. 'Perhaps it would be best if you didn't offer to help him. I'm not saying that he'd make a pass at you if you went round, but . . . to be honest, I don't know what I'm saying.'

'There's nothing to worry about, mum. If it makes you feel better, there's a boy at college I like. He's very nice and I might go out with him.'

'Oh, that's good. What's his name? When will you bring him here?'

'His name's David and I haven't even been out with him yet. If we get on OK, I'll bring him here to meet you.'

'All right. Look, I'm sorry if I seemed . . .'

'It's OK, mum. Don't worry.'

'By the way, Derek will be round later. He wants to discuss something with your dad.'

'I won't be here, I'm going to the park.'

'I just thought I'd mention it.'

Walking to the park that evening, I instinctively felt that something was going to go wrong. Why had mum said that Derek would be round? I mused as I crossed the deserted park and sat on the bench by the pond. I was sure that I'd allayed her suspicions, but why say that Derek wanted to discuss something with my dad? He was always discussing things with my dad, and mum had never mentioned it before. My anxiety rising, I imagined Derek telling my parents about me. If he said that I'd been in the woods and had stripped naked . . . No, he wouldn't do that. He'd have nothing to gain and everything to lose by getting me into trouble.

As a man walking a dog approached me, I parted my thighs and displayed the tight crotch of my white knickers. This was becoming a regular thing, I mused, looking away as he slowed his pace and gazed between my thighs. I could see him staring at me out of the corner of my eye, and I felt my womb contract with excitement. He was in his fifties, and I knew what he was thinking. Was the sight of my bulging knickers making his cock stiff? He was no doubt picturing my pussy lips, my tight crack, and I felt a wave of arousal roll through me as I imagined him fingering my hot vagina.

I was meeting John, and I didn't have the time to lead the man into the woods and . . . God, I thought, wondering whether I would have taken him to my secret spot by the fence if I'd had the time. Would I have stripped naked for him? Would I have allowed him to kiss and lick my tight pussy crack? What the hell was I becoming?

71

He finally walked away and I realised that I was going to have to be careful. Derek was my dad's boss, John was my next-door neighbour, and I felt safe enough with them. But to go into the woods with a complete stranger would be crazy. I was becoming obsessed with showing my knickers and I knew that there was no way that I could stop doing it. I also knew that I was going to have to wear my jeans now and then to keep mum happy. I'd hide my skirt in the woods, I decided. That way, I could leave the house wearing my jeans and then change.

I'd never been devious, I reflected. I'd never lied to my mother or done anything behind her back, until now. If she discovered that I'd been fucked by a middle-aged man ... My vaginal muscles tightened as I recalled John's hard cock entering me. Mum would never find out, I thought, as my clitoris swelled and my pussy milk flowed into my knickers. But I'd have to be very careful, and devious. My only real mistake had been to accept presents from Derek and John. But I'd wanted something in return for allowing them the pleasure of my young body. My thinking had changed since the day I'd opened my legs in the lounge to Derek and mum had lectured me. My body was now a commodity.

'Hi, gorgeous,' John called as he approached me from behind.

'Oh, hi,' I said, leaping up from the bench. 'Thanks for the computer.'

'My pleasure. Or it will be,' he quipped. 'Was your mum OK about it?'

'Yes, yes, she was fine,' I lied.

'That's good. I've been as hard as rock thinking about you. I wish I wasn't moving house now.'

'Are you going far away?'

'It's about forty miles. I could come and visit you now and then. If we keep in touch by email, we could arrange to meet in the park.'

'Yes, I'd like that,' I replied. Walking into the woods, I knew that John was hooked on me. 'Maybe we could meet at the weekends,' I proffered.

'That shouldn't be a problem.'

'You could bring me presents.'

'Lift your skirt up at the back,' he said, following me along the narrow path. 'I love looking at your tight knickers.'

Hoisting my skirt up, I reckoned that I could do well out of John. 'I need some money,' I sighed. 'I owe my friend twenty pounds and I've seen a pair of leather boots that I like. If you give me money every time we meet here –'

'I've just spent three hundred on you,' he cut in.

Turning as I reached the fence, I smiled. 'I'm worth it, aren't I?' I asked him impishly.

'Yes, but I don't have a never-ending supply of cash. If you're a good girl then, in a few months, I'll buy you something else.'

'A few months?' I echoed despondently. 'That's a long time.'

'Annette, I can't keep spending money on you.' He looked me up and down and shook his head. 'When we first got together, I didn't realise that you were on the game. I didn't realise that you were selling your body for sex.'

'I'm not,' I returned indignantly. 'I'm not on the game. I just like presents.'

'You could have fooled me.'

'If you don't like me . . .'

'I like you very much, Annette. It's just that you keep on about presents and money. You even suggested that I give you money every time we meet. I've had girlfriends in the past, and not one of them has wanted expensive gifts in return for sex.'

'I'm sorry, I didn't mean . . .'

73

'You remind me of Hayley Mills in those old films. Blonde hair, full, pouting lips . . .'

'That's what someone else said,' I interrupted him.

'You're a pretty little thing, Annette. You could earn yourself a lot of money from your body, if you wanted to.'

'All I meant was, I like being given presents. I mentioned the leather boots because . . .'

'If you want presents and money, then you'll have to be really dirty for me.'

'Dirty? What do you mean?'

'Do you play with yourself? Do you masturbate?'

'No, I . . .'

'Come on, Annette. Be honest with me or you won't get any presents.'

'Yes, I do,' I confessed sheepishly.

'OK, show me how you masturbate. Lie on the ground with your knickers off and masturbate for me.'

Following his instructions, I slipped my wet knickers off and lay on the ground with my skirt up over my stomach and my legs wide apart. Slipping my fingertip between my puffy sex lips and rubbing my clitoris as he knelt beside me, I pondered on his words. *I didn't realise that you were selling your body for sex.* I knew that he was right, I was selling my body for sex. But I'd never looked at it that way. To me, the whole thing was a game. Showing my knickers to men, taking presents . . . it had been an exciting game. I knew that I wouldn't be able to orgasm as I massaged my clitoris faster. The situation wasn't right, I didn't feel good about myself.

'Do you use candles?' John asked me, lifting my T-shirt up and exposing the small mounds of my firm breasts. 'Do you fuck your little cunt with a candle?'

'No,' I breathed.

'Have you ever fingered your arse?'

'No. John, I don't think . . .'

'I'm going to teach you about sex,' he said, squeezing my young breasts. 'I'm going to teach you how to be really dirty.'

He'd changed, I mused dolefully, as he leaned over and sucked my nipple into his hot mouth. I'd thought that we'd have a loving relationship and find warmth and satisfaction together. Had I really thought that? I pondered as he sucked on my other nipple. Had I wanted love, or was I deluding myself? Taking gifts in return for offering my young body to men, I knew that I'd never find anything more than cold sex. John didn't want me as a person, I mused. All he wanted was my body.

'Your tits are really hard,' he breathed, slipping my nipple out of his mouth. 'Are you going to come for me?'

'I . . . I can't,' I murmured. 'I don't feel right.'

'What do you mean?'

'I don't know. I suppose I thought that we were going to kiss and . . . I thought that we were going to love each other. I don't know what I thought.'

'Finger your cunt and make it nice and wet for me,' he said, seemingly oblivious to my words. 'Push two fingers into your tight little cunt and get it well juiced-up for me.'

Easing two fingers into the tight sheath of my vagina, I knew that I was going to have to play the role of a slut if I wanted money from him. My friends went into town on Saturday mornings and flirted with boys of their own age. They wore miniskirts and skimpy tops and behaved like tarts. But they were normal teenage girls, I decided. They were learning, experimenting and having fun with teenage boys. What the hell was I doing? I wondered as John moved down and licked the small indent of my navel. I'd been fucked by a middle-aged man. I wasn't playing the role of a slut, I was a slut.

Moaning softly through my nose as I pistoned my tight pussy with two fingers, I decided to stop worrying and try to enjoy myself. I had what men wanted, I reflected as my clitoris finally began to swell. If they gave me expensive presents and money in return for the pleasure of my young body, then there was nothing wrong with that. Why should I worry about it? None of the girls at college had been given a new television, a stereo and a computer for nothing. If I carried on like this, then I could get whatever I wanted.

My thinking was changing dramatically. Derek had only wanted my body, David had enjoyed pumping his spunk into my mouth and had then compared me with some other girl, and John was only interested in what I had between my legs. It was no wonder that my attitude towards my body was changing. It wasn't too late to turn back the clock. I could have easily stopped playing my sex games and behaved like a decent young lady. But I was in my teens and I didn't see how wrong it was of me to enjoy gifts and intimate attention from men.

'Roll over on to your front,' John ordered me. 'Keep your fingers in your cunt and roll over.'

'Why?' I asked him, rolling over on the soft grass.

'Because I'm going to teach you about real sex.'

Moving between my splayed thighs, he kissed the firm cheeks of my bottom as I continued to massage my inner flesh with my fingers. I quite liked the sensations as he ran his tongue up and down my bottom crease but, in my naivety, I thought it odd that he didn't want my pussy. Why my bum? I wondered as he parted my firm buttocks. The feel of his wet tongue running over my small brown hole driving me wild, I began to gasp and tremble. The crude act was incredibly arousing, but I wondered whether this was normal. His tongue entering my tight hole, I couldn't imagine my dad doing this to my mum. Was this normal?

I could feel his saliva running down to my pussy as I fingered myself. Quivering, breathing heavily, I closed my eyes as he slipped his wet tongue further into my bottom-hole. Did he like the taste? Had he done this to his other girlfriends? I wasn't his girlfriend, I reflected. As young and naive as I was, I knew that he was only using me for sex, using my body to satisfy his sexual needs. There was no love, no closeness, just cold, crude sex.

His tongue left my anal hole and I let out a shriek as he pushed his finger deep into the tight duct of my rectum. I could feel it deep inside me, bending, twisting, massaging the hot walls of my most private sheath. Was this normal? The sensations were heavenly, but I knew that this was wrong. My clitoris now painfully solid, desperate for the relief of orgasm, I couldn't deny the immense pleasure John was bringing me. Right, wrong . . . did it matter?

'You're a beautiful little slut,' John breathed, managing to force a second finger deep into my inflamed bottom-hole. 'Who's that slim dark girl I've seen going to your house?'

'Diana,' I gasped, grimacing as my anal ring stretched painfully around his fingers. 'She's . . . she's my friend.'

'Is she now? You'll have to bring her here to meet me. I'll bet she could do with a damned good fucking.'

'She's not like that,' I returned.

'She's not like you, you mean. She's not a dirty, filthy little slut.'

His crude words battering my mind, I wondered what Diana would think if she knew what I got up to in the woods. *She's not a dirty, filthy little slut ...* Diana was nothing like me, I reflected as I slipped my fingers out of my restricted vaginal sheath. She was a decent young lady, and I was a slut. But no one knew what I did with men in the woods. Diana hadn't been to my house for ages but, when she next came round, I wouldn't reveal my dirty little secret. We'd always told each other everything, confided in each other ... not any more.

My face pressed against the soft grass, I breathed in the scent of nature as John yanked his fingers out of my bottom-hole and moved about behind me. I'd always found peace and tranquillity in the woods, but now my secret clearing by the fence was a different place. Sex, fingering, licking and sucking, orgasms, fucking, spunk ... My hiding place in the clearing was now far removed from the tranquil spot I once knew. I was far removed from the innocent girl I once was.

John forced my legs further apart and stabbed at my tight vaginal hole with his solid knob. My second fucking, I thought, as my sex sheath yielded and allowed his huge cock shaft to penetrate me. How many times would John fuck me in the woods? How many other men would fuck me? My young body rocking back and forth on the soft grass as he began shafting my tight vagina, I gasped as he again drove two fingers into my tight rectum. It didn't matter how many men fucked me, I decided. If they gave me presents and money, and orgasms, it didn't matter.

I knew that I wasn't far away from my orgasm as John's cock swelled within my wet pussy. My solid clitoris massaged by his thrusting shaft, my erect nipples pressed hard against the ground, my entire body was alive with the beautiful sensations of illicit sex. I could never give up sex, I thought happily, as John increased his rhythm and began grunting with every thrust of his huge cock. My life had been boring before I'd discovered my body, my cunt. Reading magazines, watching television or listening to music . . . I'd now discovered life.

'You're a tight-cunted little whore,' John gasped. 'Beg me to fuck you.'

'Fuck me,' I murmured.

'Beg me, slut. Beg me to fuck you hard.'

'Please, fuck me hard,' I cried as my clitoris pulsated.

'I've a good mind to fuck your tight little arsehole once I've done your hot cunt.'

'No,' I breathed into the soft grass. 'No, please . . .'

'Tell me that you love being fucked.'

'Yes, yes, I . . . I love being fucked.'

'Tell me that you want my spunk up your young cunt.'

'I want your spunk up my cunt.'

'Young cunt,' he snapped. 'Say it.'

'I want your spunk up my young cunt.'

'That's just what you're going to get,' he said with a chuckle. 'You're a slut, aren't you?'

'No, I . . .'

'Aren't you?'

'Yes, I'm a slut,' I cried, lifting my head as I felt his spunk gushing into my tightening vagina. 'I'm a dirty, filthy little slut and I want you to fuck my cunt hard. I love your fingers up my arse and I love your hard cock fucking my girl cunt and . . .'

Resting my head on the ground again as he pumped out his spunk and breathed his crude words of sex, I imagined my mother witnessing my wicked behaviour. I was a dirty, filthy little slut, I knew, as I felt his creamy spunk running down my inner thighs. Prostitute. The word had never entered my head, until now. Whether I liked the dreadful word or not, I couldn't deny that I was a teenage prostitute.

My clitoris deflating as John fucked me, my orgasm didn't come. Harsh words battered my tormented mind as I listened to the squelching sounds of sperm. Prostitute, slut, whore, tart ... I'd been fucked twice in the woods by the middle-aged man from next-door. But I had a new computer, I tried to console myself. And a stereo system and a television and I was going to be given money and ... Did my virginity matter? I wondered as John slowed his rhythm. I'd lost my virginity to a man in his forties. Did it really matter? Half the girls at college had said that they weren't virgins. They'd been fucked and I'd been fucked, but I'd been given expensive presents. I was no fool, I thought, feeling better about myself.

'God, that was amazing,' John gasped, slipping his limp cock out of my sperm-flooded vagina. 'You really are a beautifully dirty little girl. Did you enjoy it?'

'Yes, very much,' I replied, rolling on to my back.

'Now you can clean me up,' he said, kneeling beside me. 'Go on, suck it clean,' he ordered, offering his sperm-dripping cock to my mouth.

Parting my full lips, I sucked his purple knob into my mouth and sucked hard. His sperm tasted salty, heavenly, and I found myself hoping that he'd come again and fill my mouth with his cream. This was real sex, I mused, recalling John's words. *I'm going to teach you how to be really dirty.* I loved him fucking me, I loved the taste of his cock, but I didn't like the way he'd talked about Diana as if she was just a lump of female meat to be used for his sexual gratification.

Taking his swollen knob to the back of my throat, I knew that I was nothing more than a slut to be used and abused by men. The truth hurt, I was a complete slut. But I was also an attractive and very polite young girl. I'd lead two separate lives, I decided, as John's cock fully stiffened and he began to tremble. The perfect daughter, the studious pupil ... and a dirty, filthy little slut. The notion excited me. I was sure that I could get away with it. Two separate lives, two separate identities.

'Swallow it, you dirty whore,' John gasped as his knob swelled and his sperm flooded my gobbling mouth. 'Suck my knob and swallow my spunk, slut.'

Drinking from his cock-head, I repeatedly swallowed his creamy offering as he towered above me, panting in the grip of his climax. He gasped his crude words as I wanked his solid shaft and brought out his spunk. *Mouth fuck, young whore, cum slut, dirty little slag, tight-cunted bitch* ... Running my tongue over the velveteen surface of his orgasming knob, I drank from his cock until his sperm-flow stemmed. His shaft deflating within my spunk-bubbling mouth, he finally staggered back and leaned against a tree.

'I'll do your arse when we meet again,' he breathed, zipping his trousers. 'You've got three tight holes, and I'll fuck them all.'

'Not my bottom,' I murmured, grabbing my knickers and standing up.

'If you want presents, you'll do as you're told.'

'John, I don't want ...'

'And I want you to shave your cunt.'

'What?'

'You heard me, Annette. Shave your cunt for me and I'll give you money. How much are the leather boots?'

'Fifty pounds.'

'Fifty it is. I'll meet you here tomorrow evening. Be here at six, OK?'

'OK,' I sighed as he left the clearing.

He'd not kissed me or loved me, I thought dolefully as I adjusted my clothing and brushed my long blonde hair away from my face with my fingers. He'd fucked my cunt, fucked my mouth, and then tossed me aside like a broken toy. Leaning on the fence, I watched a train snaking its way through the cutting. My knickers soaking up the sperm oozing from my inflamed vagina, I wondered where the passengers were going. Where was my life going? I mused. The people on the train knew where they were going, but I had no idea of my destiny. My bottom-hole was sore, the taste of spunk lingered on my tongue, my pussy was inflamed ... Turning, I looked at the ground, the spot where I'd been fucked. How many more men would fuck me there?

Leaving the park, I ambled home with a thousand thoughts swirling in the mist of my mind. Two separate lives? Was that possible? If I was careful, if I was devious, I knew that I could get away with it. John wouldn't say anything to my parents, and I knew that Derek would keep our dirty little secret. I just had to be very devious and cunning. The innocent young lady, and the common slut. *Shave your cunt* ...

'Annette,' my mother called as I closed the front door behind me. 'I'm up here, in your room.'

'What is it?' I asked, bounding up the stairs.

'Where have you been?'

'To the park,' I replied, sitting on my bed. 'I told you I was going to the park.'

'Who did you meet there?'

'I didn't meet anyone. We've been through this, mum. I sat by the pond and ...'

'I went next-door earlier. John was out.'

'So?'

'I saw him come back just now. He came back a few minutes before you did.'

'And?'

'Have you been with him?'

'For God's sake, mum. I was alone in the park. I walked through the woods, watched the trains . . .'

'Derek was here earlier.'

'I know. You told me that he was coming round.'

'He gave you a new stereo system, and then a new television.'

'Mum, we've talked about this before.'

'John gave you a new computer.'

'Yes, I know. You opened the door to him when he brought it round.'

'I want to know what's going on, Annette.'

'Nothing's going on,' I sighed.

'Derek came round earlier and . . .'

'Mum, you're repeating yourself. What's this all about?'

'You tell, me, Annette. You tell me.'

'I've told you everything. OK, ask me a question, and I'll answer it.'

'All right, I will. Why did Derek give you a new computer?'

'Mum, you really are confused. John gave me the computer, remember?'

'And Derek gave you one. He brought it round earlier.'

My stomach sinking, my heart racing, I stared open-mouthed at her as she waited for an explanation. Her face hot with anger, she folded her arms and cocked her head to one side. I had no idea what to say as she looked down at my short skirt, my naked thighs. I had to come across as totally innocent, I thought anxiously. I had to laugh it off, make a joke out if it.

'Well?' she said.

'What am I going to do with two computers?' I quipped with a giggle.

'It's not funny, Annette,' she snapped.

'I think it is. Two new computers? What did Derek say when he brought it round?'

'He said that he'd got it from work. Apparently, it was a spare one. I didn't want to call him a liar because he's your father's boss.'

'Why would he lie about it?'

'You tell me,' she said, unfolding her arms and sitting next to me on the bed.

'I don't understand,' I breathed, playing the innocent little girl. 'Why would he say that he'd got it from work, if he hadn't?'

'I think that he went out and bought it.'

'Why would he buy me a new computer? They cost hundreds of pounds.'

'Exactly, Annette. Why buy you a new computer? Did you ask him to buy it for you?'

'Of course not. I did mention that mine was getting old and I needed a new one. But that was ages ago. I didn't think that he'd go out and buy me one. He must have got it from work.'

'Don't you think that it's all rather odd? A stereo, a television, and now two brand-new computers ... what have you given in return?'

'You know that I don't have any money. How could I afford to ...'

'I wasn't talking about money, Annette.'

'Then how would I pay for the things?'

'In other ways,' she proffered, her eyes widening as she stared at me.

'What other ways? I have nothing that John or Derek would want.'

'You're either totally innocent and completely naive, or very clever.'

'Clever? Mum, I don't know what you're getting at. Why am I clever?'

'I hope I'm wrong about this. You must agree that it's extremely odd.'

'I'm extremely lucky, that's all I can say. There's no way people would spend hundreds of pounds on me. Derek won the stereo and TV in a competition. And you said that John's parents had given him the computer so . . .'

'I didn't tell you that, Annette. I didn't say where John had got it from.'

'You did, mum,' I said shakily. 'This afternoon, after John had brought it round, you said that his parents had given it to him.'

'I don't remember saying that, but I'll give you the benefit of the doubt. You seem innocent enough, and I'm inclined to believe you. But something's nagging me. Something about all this doesn't feel right. Why are your clothes filthy? You look as if you've been rolling around on the ground.'

'I tripped and fell over in the woods,' I lied. Reckoning that I'd won her over, I smiled. 'If you don't believe that I go to the woods alone, why not follow me one evening?'

'Don't be silly,' she said, returning my smile. Leaving the bed, she walked to the door. 'We'll leave it at that and say no more about it. However, if another new computer turns up –'

'Now you're being silly,' I cut in, forcing a giggle.

'Yes, I am. Do you have any homework?'

'Loads,' I sighed. 'I'll make a start on it now.'

'All right. I'll leave you in peace.'

As she closed the door and went downstairs, my shoulders sagged and I let out a sigh of relief. I'd been lucky to get away with my debauchery, I reflected. Maybe the time had come to put an end to my games

85

with men in the woods. Derek had obviously given me the computer with a view to fucking me, but I'd have to return the gift. If my mother did follow me to the park, if she saw John or Derek walking into the woods with me ... I dreaded to think what the outcome would be. Why had Derek not said that he was going to buy me a computer? I wondered as I grabbed a towel and went into the bathroom. It was my fault, I decided, slipping out of my clothes and stepping into the shower. I'd asked two men for a computer, and had ended up with two computers. I'd made a stupid mistake.

Washing the sperm from my pussy slit, my inner thighs, I didn't want to end my exciting games. I was enjoying my young body, the crude sex, but it had to stop. I'd have to sneak next-door and tell John that I wouldn't be meeting him again. And I'd tell Derek that I ... I'd give the computer back, and that would be the end of it.

It was at this point in Annette's story that I realised I needed more from her. She'd not contacted me for some time, and I was beginning to wonder whether she'd changed her mind about the book. I needed a lot more from her, but I didn't want to push her. When she phoned and asked me to meet her in a bar in Brighton, I feared the worst. I was sure she was going to tell me that she didn't want to go on.

'There you go,' she said, passing me a large envelope. 'That should keep you busy for a while.'

'Great,' I said with a sigh of relief. 'I thought you might have changed your mind about the book.'

'Don't be silly,' she returned with a giggle. 'I've not been in touch because I've been busy writing.' We took our drinks to a secluded corner table and sat down. 'So, where do we start?'

'You went to the park and flashed your knickers to a man walking a dog,' I prompted her.

'Yes. When I flashed my knickers at him, I felt really horny. It was like a tonic. Sitting with my legs apart and showing off my knickers sent my arousal through the roof.'

'You were more than ready for it when John arrived, then?'

'Yes, I was but . . . The way John spoke to me, the things he did . . . I should have known that he only wanted my body. After our first time in the woods when he'd made love to me, I'd expected to be loved again. Of course, he hadn't made love to me. He'd fucked me and he wanted to fuck me again, it was as simple as that. But, I was learning. All the time, I was learning about men.'

'And there were real problems when you got home.'

'The thing about the computers was a nightmare,' she began. 'I couldn't believe that Derek had brought a new computer round. How the hell could I explain why two middle-aged men had both given me computers? My mum was so suspicious. But, playing innocent, I got away with it.'

'So, again, you decided to stop playing your games?'

'I knew that I had no choice. I had to tell John that I wouldn't be seeing him again. And I had to end it with Derek. The following day . . .'

Leading Two Lives

I'd had bad dreams about my mum throwing me out of the house and I hadn't slept very well. Beneath my quilt, I'd rubbed my clitoris and fingered my tight pussy, but I'd been unable to come. My mind full of worry, I finally got up and dressed in my short skirt and a T-shirt. The sun was shining in a clear blue sky and I would have liked to walk in the woods. But I thought better of it.

During breakfast, mum was OK and dad talked about doing the garden. It seemed that the subject of middle-aged men giving me expensive gifts had been exhausted. Everything was back to normal, apart from my mind. Again thinking how lucky I was to have got away with my debauched acts in the woods, I said that I was going round to Diana's house. I needed time and space to think, to reflect.

'That's good,' my mother said. 'You've not spent any time with Diana recently. By the way, did you finish your homework last night?'

'Just about,' I lied. 'I'll probably go through it with Diana.'

'I'll set the computer up for you,' dad said. 'One of them, anyway.'

'Yes, thanks,' I breathed, leaving the room.

Was there an atmosphere? I wondered, closing the front door behind me. Perhaps it was my imagination, but I felt that they'd been talking about me. Turning as I reached the front gate, I noticed my mother at the lounge window. Was she spying on me? Checking up on me? Waving, I walked down the road in the direction of Diana's house and then turned back. I had to tell John that I wouldn't be at the park that evening. My parents were suspicious and our relationship was over. I'd miss the sex and the presents, I mused. But I'd made my decision and had to stick to it.

Hovering in the street, I was sure that my mother would still be looking out of the lounge window. I daren't risk going to John's house, I decided, as I again turned and walked away. Maybe later, on the way back from Diana's, I'd sneak round and talk to him. Riddled with anxiety, I felt my stomach churning as I imagined Derek demanding sex in return for the computer. I'd allowed things to get out of hand, I decided as I crossed the road and headed across the common. Had I taken money instead of presents, I'd have got away with it. I could have hidden the cash and . . . There was no point in looking back. What was done was done.

Unable to face Diana until I'd relaxed and composed myself, I sat on the grass beneath a tree and looked around the common. There were people walking dogs, a young couple pushing a pram. They looked happy, I thought dolefully. I should have been happy. Maybe things weren't so bad, I reflected, trying to cheer myself up. Derek would understand that I couldn't meet him again, and I was sure John would realise that I was in a difficult situation. Things would turn out all right. I had nothing to worry about.

Resting my chin on my knees as I noticed a man approaching, I reckoned that I could still play my knicker-flashing game. My stomach somersaulting, I knew that he'd see the bulging white material between my thighs as he came closer. This was only a game, I thought, as a pang of excitement coursed through my young body. I wouldn't go any further than showing my knickers to men. I wouldn't go into the woods or behind the bushes, and I certainly wouldn't sell my body for sex. I'd just enjoy the thrill and arousal of showing off my tight knickers. There was no harm in that, was there?

Moving my feet apart to make sure that the man had a good view, I looked down at the ground so that he'd think me innocent. I was aware of him standing close to me, but I didn't look up. My womb contracting, my clitoris swelling, I knew that I could never stop playing my exciting game. It was perfectly harmless, I told myself again, as I felt a wetness in my knickers. All I was doing was sitting on the common, relaxing and enjoying the warmth of the summer sun. Little Miss Innocent.

'Hello, Annette,' a male voice said.

I raised my head and looked at the man silhouetted by the sun. 'Oh ... er, hi,' I breathed shakily, bringing my feet together as I stared in horror at my teacher. 'I was just ...'

'It's a lovely day,' he said, sitting on the grass in front of me.

'Yes, yes, it is.'

'Are you meeting someone?'

'No, I was on my way to Diana's house. I thought I'd sit down for a while.'

'Ah, yes, Diana. She's doing very well at college. Her course work is excellent.'

'Yes, she's very clever.'

'So are you, Annette. Your course work was very good, until recently.' He looked awkward as he gazed at me. 'Is there anything worrying you?' he asked me.

'No, not at all. I thought my work was OK.'

'Yes, it's been very good. It's just that, for a while now, it seems as though you've been distracted. Are you sure everything's all right? No worries at home or anything?'

'Everything's fine,' I lied, wishing he'd go away and leave me in peace.

'I'm sorry. It's the weekend and I shouldn't be talking about your college work. So, you're off to see Diana?'

'Yes, I am. Well, I was. I don't think I'll bother now. I haven't done my homework so I suppose I'd better . . .'

'It's due in tomorrow morning.'

'Yes, I know,' I sighed, wishing I hadn't mentioned it.

'Are you having problems with the work?'

'No, it's just that the weekend goes so quickly. I was going to do it yesterday, and then I thought I'd do it today . . .'

'It's your last year, Annette. In fact, it's your last couple of weeks. As you know, your course work is part and parcel of your exam results. Do you need any help?'

'No, no, it's OK.'

'Actually, I'm glad I bumped into you. I'll be honest with you, Annette. I was going to ring your parents.'

'Why?'

'As I said, you've been distracted recently. You obviously have something on your mind, and I thought it might be an idea to ask your parents whether you were all right.'

'No, please don't ring them. Everything is fine, honestly.'

'All right, if you say so. A lot of girls of your age have boyfriend problems. Is that the case with you?'

'Yes,' I said, hoping that would appease him. 'It's OK now, though. It's all over, so I'm fine now.'

He looked down at my legs and smiled. 'Do you spend a lot of time outdoors?' he asked me, reaching out and stroking my shin. 'You have a lovely suntan.'

'Yes, I . . . I like the sun.'

'Blondes always look good with tanned skin. You're a very attractive girl, Annette.'

'Thanks.'

'Going back to your exams . . . I could help you out with your results.'

'How?'

'I'll be there when you sit the exams. If you get stuck, I could help you out.'

'That would be great,' I said, forcing a grin. As he stroked my cheek, I knew what was coming next.

'We could have a little arrangement,' he began. Looking around the common, he moved closer to me. 'We could work together, just you and me.'

'Work together?' I echoed.

'I'll explain in a minute,' he said as a young couple approached.

I knew exactly what he was getting at, but I could hardly believe it. He was in his fifties, and he was my teacher. Did all men want me? I wondered, feeling rather flattered. Did he want to have sex with me? I'd narrowly avoided trouble with my parents, and wasn't going to risk more problems. If I allowed my teacher to strip me naked in the woods and . . . I'd made my decision, I reflected, and I had to stick to it.

As he smiled at me, I knew that I was weakening. I really did need good exam results if I was going on to university but . . . I'd heard about relationships between teachers and pupils. I'd seen things on the television news. It wouldn't be dangerous for me, I thought as he eyed my naked legs. If there was any trouble, he'd be the culprit. I'd be the innocent virgin girl, wouldn't I? My mind was torn. If I played the exciting game, it could be extremely rewarding. But I knew that I'd be heading for trouble.

I'd never had so much attention before, I reflected, as he again stroked my cheek. Visitors to my house, teachers, men in the park ... No one had taken a great deal of interest in me. Until now. Parting my feet, exposing the white material between my thighs, I knew that I couldn't help myself. I was hooked on my games, addicted to showing my knickers to men. I wouldn't allow my teacher to fuck me, I decided. He'd be happy enough just looking at my pussy, stroking me and ...

'As I was saying,' he whispered once the young couple were out of earshot, 'we could work together.' Gazing longingly at my knickers, he looked up and winked at me. 'I've always liked you, Annette. You're not like the other girls. They're silly most of the time. You're a sensible girl, and ... I think that we could have an arrangement where we help each other out.'

'I don't know what you mean,' I said. I didn't want to make it too difficult for him, but I did want to appear innocent. 'How could I help you? I don't understand.'

'Your homework is due in tomorrow. What if I gave you more time? Say, until Friday?'

Yes, that would be great. But how can *I* help *you*?'

'I'll come to that in a minute. I don't want you telling the others about this, Annette. Our arrangement will be between us, OK?'

'Yes, of course.' Parting my feet further, I knew that he had a perfect view of my wet knickers. 'I won't say anything to anyone, I promise.'

'That's good. Look, I won't beat around the bush. I like you, Annette. And I'd like to see more of you.'

'You want to meet me here, on the common?' I asked naively.

'Yes, I do. We could meet here after college or in the evenings.'

'OK,' I said, smiling at him. 'I don't mind meeting you here. We can chat about –'

'I ... I wasn't thinking of chatting, Annette,' he interrupted with a chuckle. 'Give it some thought.'

'Yes, but ... what am I supposed to be thinking about? I said that I'd meet you here.'

'I think you know what I'm suggesting, Annette. You'll leave college with top exam results, I can promise you that. You're a very clever girl, and I'm sure you know what I'm getting at. As I said, give it some thought.'

'Yes, I will,' I breathed.

He fixed his eyes on mine. 'You know what I mean, don't you?'

'Yes, I do.'

'Would you be all right with that?'

'I'll think about it.'

'I'll tell you what I'll do. I'll be here at seven o'clock this evening. You think about it this afternoon and, if you agree, meet me here at seven.'

'All right, I'll think about it this afternoon.'

'Good girl. I hope to see you later.'

As he climbed to his feet and walked away, I knew that I'd have to reconsider my decision about meeting men. I was far from brilliant at college, and I knew that my exam results were going to be dismal. It wasn't that I was stupid or thick. I just had trouble concentrating and remembering what I'd been taught. If I had help during the exams, if my results were excellent ... that would make my parents happy. But at what price? Showing my pussy to my teacher? Allowing him to stroke me or even go as far as fingering me? That was a small price to pay, I thought happily. Deciding to go for it, I leapt to my feet and headed for John's house. I didn't want to meet him in the woods again. What with my mum's suspicions, the whole thing was too risky. Besides, I now had my teacher to keep happy.

I walked slowly towards John's house and slipped into his front garden. Screened from my house by the bushes, I felt like a thief in the night as I crept up to his front door and rang the bell. My heart racing, I imagined my mother coming out of our house and finding me on John's doorstep. God, I thought, ringing the bell again. If she caught me . . . Trying to calm myself, I decided to tell John the news quickly and then go home. It would only take a minute to explain things, and then it would all be over. Hearing movements in the hall, I breathed a sigh of relief. He opened the door and grinned at me. He was wearing a T-shirt and shorts, and I tried not to think of his cock as he invited me in.

'What a nice surprise,' he said. 'Come in, come in.'

'Thanks,' I breathed softly.

'Sorry about the mess, but I'm in the middle of packing.'

'I can't stay,' I said, following him into the lounge. 'I've just come round to say that . . .'

'You can stay for a while, surely?'

'No, I can't. My mum's suspicious.'

'Suspicious? What do you mean?'

'She had a go at me last night. She thinks that I'm meeting a man in the woods and . . .'

'What the hell have you said to her?' he snapped.

'Nothing, I've said nothing.'

'You must have said something, Annette. Why would she think that you're meeting a man in the woods? She must have got the idea from somewhere.'

'Someone else gave me a new computer yesterday, and she thought it odd.'

'Who was it? Another man?'

'No, no . . . a friend of the family. I go to the park most evenings and she thought . . . Anyway, I can't meet you there again.'

'In that case, come round here to see me.'

'No, I can't.'

'Why not? You're here now.'

'I had to sneak round here. If she finds out . . .'

'She won't find out, don't worry. Did you shave your sweet cunt for me?'

'No, no, I didn't. John, I . . .'

'I have an idea,' he said excitedly, grinning at me. 'I'll shave your cunt for you.'

'John, you don't understand,' I persisted. 'I can't see you again.'

'No, no, no. You don't understand, Annette. I spent a hell of a lot of money on you. The deal was that we meet several times. And, when I've moved, we'll meet once a week. If we can't go to the woods, then you'll come here. Once I've moved, we'll find somewhere else to meet.'

'No,' I said firmly. 'How many times do I have to tell you? I can't meet you again. It's too risky.'

'Would you like me to talk to your mum and explain about the computer I bought you?'

'I've already explained things and I think she's all right about it. If you talk to her, she'll know that I've spoken to you and . . .'

'If I talk to her, she'll discover exactly why I bought you the computer.'

'What do you mean?'

'I'll tell her that you asked me for a new computer in return for allowing me to fuck you.'

'What?' I gasped, unable to believe what he'd said.

'I'm moving soon, Annette. I have nothing to lose by telling your mother the truth. Of course, you have everything to lose. Take your skirt off and we'll have some fun.'

'John, please . . . I can't . . . If you tell my mum . . .'

'There's no need for me to say anything to her. Why spoil what we have together?'

'Because she's suspicious. Would you really tell her the truth?'

'If I have to, yes. I'm not trying to be nasty, Annette. I've spent a lot of money on you, and I want you to stick to your side of the bargain. If you don't . . . Look, this is easy to work out. We'll stick to our original arrangement, and no one will ever find out.'

'I can't. I'll have to give the computer back to you.'

'I sold that computer to you, Annette.'

'No, you didn't.'

'It wasn't a present, a free gift. You bought it from me, and you can't return it.'

'I didn't buy it. I don't know what you're talking about.'

'You didn't use money to buy it. You bought it with your body. You're paying by instalments, Annette. I've had a couple of payments from you, and it's only right that you continue to pay me by instalments. That's what we agreed, isn't it?'

'Well, yes, but . . .'

'But what? You can't buy something from a shop on credit, pay a couple of instalments, and then say you want to return the goods. Is the computer faulty?'

'Well, no . . . I mean, I haven't tried it yet.'

'If there's something wrong with it, I'll take it back and have it changed for another one. I'm doing all I can to help you, Annette. You wanted a new computer, and I got you one. Now I want you to pay me for it. Take your skirt off.'

'All right,' I finally conceded, unzipping my skirt. 'But I can't see you again after this.'

'Have you heard of the small claims court?'

'Yes, I think so.'

'That would be a last resort, of course. I don't think we'll end up going down that road. Now, take your skirt off and we'll have some fun.'

I couldn't believe what he'd said as I dropped my skirt and kicked it aside. Take me to court? I hadn't signed anything, but ... could he do that? Imagining my name in the local paper, I recalled my dad saying something about a client at work and a verbal agreement. He'd said that verbal agreements were legally binding, and I knew that I couldn't go back on my word. Maybe I could sneak round to John's house, I thought, as he ordered me to take my T-shirt off. Once he'd moved, we could find another park or go to the woods on the common. Whatever happened, I had to keep my side of the deal with John.

When I'd started my games, I'd wanted to be in control. For a while, at least, I had been in control. But now everything had gone wrong. Tugging my T-shirt over my head, I decided not to meet my teacher on the common. I'd just be digging myself deeper into a hole I'd never get out of. I'd just have to keep up with my homework and try to do my best in the exams. But, as John squeezed my naked breasts, a terrible thought struck me. If I didn't do what my teacher wanted, he might make sure that I got bad results. This was worse than a nightmare, I thought, as John leaned forward and sucked on each nipple in turn. Kneeling before me, he pulled my wet knickers down and kissed the puffy lips of my pussy.

'I can't stop thinking about your sweet little cunt,' he breathed. 'You're nice and slim. Slim girls have narrow hips, and narrow hips mean a tight little cunt.'

'I have to go now,' I murmured.

'You have to come now,' he quipped.

'I'll wank you and make you come and then I must go.'

'Turn round,' he ordered me. 'I want to look at your tight little buttocks.'

'All right,' I sighed, spinning round on my heels. 'And then I must go.'

The feel of his wet tongue running up and down my bottom crease sent quivers through my pelvis. I tried to deny the immense pleasure he was bringing me. I began to tremble as he parted the firm cheeks of my buttocks and licked my private hole. The sensations were heavenly, but my mind was riddled with anxiety. If my mother rang Diana and asked to speak to me . . . I had to get home and tell her that I'd not gone to see Diana after all. If I was away for too long, she'd become suspicious and start asking me awkward questions.

As John's tongue slipped into my anal hole, I let out a rush of breath. I could feel my clitoris swelling as he drove two fingers deep into my tightening vagina, and I imagined my teacher fingering me behind the bushes on the common. I knew that I had to put a stop to my illicit activities but it seemed there was no way out. If I didn't give my young body to John, he'd speak to my mother. If I didn't allow my teacher to strip me naked, he'd give me bad exam results. And I had Derek to satisfy, I reflected dolefully. I really had dug myself into the mire, and there was no way out.

Ordering me to stand with my feet wide apart, John told me to bend over and touch my toes. I did as he'd asked and gazed between my legs at his upside-down face. He licked my bottom-hole and then again pushed his tongue deep into my rectum. I could feel his hot breath between my buttocks, his saliva running down to my finger-stuffed pussy. He lapped and slurped and breathed heavily as he massaged the hot inner flesh of my vagina. My clitoris was painfully solid, the sensitive tip massaged by his thrusting fingers. I knew that I was nearing my orgasm.

Yanking his fingers out of my hot pussy, John leapt to his feet and dropped his shorts. I could see his heavy balls swinging below his solid cock as he pressed his purple knob between the puffy lips of my vagina. My juices of lust streaming from my open hole, I grimaced as his cock shaft drove deep into my quivering body and impaled me completely. He grabbed my hips and began his shafting. Fucking my tight pussy, gasping with every lunge of his huge cock, he repeatedly pulled me towards him to meet his thrusts.

'Tight-cunted little whore,' he breathed as I flopped back and forth like a rag doll. 'I want you to shave your pubes off when you get home. Then tomorrow after college, you'll come round here and show me your hairless little cunt. I'm going to fuck you every day and . . .'

As he breathed his crude words and fucked me harder, I knew that my orgasm wouldn't come. *Tight-cunted little whore. I want you to shave your pubes off . . . I'm going to fuck you every day . . .* I didn't want to shave, and I certainly couldn't see him every day. There was no way I could go to his house after college. Mum would wonder where the hell I'd got to, and she'd become incredibly suspicious. Praying for the day to come when John moved away, I felt his spunk gushing into the inflamed sheath of my vagina.

He let out low moans of pleasure as he repeatedly rammed his solid cock deep into my sex-drenched pussy. He'd done it, I thought happily. He'd satisfied his craving for crude sex, and now he'd allow me to leave. Watching his glistening shaft gliding in and out of my spermed pussy, I listened to the sounds of my squelching juices and his spunk. He'd nearly finished, I thought with relief. I was almost free to go home.

'God, that was amazing,' he gasped, finally slipping his deflating cock out of my sperm-bubbling pussy.

'I have to go,' I said, hauling my abused body upright. 'I have to . . .'

'Not yet,' he said, spinning me round and kissing my full lips. 'I want to watch you bring yourself off.'

'John, I can't,' I stated firmly, pulling away from him and grabbing my clothes. 'There's been enough trouble with my mum as it is.'

'All right,' he conceded as I dressed. 'Come round tomorrow, after college.'

'I'll see what I can do.'

'Promise me that you'll . . .'

'I said, I'll see what I can do,' I snapped.

Fully dressed, I brushed my long blonde hair back with my fingers and left his house. I could feel his sperm filling the tight crotch of my knickers as I slipped along the front path to the street. Composing myself, taking a deep breath, I walked up to my front door and rang the bell. Wishing that I'd taken my key, I hoped my mother wouldn't start asking questions the minute I stepped into the hall.

'Oh, hi,' she said as she opened the door. 'Did you see Diana?'

'No,' I replied, walking past her into the hall. 'I changed my mind.'

'I'm pleased you said that,' she breathed softy, closing the door. 'I rang Diana's mother, and she said that you'd not been there.'

'Were you checking up on me?' I asked her accusingly.

'No, Annette, of course I wasn't. I just wanted to let you know that dinner will be at six o'clock. So, where have you been?'

'I got halfway across the common and I bumped into David.'

'David?'

'The boy I told you about.'

'Oh, yes. So, er . . . are you going to see him again?'

'Yes, this evening. If that's all right with you?'

'Yes, yes, of course it is.'

'We're going to walk into town and have a coffee or something.'

'That is good, Annette. I'm really pleased. And you'll be pleased to know that no more computers have turned up.'

'That's not funny, mum,' I said, climbing the stairs.

'Sorry, it was only a joke.'

I closed my bedroom door and slipped my wet knickers off. The crotch was full of thick, creamy sperm, and I knew that I daren't let mum see them. Hiding them beneath the bed, I wandered into the bathroom and turned the shower on. I had no intention of shaving my blonde pubes off, until I noticed dad's razor on the shelf. Grabbing the tin of shaving cream, I hesitated. Which way was my life going? Could I lead two separate lives? The dirty little slut and the innocent college girl?

Placing the can on the shelf, I stepped into the shower and washed my hair. I was going to have to make my mind up, I knew, as I again considered shaving my pussy. John wanted me, Derek wanted me, and my teacher . . . I either ended my games now, I thought, or I carried on. If I was to continue, then I'd have to plan my sexual exploits properly. I couldn't go sneaking around the woods and the common, or creep round to John's house or keep wondering when Derek would next turn up and want sex ... I couldn't sit on the fence for a moment longer.

Taking the tin from the shelf, I squirted the foam over the fleshy swell of my pussy lips, the gentle rise of my mons. Massaging the cream into my vulval area, rubbing, caressing, I breathed heavily as the beautiful sensations rippled through my pelvis. My clitoris responding to my intimate touch, my inner lips engorging, my outer labia inflating, I felt sexually alive as never before. My nipples were becoming acutely sensitive and I knew that I needed the relief of orgasm. But I wanted to shave my pubic hair first.

It was easier than I thought. Dragging the razor over my mons, I gazed at the smooth white flesh left in its wake. Smooth, unblemished, alluring ... Pulling my outer lips up and apart, running the razor carefully over my sensitive flesh, I removed the fleece of blonde curls I'd once been so proud of. When they'd first sprouted, I'd deemed them a sign of womanhood. My pubes had grown, my breasts had developed, and I'd thought that I was a woman. Didn't men like pubic hair? I wondered, finishing the job and washing away the foam.

Drying my body, I gazed at my reflection in the mirror. God, I thought, staring at my hairless crack. I'd stripped away the years and now looked like a young girl. Was that what men wanted? Did they really want a schoolgirl look-alike? Turning this way and that, admiring my reflection, I grinned. I had what men wanted, I mused happily as I wrapped the towel around my naked body and dashed back to my bedroom.

Sitting at my dressing table, I felt funny inside, sort of nervous and guilty. Brushing my hair, I knew that I shouldn't meet my teacher that evening. How would

I face him in class, having allowed him to see me naked? If he fingered me, kissed my pussy and ... He'd realise that I'd shaved, he'd think me a slut and ... Again thinking of my exam results, I knew that I had no choice. I'd finally come to a decision. From that moment on, I'd lead two separate lives.

Taking a pair of white knickers from my drawer, I had an idea as I gazed at the crotch. The strip of material was obviously wide enough to allow the elastic to settle in the creases between my pussy lips and the tops of my thighs. If I made the crotch narrower, the elastic would sink into each lip, causing them to bulge either side of the kickers. That would excite the men, I thought in my rising wickedness. Grabbing mum's sewing box from her bedroom, I made the adjustments to the crotch.

Pulling my knickers up and standing before my mirror, I grinned. Perfect, I thought happily, as I focused on the smooth flesh of my hairless outer lips bulging either side of the narrow crotch. Men would be delighted to peek up my skirt, and I'd be totally innocent. It wasn't my fault that my knickers were too small for me, was it? Little Miss Innocent, sitting with thighs parted, pussy lips bulging ... Little Miss Guilty.

Dressed in my denim miniskirt and T-shirt, I applied a little make-up and finally went downstairs to dinner. Dad said how pretty I looked and mum reckoned that David was a lucky boy. They asked questions about him, and I lied as best I could. Leaving half my dinner, I cringed when mum suggested that I'd probably gone off my food because I was in love. A barrage of words hit me, and I couldn't wait to get out of the house. *What colour is David's hair? How tall is he? Where does he live? What does his father do for a living?*

'What time will you be home?' mum asked me as I was about to make my escape.

'I'll only be a couple of hours,' I replied. 'That should be long enough to . . . to walk into town and back.'

'Well, have a good time,' dad said, seeing me to the front door.

'Yes, yes, I will.'

Walking down the street, I felt guilty as never before. I was going to meet my teacher behind the bushes on the common. He'd strip me naked, finger my pussy . . . and probably fuck me. The lies I'd told my parents were hurting my mind, but I'd come to a decision and was determined to stick to it. This was my other life, I thought as a passing car tooted at me. Innocent little Annette was at home studying and doing her homework. The other Annette had shaved her cunt and adjusted her knickers and was strutting down the street like a tart. And she'd probably end up getting fucked by a man in his fifties.

Annette met me at Brighton station and we walked down to the sea front and found a quiet pub. I passed her the latest chapter of her book and she read it without comment. I got the impression that she was nervous, so I didn't mention the book until she'd finished her second glass of red wine. She seemed to relax as I talked about her mother's suspicion. But I then mentioned her college teacher.

'What must you think of my story?' she sighed.

'I think it's going to make a great book,' I replied.

'I mean, my teacher. I wanted to do well at college and he . . . he offered me the opportunity to do very well. Have you read the next chapter yet?'

'No, I haven't,' I lied. 'I don't know what happened between you and your teacher.'

'Oh, right. When I left the common and went to John's house, I was very confused. My teacher's proposition had thrown me into turmoil. I mean, he was my teacher and ... I suppose he was a normal man. John was a normal man, too. He wouldn't give up and went on and on until I agreed to his demands. I must have been crazy to believe that he'd take me to court, but I was young and naive.'

'What with Derek and John and your teacher ... and the episode with David, It's no wonder you were confused.'

'I was so confused that I went and shaved my pussy. Had John lovingly asked me to shave ... no, that sounds daft. John was a crude man who loved crude sex. And I was becoming cruder by the minute. I was also becoming a prostitute.'

'How much did that bother you at that point?'

'I don't think it bothered me at all because, at that age, I thought that prostitutes were dirty women who hung around on street corners. I suppose I didn't really think of myself as a prostitute. I knew that what I was doing was wrong – that's why I wanted to stop it. But every time I tried I was dragged into another sex session. To be honest, I loved sex. I loved being licked and fingered. I loved coming and ... well, I loved being fucked.'

'And you loved the presents?'

'Oh, yes. I must have been the only girl at college who had two new computers, a new stereo and a television ... I hadn't taken any money. I think that's why I didn't consider myself a prostitute. What did upset me was having to lie to my mum. I'd never lied to her in the past, but I found that I had no choice. I'd already mentioned to her that I was interested in a boy at college. So, when I went out that evening to meet my teacher, David was the perfect alibi. He had his uses, even though he wasn't interested in me.'

'You managed to get out of the house with no trouble, and you walked to the common. What were your thoughts at that time?'

'I thought that I was in control. I thought that I knew everything and I could handle everything. Until I reached the common.'

Lesbian Encounter

There were a few people walking on the common when I arrived, but there was no sign of my teacher. My hands trembling, my heart beating fast, I wasn't sure whether I wanted him to turn up. Although I'd come to a decision, I was still battling with my guilt over lying to my parents. But I was winning the battle between right and wrong. Who's to say what's right or wrong? I mused as I sat beneath the tree. Male and female together is right, age doesn't matter.

Trying to convince myself that I was in control, I looked upon my teacher as just another man who wanted my young body in return for giving me something. Recalling his words, I smiled. *You'll leave college with top exam results, I can promise you that.* He wanted my body, my pussy. It was a small price to pay, I thought happily. I then recalled Derek's words. *You've not got anything that every other girl in the world hasn't got.* In my musings beneath the tree, I realised that my pussy wasn't anything special. Every girl had a crack, there was nothing unique or special about mine.

My parents had always said that I was special, and I'd been brought up to believe in self-worth, self-respect. What I didn't realise as I waited for my teacher was that my thoughts were destroying my self-worth. I had no respect for my young body. My pussy was a commodity to be traded for the things I wanted. At my age, thoughts of finding love should have flooded my mind. Thoughts of meeting a nice boy, building a relationship and . . .

'Hey, it's great to see you,' my teacher said, making me jump.

'Oh, hi,' I breathed, holding my hand to my mouth. 'Sorry, I was dreaming.'

'And I've been dreaming, Annette. Dreaming about you.'

'Well, here I am.'

'I took a look around earlier. You see that litter bin over there?'

'Yes.'

'There's a narrow track behind the bin. It leads to a small clearing in the bushes. You go there, and I'll join you in a few minutes.'

'OK,' I said, clambering to my feet. Should I call him Mr Williams? I wondered. No, we were out of college. 'Why don't you come with me now?' I asked him.

'I don't want to be seen with you. People might get the wrong idea.'

'Or the right idea?' I said, cocking my head to one side.

'Well, yes . . . Off you go. I'll be there in a while.'

The small clearing was surrounded by bushes. It was an ideal place to take my clothes off and show my young body to my teacher. A perfect place to trade my body for good exam results. I had to remain in control, I thought as I waited. I'd been threatened with blackmail by John, and I wasn't going to allow that to happen again. I wasn't going to allow myself to be cornered and end up having to offer my body to a man for nothing in return. I might to able to get more than good exam results, I mused, as I heard the bushes rustling. Money?

'All right?' my teacher asked my as he joined me in the clearing.

'I'm fine,' I replied. 'This is a nice spot.'

'You're a beautiful girl, Annette. I can't wait to see more of your beautiful body. Why don't you start by taking your T-shirt off?'

I was getting used to this, I thought, mechanically tugging my T-shirt over my head. Showing my young body to men was becoming a way of life. But it was a separate life, I reminded myself as he gazed longingly at the firm mounds of my petite breasts. I was now leading two lives. Annette, the innocent college girl and perfect daughter; Annette, the slut.

'You're amazing,' my teacher breathed, his eyes fixed upon my erect nipples. 'You're absolutely beautiful, Annette.'

'Thank you,' I said softly.

'Are you going to take your skirt off for me?'

Saying nothing, I released my skirt and allowed it to fall down my legs and crumple around my feet. Kicking my shoes and skirt aside, I stood before my teacher wearing nothing but my white knickers, with the crotch so narrow that my hairless lips swelled either side of the tight material. I felt good, proud of my young body, as he looked me up and down approvingly. Feeling no shame or guilt, no embarrassment, I knew that I was becoming used to my new and rewarding secret life. My hairless pussy lips swelling within my tight knickers, my clitoris calling for my intimate attention, I smiled as he asked me to complete my disrobing.

Turing my back to him, I slipped my knickers down and exposed the firm cheeks of my bottom. I was teasing him, making him wait before facing him and allowing him to gaze at my hairless pussy. Although I had no self-respect, no self-worth, I was extremely proud of my body. Petite and very firm breasts, curvaceous hips, smooth pussy lips rising either side of my tight crack ... I had every reason to be proud.

'God,' he breathed as I turned and faced him. 'I had no idea how ... how beautiful you were. I've always thought you extremely attractive but ... you're an angel.'

'How do I know that you'll help me during the exams?' I asked him.

'I promise you I will, Annette. I'll do everything I can for you.'

'Good. Well, you've seen me naked so I'd better get dressed and –'

'No, not yet,' he interrupted. 'I mean ...'

'What do you mean?'

'I thought ... I'd like to touch you.'

'All right,' I conceded, trying to hide my excitement. 'You may touch me.'

Pleased that I was in control, I knew that things between us at college were going to be very different. I'd have to do my best to come across as normal, I mused, as he reached out and squeezed each breast in turn. The feel of his hand sending quivers through my young womb, I decided to allow him to go only so far. If I gave him everything on our first meeting, he'd be chasing me at college and asking me for more. If I wanted more than good exam results, I was going to have to dangle a carrot in front of him. Tease him, allow him to look and touch, and he'd give me everything in return for more.

Kneeling before me, he ran his fingertip up and down my tightly closed sex crack. Pressing the firm swell of my hairless pussy lips, he reached behind me with his free hand and clutched my rounded buttock. He was exploring, I thought dreamily, as he leaned forward and kissed the gentle rise of my stomach. In his fifties, he was probably recalling his youth, his time with teenage girls. Until now, all he'd been able to do was look at the girls in class and try to remember. He was a lucky man to have me. But it would cost him.

'Annette,' he began, his dark eyes reflecting a longing as he looked up at me. 'May I . . . would you mind if I put my finger in you?'

'Well, I . . . I don't know,' I replied as sheepishly as I could. 'I have to go home soon and . . .'

'Please, it won't take long and I'll be very gentle.'

'The thing is I have to do the ironing for my mum. I mean, I don't have to but . . . she pays me ten pounds. I really need the money.'

'I have ten pounds,' he offered eagerly, thrusting his hand into his pocket. 'There,' he said, grinning, as he passed me a note.

'Well, all right,' I agreed, taking the cash without grabbing it.

As he parted the fleshy swell of my outer lips and gazed at my pink inner folds, I knew that I had him exactly where I wanted him. My lie about the ironing had been perfect, I reflected. I'd not asked him for money, he'd offered to pay me. And it wasn't in return for fingering my pussy, it was to make up the money I'd lose from not helping my mum. He wouldn't think me a prostitute, I thought happily, as his fingertip slipped into my very tight and creamy-wet sex hole.

'You're so hot,' he breathed shakily as he pushed his finger deeper into my tightening sheath.

'Am I?' I said, concealing a grin as I clutched the ten-pound note in my hand.

'God, yes. And so incredibly tight. It's been a long time since I've slipped my finger into a virgin girl.'

A virgin girl? I mused in my wickedness. That's what I wanted him to believe, I thought, as he massaged the wet inner flesh of my tight vagina. I wanted him to think me an innocent little virgin girl who was desperate to pass her exams with excellent results. I should have come across as shy when I'd stripped naked, I reflected. I should have looked anxious and . . . I'd been far too quick to strip naked in front of him. But it was too late to change things now. I wasn't yet practised in the fine art of deception. But I was learning fast.

My erect clitoris massaged by his inquisitive finger, I knew that I daren't gasp or show any signs of pleasure. Although I was desperate to come, I had to remain calm. Looking down at his greying hair, the small bald patch on the top of his head, I again wondered how things would be between us at college. Our teacher-pupil relationship had changed, but we'd have to behave normally. Would he smile at me in class? I mused as he slipped a second finger into my moistening vagina. Would he look at me and think of my cunt?

'I have to go now,' I said as he again kissed my lower stomach.

'Annette, I . . . Have you ever been with a boy?'

'No, I haven't.'

'Do you know about . . . what I mean is . . . do you know about wanking?'

'Well, I've heard of it,' I breathed softly.

'Do you know how to do it?' he asked me, slipping his wet fingers out of my hot pussy and licking them. 'God, you taste wonderful. So, do you know how to wank a boy?'

I reached down and grabbed my clothes as he gazed at me with expectation reflected in his dark eyes. 'I suppose I do,' I replied. 'I mean . . . I've never done it, but I know how.'

'Would you do it to me?' he asked me. 'It won't take long.'

'Well, I . . . I don't think so,' I breathed, desperate to feel the hardness of his cock in my hand. 'No, I don't want to,' I finally stated.

'Why not? I know that you have to get home, but it won't take long. After looking at you and touching you . . . I'd give anything if you'd do it, Annette.'

'I already feel bad,' I sighed, pulling my T-shirt over my head. 'I shouldn't have taken my clothes off and let you touch me. It's wrong, and I wish I hadn't done it.'

'Didn't you like it?'

'I don't know. It's not right to . . .'

'You will meet me here again, won't you?'

'Well, I . . . I can't. I'm getting a job, so I won't be able to come here after college. I'm saving up for a new computer and I need the money.'

'I have an idea,' he said, smiling at me. 'You could meet me here instead of getting a job.'

'But I need the money.'

'I'll pay you.'

'Pay me?' I echoed, tugging my skirt up. This was going well, I thought happily. 'Pay me for what? I don't understand.'

'How much will you get from this job?'

'Ten pounds for two hours, three times each week.'

'Meet me here three times each week, and I'll pay you the same,' he persisted.

'Well, I suppose I could.'

'Here,' he said, reaching into his pocket. 'This is the first ten pounds. The other money made up for the ironing, OK?'

'OK,' I breathed softly. 'Shall I meet you here tomorrow?'

'Yes, yes. But, now that I've paid you . . . will you wank me?'

'I've never done it before,' I sighed. 'I suppose I could . . . All right, I will.'

I'd kept him waiting long enough, I thought, stuffing the money into my skirt pocket as he unzipped his trousers and pulled out his erect cock. I'd kept myself waiting long enough. Gazing at his huge cock, I imagined slipping it into my mouth and sucking it. I'd already tasted sperm and I'd loved it. But I didn't want to go too far on our first meeting. Dangle the carrot, I thought, wrapping my fingers around his hard shaft. Moving my hand up and down, I watched his purple knob appear and disappear as I wanked him. He groaned as if in pain, but I knew that he was enjoying it.

Never would I have dreamed that I'd be wanking my teacher, I reflected, as he trembled and gasped. He'd given me ten pounds for showing him my naked body and allowing him to finger my pussy. And another ten for wanking his huge cock. I'd got things right at last, I was sure, as his warm shaft swelled in my hand. My parents didn't know him, he wouldn't visit my house or bring me presents, he didn't live next-door . . . I'd got things right.

He groaned and thrust his hips forward and his spunk shot from his purple knob and rained over the front of my skirt. His shaft was as hard as rock, and I knew that he'd been desperate for me to wank him and bring out his creamy spunk. Had I not agreed, he'd have waited until I'd left the clearing and then done the job himself. He was a lucky man to have me. With the white liquid running over my fingers and splattering my skirt, I thought how lucky I was. And how easy it was to earn money.

'I needed that,' he gasped as his spunk flow stemmed.

'Was it all right?' I asked him, releasing his cock and watching a long thread of sperm hanging from his purple knob. 'I mean, did I do it properly?'

'God, yes, you did. You were amazing.'

'I have to go now,' I breathed, discreetly licking my fingers clean.

The taste of fresh spunk sending my arousal soaring, I was desperate for an orgasm. But I knew that I'd have to wait until I got home before masturbating. I'd have loved him to lick and suck my clitoris, but I didn't want to allow him too much pleasure too soon. I straightened my clothes and brushed my long blonde hair back with my fingers, then gazed with triumph at the crumpled ten-pound notes. I'd done well, I thought. And I'd do even better.

'You go first, and I'll see you in the morning,' he said.

'All right,' I breathed, turning to leave.

'You will meet me here tomorrow, won't you?'

'Yes, I will.'

'What time is best for you?'

'I don't know,' I sighed, trying not to show my eagerness. 'I suppose straight from college would be best.'

'Four o'clock, then?'

'Yes, I'll be here at four.'

'And . . . don't tell anyone.'

'I won't.'

I emerged from the bushes and walked briskly across the common. I'd hide the money I'd earned behind my wardrobe in my room, I decided. Unlike a computer or a television, I could hide the money and no one would ever discover it. Thirty pounds each week, I mused, wondering what to buy. Clothes? I'd have to tell my mum that I'd got a part-time job, otherwise she'd wonder where I was getting money from. Everything was going according to plan.

'Annette,' someone called as I reached the edge of the common.

'Diana,' I said, turning and smiling as she ran up to me. 'Where are you going?'

'To your house. I was going to come and see you.'

'Great. You can walk with me.'

'Where have you been?' she asked me accusingly.

'Nowhere, just on the common.'

'I saw you,' she said, grabbing my arm as I walked on. Spinning me round, she stared hard at me. 'I saw you go into the bushes.'

'So?'

'What were you doing?'

'Having a wee, if you must know.'

'I saw Mr Williams go in after you.'

'Yes, we were . . .' I needed an instant lie, and a good one. 'We were talking about . . . about college and stuff,' I stammered.

'In the bushes? I thought you went in there to have a wee?'

'Well, I . . .'

'You were in there for ages, Annette.'

'I went in there for a wee, Mr Williams saw me and followed me and . . . and we chatted. Luckily, I'd pulled my knickers up by the time he found me,' I added with a giggle.

'I went into the bushes,' she breathed. 'I saw what you were doing, Annette.'

'It's not what you think,' I said stupidly.

'You were naked.'

I had no idea what to say as she waited for an explanation. She'd obviously seen everything, so what could I say? I could feel my stomach churning, my hands trembling, as I tried to think of a plausible

117

excuse for my debauched behaviour. There was no excuse for standing naked before our teacher, let alone allowing him to finger my pussy. She must have seen me wanking his cock, seen the spunk shooting down my skirt and . . . Things had been going so well, I reflected anxiously. And now I had this nightmare to deal with.

'I can't believe this,' she sighed, tossing her long black hair over her shoulder. 'I thought I knew you well. Obviously, I don't know you at all. Did he touch you?'

'I thought you were watching?'

'I didn't hang around. I saw you without your clothes on, saw him looking at you, so I left.'

'He only looked at me,' I breathed with relief. 'I'd never let him touch me. He only looked.'

'Why did you do it? Why strip naked in front of him? What if he'd touched you?'

'He wouldn't do that.'

'Had you arranged to meet him there?'

'I'll tell you the truth,' I sighed, sitting on the grass. Joining me, she locked her blue eyes to mine. 'Go on,' she said.

'I'd not gone in there for a wee. I was . . . I'd taken my clothes off because I was going to play with myself.'

'Wow. You mean . . .'

'I was going to play with my pussy, OK? He must have seen me go into the bushes and he followed me. He saw me naked and . . .'

'God, weren't you embarrassed?'

'Of course I was embarrassed. He saw me doing it, he saw me fingering my pussy. I've never been so embarrassed in all my life.'

'Why didn't you tell me the truth in the first place?'

'Because I didn't want you to know that I'd taken my clothes off in the bushes because . . . I didn't want to tell you that I'd gone in there to masturbate. I mean, it's not the sort of thing you tell people.'

'You could have told me, I'm your best friend. Why were you in the bushes for so long?'

'He was lecturing me. I got dressed and he started lecturing me about sex and stuff. It was awful.'

Thanking God that she'd not spied on me for longer and discovered the truth, I knew that I'd had a narrow escape. Had she seen him fingering my pussy, had she seen me wanking his cock ... I dreaded to think what would have happened. Was there nowhere I could play my sex games? I was going to have to find another place to meet my teacher. Somewhere secluded and perfectly safe. But where?

'Why not play with yourself at home?' she asked me.

'I don't know. I like being naked with the feel on the hot sun on my skin and ... I just like being outdoors.'

'I do it in my room,' she informed me.

'You ... you masturbate?' I asked, my eyes wide as I gazed at her.

'Of course I do. Doesn't everyone?'

'Well, I ... I don't know.'

'I've been doing it for years.'

'Have you been with a boy?'

'No, I haven't. How about you, Annette?'

'No,' I lied.

'I noticed that you've shaved,' she said, her pretty face grinning at me. 'When I saw you in the bushes ... How long have you been doing that?'

'Well, not long. I just thought I'd see what it was like.'

'I've been shaving forever,' she said with a giggle. 'I started shaving from the day the first hairs appeared. I don't like hair all over my pussy.'

119

'I had no idea,' I gasped. 'We've been best friends for ages, Diana. But we don't know anything about each other.'

'I was just thinking the same. Fancy getting caught naked in the bushes by old Williams.'

'It was awful. He must have seen me walk into the bushes and ... God knows what he must think of me.'

'Just forget about it, if you can. And the next time you want to play with your clitty, do it in your bedroom.'

'Yes, yes, I will.'

'Shall we go to your house, then?'

'OK,' I replied, leaping to my feet.

Walking with Diana, I couldn't believe that she shaved her pussy and masturbated regularly. I'd thought that I was the only girl of my age in the world who did such naughty things. Did all the girls at college masturbate? I liked Diana and was pleased that she hadn't discovered the truth about me. If she discovered that middle-aged men paid me to have sex with them ... that would have been the end of our friendship, I was sure.

We reached my house to find that my parents were out, which was a relief. The last thing I needed was mum asking me questions about my meeting David in front of Diana. My lies were going to get me into trouble before long, I was sure. It seemed that, no matter how careful I was, no matter how good my planning, I ended up in awkward situations. Mum had accepted my lie about meeting David. But Diana had caught me in the bushes with our teacher. God, I'd had a lucky escape. I had to find somewhere safe to have sex with men.

Diana followed me upstairs to my room, flopped on to my bed and immediately started talking about masturbation and orgasms. Things had changed between us, I mused, eyeing her miniskirt, her long legs. I'd never thought of her in a sexual way but now I couldn't help imagining her rubbing her clitty and fingering her pussy. In the past, we'd talked about college work, listened to music or watched television. Boring in comparison, I thought happily, eyeing the triangular patch of her white knickers as she lay back on the bed.

'How many times can you come?' she asked me unashamedly.

'Well, once or twice,' I replied a little sheepishly. 'How about you?'

'The most ever was six,' she trilled excitedly. 'I usually manage to come three times. Do you finger yourself or just rub your clit?'

'I finger myself. I didn't know that you were like this,' I said with a giggle. 'You've never talked about it before.'

'I've never seen you standing naked in the bushes before,' she returned laughingly. 'What a coincidence. I was walking across the common to your house, and you went into the bushes to masturbate. If I hadn't followed you, we'd never have talked about orgasms and stuff.'

'No, we wouldn't,' I replied softly.

'What's that down the front of your skirt?' she asked me, propping herself up on her elbows.

'Oh, er . . . I spilled something earlier.'

I'd forgotten about my spunk-splattered skirt. I should have wiped it, cleaned away the evidence of my debauchery. Gazing at Diana's naked legs, I imagined her standing naked in front of our teacher. She would never do anything like that, I knew. She'd never been with a boy, let alone a man in his fifties. She was a decent young lady, and I was a slut. How was I going to face my teacher in the morning? I wondered anxiously. He'd fingered my pussy, I'd wanked him and watched his spunk shoot out . . . but I'd earned some money.

Noticing a wet patch on the bulging crotch of Diana's knickers as she lay back on the bed, I became aware of my own sex-milk seeping into mine. My arousal running high from the illicit fingering in the bushes, I'd hoped to masturbate when I got home. Diana would probably stay for a couple of hours, and my clitoris was swelling, demanding my intimate attention. Maybe I should slip into the bathroom and appease it, I thought as Diana's legs parted.

'I can't stop thinking about old Williams catching you naked in the bushes,' she said with a giggle.

'Neither can I,' I sighed. 'God knows what he must think of me.'

'I reckon he's thinking about you now.'

'What do you mean?'

'He's probably wanking and thinking about your tits and shaved pussy. Did he ask you why you'd shaved?'

'No, he didn't. I dressed quickly when he turned up.'

'He'll be looking at you in class tomorrow,' she taunted me. 'He'll be thinking about your naked body.'

I didn't need reminding, I reflected, as she parted her legs further. Little did she know that he'd also be looking forward to meeting me on the common. He'd want to finger me again, rub my clitoris and take me to orgasm. He'd also want me to wank him again. And suck his purple knob? Gazing at Diana's wet knickers again, as I thought about my teacher licking and fingering me, I wondered whether she was deliberately opening her legs. Her skirt had ridden up

122

her thighs, and she was blatantly exposing the triangular patch of white material bulging to contain her sex lips.

This was knicker flashing in reverse, I mused. On the receiving end for once, I could now see what the men saw, what excited them so much. Did she know about flashing? Had she parted her legs and exposed her tight knickers to excite middle-aged men? Gazing at the taut material, imaging her tight little crack, I wondered why I was feeling excited. This wasn't supposed to work on other girls, and yet . . . Was she feeling sexy? Perhaps all the talk about Mr Williams had excited her. Maybe that's what had excited me.

'Do you know Deborah Jones?' she asked.

'She's in Johnson's class, isn't she?'

'Yes, that's right.' She grinned at me. 'We've done it together,' she revealed.

'Done what?' I asked.

'Come,' she explained. 'We've come together.'

'You mean, you've watched each other masturbate?'

'No, silly. We did it to each other.'

'You did it . . .'

'Yes, why not?'

Unable to believe what she was saying, I stared at her with my mouth hanging open. This wasn't the Diana I knew, I reflected incredulously. She'd masturbated Deborah Jones? What was she leading up to? I wondered, again eyeing her tight knickers. I had no idea what to say as she gazed at me with expectation reflected in the blue pools of her wide eyes. I'd heard about lesbians, and I'd heard rumours about some of the girls at college. But I'd never believed that some girls actually fingered each other. Deborah Jones? I'd always thought her to be quiet and shy. There again, I'd always been quiet and shy.

'Shall we do it?' she asked me. 'Your mum and dad are out, so how about it?'

'God, Diana,' I breathed. 'I'm not a lesbian.'

'Neither am I,' she returned. 'It has nothing to do with being a lesbian. It's just two girls making each other come. Some of the boys wank each other, I've seen them.'

'Where?'

'In the changing rooms. They're not gay. They just like wanking each other. I had a great time with Deborah the other day at her house.'

'God, weren't you embarrassed?'

'No, not at all. To have someone else bring you off is amazing. You don't know what you're missing. You should try it.'

Twisting my long blonde hair nervously around my fingers, I realised just how much my life had been turned upside down. My dad's boss, the man next door, David from college, my teacher . . . and now my best friend was suggesting that I try lesbian sex. Gazing at her slender legs, the smoothness of her shapely thighs, I focused on the bulge of her tight knickers for the umpteenth time. What the hell was I thinking? I wondered, picturing her hairless lips, her tight crack. I wasn't a bloody lesbian.

'Get on the bed,' she said, leaping to her feet.

'No, I don't want . . .'

'Come on, Annette.'

'I'm not going to let you do anything to me,' I breathed, lying on my back on the bed.

'Don't worry, I won't touch you,' she assured me.

'If you do, I'll never speak to you again.'

'Annette, I won't touch you, I promise. I just want to look at your legs. I've always been envious of your legs.'

Sitting beside me, she ran her fingers up and down my shins and around my knees. I knew that she wanted to get her hands inside my knickers, but I wasn't going to indulge in lesbian sex. And yet, somewhere deep within my mind, something was stirring. Another monster? I wasn't a lesbian, but . . . it would be interesting to see another girl's pussy, I mused dreamily, as Diana's fingers worked their way up to my thighs. I was curious, but nothing more.

Closing my eyes, I felt sleepy as she tickled my inner thighs. The sensations were beautiful, arousing. I quite enjoyed her tickling me, but I didn't want her to go any further. Although I was desperate for the relief of orgasm, there was no way I'd allow another girl to masturbate me. Her fingers moving higher, dangerously close to the triangular patch of my knickers, she eased my thighs apart. No, I thought. Nice though her tickling was, I didn't want this.

My mind flooded with a thousand thoughts as she stroked the small indentations at the tops of my thighs. She was so close to my knickers, to my swelling pussy lips. And I was so close to giving her what she wanted. Was it what I wanted? Lost in confusion as I felt my clitoris inflate, my knickers soak up my flowing sex-milk, I knew that I had to make another major decision. I was already leading two separate lives, the innocent college girl and the dirty little slut. Now I had to decide whether to expand my sexual experience, my exploits, to include lesbian acts.

Letting out a gasp as Diana pressed her fingertips into the swelling material of my tight knickers, I knew that I had a matter of seconds to decide what it was that I wanted. I could stop her now, I thought, as my young womb contracted. I could halt the imminent lesbian sex act, or allow her to masturbate me and bring me a much-needed orgasm. My mind torn between right and wrong, I recalled my earlier thoughts about my body. My pussy was a commodity, something to bring me pleasure and money. Diana could bring me pleasure, I thought dreamily, as her fingertip ran up and down my crack through the wet material of my knickers.

Her finger slipped through the leg hole of my knickers and massaged my wet outer lips. I knew that the decision had been made for me. I could no longer fight my desire for an orgasm. Whether it was a male or female finger massaging between my legs no longer mattered. I needed to come. Would I mind a female tongue lapping between my sex lips? I wondered as Diana yanked my skirt up over my stomach and tugged the front of my knickers down. I wasn't a lesbian, I repeatedly thought, as I felt her slipping my knickers down my thighs. Taking my shoes off and pulling my knickers over my feet, she pushed my legs wide apart and ran her fingertip up and down my very wet crack. I felt as though I was removed, somehow not there, as she peeled my fleshy sex lips open and massaged my pink inner lips. Was I dreaming?

I'd been confused enough by the middle-aged men and my teacher. Now my mind was in complete turmoil. Pulling on my pink inner lips, she was obviously examining me. She'd be looking at me, gazing at the most private part of my young body, scrutinising the pink cone of flesh surrounding my vaginal entrance ... I could feel her finger entering the tight sheath of my vagina and massaging my creamy wet inner flesh. Trembling, breathing deeply, I arched my back. I was weakening in my longing. But this was wrong, I thought guiltily. Wrong, but beautiful.

A female finger, I thought anxiously. It didn't matter, didn't it? Had she been a male, I'd have felt easier. But this was another girl, my best friend. Things had happened so quickly. We'd been talking one minute and the next she was stroking my legs and then pulling my knickers off and fingering me ... There was no way I'd be able to enjoy an orgasm, I was sure, as she twisted and bent her finger deep within the hot wetness of my tight vagina. Another monster had risen from the deep and had me in its grip.

Massaging the swollen bulb of my clitoris with her free hand, she eased a second finger into the wet heat of my tightening vagina. Why was I allowing her to do this to me? I wondered guiltily as my womb contracted. Was I a lesbian? Or had I gone crazy? I could feel her long black hair tickling my inner thighs as she massaged my clitoris expertly. My vagina was stretched even wider open, and I knew that she'd managed to force a third finger into my hot sex sheath. The sensations were amazing, heavenly, but this was wrong.

No words passed between us as I came closer to my orgasm. I'd thought I wouldn't be able to come, but now, the sensations building, my clitoris swelling, I knew that I couldn't halt the imminent explosion of sexual bliss. Another girl, I again thought, covering my face with my hands. A girl's fingers, a girl was masturbating me and I was about to come. Girl, girl ... No, I thought, desperately trying to deny the immense pleasure she was bringing me. This was another girl, a lesbian. No, this was wrong.

'Stop,' I murmured shakily.

'Come for me,' she breathed, increasing her massaging rhythm, her finger thrusting.

'Diana, no ...'

Orgasm erupted within my pulsating clitoris. My vaginal muscles contracting and gripping her

127

pistoning fingers, I shook uncontrollably in the grip of a powerful climax. With my head lolling from side to side, I dug my fingernails into the quilt as she sustained my incredible pleasure. Again and again, waves of pure sexual ecstasy rolled through my young body as she fingered my contracting vagina and expertly massaged my orgasming clitoris. Never had I known a climax of such strength and duration. Was my pleasure heightened because this was another girl masturbating me? Lost in my coming, I couldn't think straight. Lesbian, slut, prostitute ... I didn't know what I was.

My orgasm began to fade as I realised that Diana would want me to masturbate her in return. Listening to her fingers squelching my cream as she continued to massage my pulsating clitoris, I knew that I couldn't bring myself to finger another girl's vagina. Whatever I was, a slut, a whore ... I wasn't a lesbian. Finally leaving my pussy and sitting upright, she fixed her sparkling blue eyes on mine and smiled at me.

'Well?' she breathed. 'Was that OK?'

'Yes,' I replied softly. 'It was nice, but –'

'Yes, I know,' she cut in. 'But I'm a girl.'

'Yes.'

'I need to come now, Annette,' she said. 'Let's swap places and ...'

'Annette,' my mum called up the stairs. 'We're home.'

'OK,' I said, leaping off the bed. Gazing at Diana, I tried to look disappointed. 'Sorry,' I whispered.'

'So am I,' she sighed. 'Another time, OK?'

'Yes ... another time.'

I'd thought that Annette wouldn't want to talk about the episode with her teacher, but she seemed quite happy to do so. Rather than come across as embarrassed, as I'd expected, she gave me the impression that she felt rather proud of her conquest.

'The sex game with my teacher was amazing. I played little Miss Innocent and he coaxed me gently and . . . it was such a thrill. Taking my clothes off slowly, revealing my breasts, my bum and finally my hairless crack . . . I felt powerful and sexy as never before. The power thing, the need to be in control, really came into its own. I was the sweet little virgin girl. I was Little Miss Innocent.'

'That was the first time you'd taken money in exchange for sex. Did you then consider yourself a prostitute?'

'I was so excited about the prospect of earning thirty pounds a week that I didn't think about anything else. I mean, I knew that it was prostitution, but . . . the way I looked at it was that my teacher wanted me to wank him and let him finger me and stuff, and I wanted money and good exam results. The arrangement was perfect. It couldn't have worked out better.'

'Until you met Diana on the way home.'

'God, that was awful. I thought that she'd seen everything. It was such a relief when she said that she'd not stayed to watch. When we got back to my house . . . Diana and I had been friends forever, she was my only friend, but I didn't know her at all. I'd thought that I was the only girl in the world who masturbated but, when she started talking about rubbing her clit and having orgasms, I felt so much better about it.'

'Why worry about masturbating? Surely your other sexual exploits were far more worrying?'

'It's an old-fashioned thing, isn't it? Masturbation is bad, it makes you go blind, it's self-abuse . . . Sex with men was normal. Rubbing my clit and coming in my bed was wrong.'

'You then had your first lesbian encounter.'

'That was really strange. Gazing at Diana's knickers as she moved about on my bed . . . As I said in the book, it was knicker-flashing in reverse. Then I realised that the sight of her knickers was turning me on. I couldn't comprehend my feelings as I thought about her shaved crack. I found myself in the middle of another battle. Was I a lesbian? My previous battles had been nothing in comparison. I mean, I was having sexual thoughts about another girl.'

'You had more than just thoughts.'

'I can't describe the feelings I had as she pushed her finger into my pussy, because they were so mixed up. I was being bombarded by thoughts from all directions. Right, wrong, lesbian sex, a female finger . . . My mind just kind of imploded with confusion. And then I had an amazing orgasm. Someone once said that only a girl knows how to pleasure another girl. I think that's true.'

'Do you still have lesbian relationships?' I dared to ask her.

'I'll answer that the way a politician would. Quite a few heterosexual women enjoy lesbian sex now and then.'

'Did your time with Diana affect your decision to lead two separate lives?'

'It confused my decision. When I woke up the following morning. . . .'

My First Real Client

Unable to face my teacher, or Diana, I didn't go to college. Dad was at work and mum was out, so I had the freedom to pace the lounge floor with my thoughts. A removal lorry pulled up next door, and I knew that John would be out of my way within hours. I could easily avoid Diana in the evenings and at weekends, and I'd make sure that I wasn't around when Derek called at the house. That left only my teacher to worry about. He wasn't a worry, I decided. Thirty pounds each week and good exam results? That was nothing to worry about.

I'd come to a decision, I reflected. I was going to lead two separate lives. So why was I confused? Why were thoughts nagging me? Why was guilt stabbing my conscience? My teacher was in his fifties, so what? Diana was a girl, so what? Sex was sex, wasn't it? To get my head sorted out, I needed to go to the park and sit by the pond. I'd told mum that I might go for a walk to get some fresh air, so she wouldn't worry about me when she got home. Determined to make my decision final, I needed to show off my knickers to passing men to establish my secret life.

Walking down the street in a short red dress, I instinctively knew that today would see an end to my worries. I was out of the house, heading for the park, and I was Annette the slut. Annette the prostitute? This was the final test, I thought as I reached the pond. The sun warming me, I sat on the bench and looked around the park. It was a lovely summer day, a day for exposing my specially adjusted knickers to men and confirming my decision once and for all.

After an hour, I was feeling despondent. Apart from a woman walking a dog, the park had been deserted, and I began to wonder whether I would have been better off going to the common. As I was about to leave the bench, I noticed a man heading my way. This was my chance, I thought anxiously. My stomach churning, my heart racing, I looked the other way as he neared the bench. I was no good at this, I thought. Rather than relaxed and composed, I was quivering with nerves.

'Hi,' he said, standing before me. 'I've seen you here before, haven't I?'

'Probably,' I replied, looking up at him.

He gazed at the triangular patch of my white knickers and smiled. 'Mind if I join you?' he asked.

'No, I don't mind,' I breathed, parting my thighs further.

'I'm retired and I often walk in the park.' Rather than join me, he stayed where he was and stared at my knickers. 'I like it here during the week, it's quiet.'

He was in his fifties and not bad looking, and I wondered whether his cock was hard. As he talked about the park, he was unable to take his eyes off my knickers. I felt my outer lips swelling either side of the narrow crotch, my sex-milk seeping, as he finally joined me on the bench. I wasn't sure what I wanted to do as he said how pretty I was. He commented on my blonde hair and my slender legs, and I reckoned that he wanted to see more of me. Did I want to wank him in return for cash? Would he pay me to show him my hairless crack? I had no idea how to start the ball rolling.

'Are you working?' he asked me.

'Yes, I am,' I replied, knowing exactly what he meant.

I was about to become a full-fledged prostitute, I thought. How much should I charge to wank him? I pondered. Did he want to fuck me? As he ran his hand up my leg, I had a change of mind. I couldn't do it, I couldn't wank a complete stranger. I couldn't take him into the woods and strip naked and ... I must have been mad, I reflected. I should have been at college and ... His fingers were wandering further up my leg towards my knickers. I grabbed his hand.

'Money first, I suppose,' he said with a chuckle. 'What do you charge?'

'What do you mean?' I asked.

'You said that you were working. How much for ...'

'Yes, I am working today. This is my break. I always come here during my break.'

'I'm so sorry,' he said. 'I thought you looked rather young to be ... God, I'm sorry.'

'Young to be what?'

'Nothing, it's all right. Look, I'd better be going.'

'You can stay for a while, I don't mind.'

'Well, just for a minute. A word of advice ... I'm Paul, by the way.'

'I'm Annette.'

'A word of advice, Annette. You're an extremely attractive young girl. You shouldn't sit that way with your ... you shouldn't sit with your knickers showing.'

'God,' I breathed, looking down at my naked thighs. Having second thoughts about wanking him, I wondered where to go from here. 'I didn't realise.'

133

'Men will get the wrong idea if you sit like that.'

'Did you get the wrong idea?'

'Yes, yes, I did. I've seen you here before and I thought . . . Let's change the subject.'

'No, I'm interested,' I said with a giggle. 'Do you pay girls?'

'Yes, I have done. I live alone and . . . you wouldn't understand.'

'Tell me,' I persisted.

'A man needs certain things. I don't have a lady friend, I'm not married, and I get pretty lonely at times. Seeing your knickers like that, I thought that you might show me more.'

'Wow,' I gasped. 'You mean, you pay girls to pull their knickers down?'

'Yes, I suppose you could put it that way,' he replied with a chuckle. 'I'll never see a girl's body again unless I pay.'

'If you just want to look at a girl, I'm sure that someone would let you.'

'Not without paying.'

'That's amazing.'

'Not really, Annette. You wouldn't show your body to men for nothing, would you?'

'I've never thought about it. So, just to look at a girl with no clothes on, you'd pay her?'

'Yes, I would. And I have a couple of friends who would pay. We're trying to find a girl who would be willing to . . .'

'Take her clothes off? How much do you have to pay?'

'That depends on what the girl does. We did have a regular girl, but she moved away. Look, I don't think we should be talking about it. You're obviously very young, and I don't think we should discuss it.'

'I'm not shy,' I said, smiling at him.

'I know you're not, but we shouldn't be talking about . . .'

'No, no, I mean . . . if you just want to look, I'll show you.'

His eyes widened. 'Really?' he said.

'Yes, why not? I'm not shy, I wouldn't mind you looking at me.'

'Hang on, hang on. Why are you doing this? Why offer to show me your body?'

'I feel sorry for you,' I sighed. 'You said that you'll never see a girl's body again unless you pay. That's sad, and not fair.'

'Well, if you're sure?'

'Of course I'm sure. We'll go into the woods,' I proffered, leaping to my feet. 'I have about half an hour.'

'Right,' he said eagerly, leaving the bench. 'Let's go.'

Leading him into the woods, I had no intention of stripping naked for nothing. I'd show him my tits, tempt him and, if he wanted more, charge him. He was bound to want to meet me again, I thought as we reached the clearing. And no doubt his friends would be keen to feast their eyes on my young body. My knicker-flashing had worked yet again, I thought happily, as I turned and faced him. Beaming, he swept back his crop of greying hair and looked me up and down.

'I can't believe my luck,' he said excitedly as I released the top buttons of my dress.

'I like to make people happy,' I trilled, opening the front of my dress and exposing the firm mounds of my petite breasts. 'There, what do you think?'

'God,' he breathed, gazing longingly at my erect nipples. 'So firm and . . . You're beautiful, Annette.'

'Thank you, you're very kind.'

'I can't wait to see the rest of your beautiful body. Take your dress off for me and . . .'

'Oh,' I sighed. It was time to play naive. 'I . . . I didn't think you wanted me to take all my clothes off.'

'I'm sorry, I thought that's what you meant.'

'I meant that I'd show you my top half.'

'Look, I'll pay you.'

'Pay me? I'm not a prostitute.'

'I know you're not. Look upon it as a gift. Say, twenty pounds?'

'To take all my clothes off?'

'Yes.'

'Well, I suppose I could do with some money,' I breathed softly. 'Well, all right,' I finally conceded.

'Good girl,' he said, taking the money from his pocket and passing it to me.

Tugging my dress over my head, I stood before the old man in nothing but my knickers and shoes. He looked me up and down appreciatively, grinning as he focused on the tight crotch of my knickers. I loved playing the innocent little girl. To have asked him for cash and shown myself to be a prostitute would have spoiled the game. Little Miss Innocent, seduced by a dirty old man. Eyeing my curves, he licked his lips and waited for me to pull my knickers down and expose the tight crack of my hairless pussy.

Pulling my knickers down, allowing them to fall down my legs and crumple around my ankles, I stood upright and did my best to look incredibly embarrassed. Biting my lip, twisting my long hair around my fingers, I hung my head as he knelt before me and stared in disbelief at my tightly closed sex crack. Without a hair in sight, he could see everything I'd got, and he obviously liked it. As he moved further forward, I stepped back and clasped my hands in front of my pussy.

'I'd better get dressed,' I said softly, hoping that he'd offer me more money.

'Not yet,' he breathed. There was a longing reflected in the dark pools of his eyes. 'Please, let me look at you for a while longer.'

'Well, all right,' I replied. My hands by my sides, I stepped forward. 'There.'

'Your hair . . .,' he began. 'Did you shave or . . .'

'I use cream. I like it that way.'

'God, you look so . . . May I stroke you there?'

'No, I don't think so. You've looked, so I'd better get dressed.'

Thrusting his hand into his trouser pocket, he pulled out a twenty-pound note. 'If I give you this, will you let me?' he asked me.

With one note in my hand, I was eager to get hold of the other one. 'I don't think so,' I said. 'Well, maybe . . .'

'Please, I only want to feel you.'

'All right,' I murmured, taking the money.

This was too easy, I thought, as he ran his fingertip up and down my tightly closed crack. Forty pounds was a hell of a lot of money for standing there naked and allowing him to stroke me. The sensations sending quivers through my contracting womb, I began to think that I needn't bother going to university. If I could earn this sort of money, why bother with exams and get a job? If the old man's friends paid me to allow them to touch me, and my teacher gave me thirty pounds each week, I'd have plenty of money.

Running his hands over my hips, he reached up and squeezed the firm mounds of my breasts. My arousal was soaring as he encircled my sensitive nipples with his fingertips, but I daren't show it. My naked body beginning to tremble as he pulled on my

137

erect nipples, I could feel my pussy-milk seeping between my engorged inner lips. I needed to come, but I daren't suggest that he finger me. I was Little Miss Innocent, wasn't I?

'I have a proposition,' he said, cupping my outer lips in his hand as he looked up at me. 'Do you have a boyfriend?'

'Well, no,' I breathed. I could feel his middle finger close to my bottom-hole as he squeezed me. 'Not at the moment.'

'I was wondering . . . I mentioned my friends earlier. Would you do this for them, if they paid you?'

'What, take my clothes off?'

'Yes.'

'Well, I suppose I could.'

'If you came to my house –'

'No,' I cut in. 'I don't mind doing it here, but not at your house.'

'All right, that's fine. How much would you want?'

'Well, the same as you gave me.'

'That's rather a lot of money. If you let them do more than just touch you, they'd probably be OK with that.'

'Forty pounds?'

'Yes.'

'What would I have to do?'

'I'll be straight with you, Annette. They'd want to finger you and lick you.'

'Well, I suppose that would be all right.'

'And would you . . . would you touch them?'

'You mean, their cocks?'

'Yes. Nothing bad, just wanking.'

'How often would I have to meet them here?'

'Once a week.'

'All together? I mean, all of you together?'

'Yes, if that's OK?'

'All right,' I agreed, trying to conceal my delight. One hundred and twenty a week? God, I'd be rich. 'It will have to be an evening.'

'Yes, whenever you say. Tomorrow night, if you're free?'

'OK, tomorrow at seven o'clock.'

'All right, I'll be here.'

'That's great. Look, as I've already paid you –'

'You can lick me and stuff if you want,' I interrupted.

Wasting no time, he pressed his mouth to my swollen pussy lips and pushed his tongue into my wet crack. Licking my solid clitoris, he reached behind my naked body and clutched my firm buttocks and pulled my pussy hard against his face. I looked up at the sun sparkling through the foliage high above me as he moved down my crack and slipped his tongue deep into my vagina. This was my secret place in the woods, this was where I'd earn some real money,

I recalled my time in the woods with Derek and John. I'd been licked, fucked, spunked ... and I'd sucked the spunk out of David's cock. Although I'd decided never to go to the small clearing again, I reckoned that I'd be safe enough there. My mum wouldn't bother to follow me to the park, and I doubted that Derek or John would come looking for me. I'd meet the old men there, and meet my teacher in the bushes on the common. Things were looking good.

Slurping, sucking, drinking my cream, the old man slipped his fingers between my buttocks and toyed with my sensitive anal hole. He was obviously enjoying himself, I thought happily. Still clutching the forty pounds, I realised more than ever that my pussy was a commodity to be traded. My knickers were my shop window, they brought people inside. Once I'd enticed them into my shop, I'd grab their money and sell them my goods. It was all too easy, I again reflected. Money for nothing.

'May I ask you to do something?' he said, looking up at me.

'I suppose so,' I replied softly, not wanting to show my excitement.

Lying on the ground on his back, he smiled at me. 'Would you kneel astride my face?'

I frowned at him as if I didn't understand. 'What do you mean?'

'Put your knees either side of my head so that I can lick you.'

'Er . . . like this?' I breathed, taking my position with my open pussy hovering above his face. 'Is that OK?'

'God, yes,' he gasped. 'Thank you, thank you so much.'

His tongue delving deep into the creamy wetness of my vaginal hole, his nose pressed hard against the delicate tissue surrounding my anus, he slurped and sucked wildly in his sexual frenzy. Peeling my hairless outer lips wide open, exposing the intricate folds of my inner lips, the bulb of my erect clitoris, he drank the hot cream flowing from my vagina. The sensations were beautiful, but the power I felt over the old man was amazing. Although he was using me to satisfy his craving for young girls, I was in control. I was using him.

Pleased that I'd at last made a decision, I decided to keep a diary of my appointments. My teacher at four o'clock after college three times each week, the old man and his friends once a week . . . my secret diary, my dirty diary. I felt as though I had a purpose in life. I'd been studying, working towards the exams, preparing for university . . . Why bother? I wondered

140

as the old man sucked my solid clitoris into his hot mouth. I could earn more than enough money from my young body, so why study?

The old man unzipped his trousers and hauled out his erect cock as his tongue again slipped into my wet sheath. I gazed in awe at his huge veined shaft, the purple globe of his succulent knob. He'd want me to wank him, I knew, as he ran his hand up and down the length of his solid rod. But I wanted to suck his knob, bring out his spunk and swallow the creamy liquid. Would he give me more money to allow him to come in my mouth?

'Wank me,' he gasped through a mouthful of vaginal flesh. 'Please, I need to spunk.'

Leaning forward and wrapping my fingers around his solid shaft, I began my wanking motions. My hand moved slowly, up and down, up and down, wanking gently. As he moved away from the drenched entrance of my vagina and began tonguing my anus, I gasped and quivered. He was good, I thought as the tip of his tongue slipped into my small brown hole. The feel of his hot breath, his delving tongue, taking me to the brink of my climax, I leant further forward and sucked his swollen knob into my wet mouth. His body became rigid as I ran my tongue over the velveteen surface of his beautiful knob, and I knew that his sperm pump would soon spring into action and my thirsty mouth would flood with his male cream.

Strangely, I had no qualms about sucking off a stranger. This was business, I mused happily, taking his bulbous knob to the back of my throat and sinking my teeth gently into his rock-hard shaft. But, although I was making good money from selling my young body, my sexual services, I was also deriving immense pleasure from my exploits. Thinking that

141

there was no other work that would bring me so much money and pleasure, I knew that I was now firmly on the road to prostitution. The thought didn't bother me. This was my other life, my separate life away from Annette the innocent young girl. So why should it bother me?

The old man slurped and sucked between the swollen lips of my pussy as his sperm jetted from his throbbing cock and filled my gobbling mouth. The salty taste was delicious, and I swallowed repeatedly as his body trembled and he sucked my orgasm from my aching clitoris. Would he realise that I'd had sexual experience? I wondered as I wanked his solid shaft to sustain his orgasm. He'd not asked me to suck his cock. He might think me a slut and . . . Did it matter? If anything, he'd be pleased with me, think me worth every penny of his money.

My orgasm receding, his sperm-flow stemming, I finally slipped his deflating cock out of my mouth and licked my spunk-glossed lips. I'd done it, I thought happily as he sucked the last ripples of sex out of my clitoris. I'd sold my young body to a stranger, my first real client. I felt good inside, powerful, wicked, sexually alive as never before. His tongue lapping at my vaginal entrance, he sucked out the remnants of my orgasmic cream before easing me off his face.

'You're wonderful,' he breathed as I sat beside him on the soft grass. 'So young and fresh and . . . you're perfect.'

'Thank you,' I said softly, grabbing my clothes as his zipped his trousers and clambered to his feet. Taking my hand and helping me up, he locked his eyes on my firm breasts and smiled. 'My friends will be delighted,' he said, licking his creamed lips.

'How many friends will you bring?' I asked him.

'Only two, to begin with. I may bring more at some stage, if that's all right?'

'That's OK.'

'The way you sucked me and ... have you done this before?'

'Never,' I lied as I finished dressing. 'I'm a virgin.'

'May I be the first?'

'I don't want that,' I breathed, wondering whether he'd pay heavily if he believed that he was to strip me of my virginity. 'I don't want to do that.'

'Annette, you're an angel, heaven-sent. I'd give anything to be the first man to –'

'I've never done anything sexual before,' I cut in. 'This is all new to me and I don't want to lose my virginity to ...'

'Here,' he said, taking a wad of notes from his trousers pocket. 'One hundred pounds.'

'Wow,' I gasped as he pressed the money into my hand. 'Where did you get all this cash from?'

'I was out looking for a girl. I always carry a lot of cash when I'm looking for a girl. So, will you do it?'

'I suppose so,' I replied softly.

'That's great. Take your knickers off and bend over that fallen tree,' he instructed me. 'I'll take you from behind.'

'Well, I ... I don't know.'

'I'll be gentle with you,' he said with a chuckle.

Slipping my wet knickers off, I took my position over the fallen tree and waited in anticipation. He moved about behind me, lifting my dress up and stroking the firm cheeks of my bottom and I stared at the ground. The rough bark squashing my young breasts through my dress, I closed my eyes as I felt his bulbous knob running up and down the hairless crack of my teenage pussy. One hundred pounds for a quick fuck? I thought dreamily as his knob slipped between the wet petals of my inner lips and pressed against the hot flesh surrounding the entrance to my vagina. This was easy money.

His solid shaft entered me, his swollen knob gliding along my tight sex sheath to my cervix. He grabbed my hips and rammed his huge cock fully home. The stretching sensations were incredible, and I let out a gasp as he pulled me hard against his body. I could feel his heavy balls against my hairless mons, his lower belly against my rounded buttocks, and I knew that he'd dropped his trousers and lifted his shirt up. Withdrawing, he rammed into me again with such force that I almost went head-first over the fallen tree.

'God, you're so tight,' he gasped, finding his fucking rhythm as a train rumbled through the cutting far below. 'You're not a virgin any more. Do you like it?'

'I'm not sure,' I lied, the sensations driving me wild as he fucked me.

'God, you're hot and tight.'

My long blonde hair cascading over my face and dragging on the ground as I flopped back and forth like a rag doll, I listened to the squelching sounds of my pussy-milk as his huge cock repeatedly glided in and out of my teenage vagina. My young body, my hairless pussy, my teenage cunt . . . a commodity to earn me money. The old man had been happy enough to part with his cash, and I'd been more than happy to grab it. A business arrangement, I thought, imagining three men queuing up to fuck me from behind. I might as well make money while I was young and fresh. Besides, my pussy would hardly wear out.

His sperm jetting from his orgasming knob and flooding my tight vagina, he repeatedly battered my cervix with his purple crown as his balls drained for the second time. My own orgasm erupting within the pulsating bulb of my clitoris, I cried out and shook uncontrollably. My mind blown away as my pleasure gripped me, the slapping of flesh meeting flesh and the gasps of orgasm filled the warm summer air. I was in my sexual heaven, and I never wanted to come down from the most beautiful climax I'd experienced.

Clutching my money, I knew that I was now a fully-fledged prostitute. But the notion didn't bother me at all. I'd been stripped of my virginity by my next-door neighbour and stripped of my morals by all the men I'd been with. A teenage prostitute, keeping men happy and earning a fortune, was now my role in life. I could feel warm spunk overflowing from my vagina and streaming down my inner thighs. Again, I contemplated my cunt as a commodity. It was nothing more than a creamy-wet hole between my legs, I reflected as my orgasm began to wane. My cunt was simply a hot, tight and very wet hole to be sold to old men to make them happy.

'Bloody hell,' the man gasped as he slowed his fucking rhythm. 'I can't believe how tight you are. It's been decades since I fucked a virgin.'

'You were amazing,' I breathed, shuddering my last shudder as he slipped his spent cock out of my inflamed vagina. 'I hope your friends are as good.'

'Oh, yes,' he said with a chuckle as I hauled my quivering body upright. 'They're going to love you.'

'They'll pay the same as you, of course.'

'Well, now that you're not a virgin . . . I don't think they'll pay one hundred.'

'In that case, I'll have to think about it,' I murmured, adjusting my dress. 'I don't like the idea of being used by three men at once. Not for less than one hundred each.'

'All right, I'll speak to them about it.'

'If they agree, shall we meet tomorrow evening? Say, seven o'clock?'

'We'll be here, I assure you. Thanks, Annette. You really are an amazing girl. I'll walk with you.'

'No, I'll stay here for a while. You go, and I'll see you tomorrow evening.'

'OK. And, thanks.'

As he left the clearing, I gazed at the wad of notes in my hand. I could hardly believe that I'd earned a hundred and forty pounds from one trip to the woods. I'd collect money from my teacher that afternoon, and then another three hundred from the old man and his friends tomorrow evening. I'd soon be rich, I thought, wondering how many more men would pay to use my young body. My mind was buzzing with thoughts of the cash I could earn in one month, one year. This was better than to university, exams and getting a proper job . . .

'I thought I'd find you here, Annette.' Recognising my mother's voice, I spun round on my heels. 'What on earth are you up to?'

'I'm not up to anything,' I replied, my heart banging hard against my chest. 'I've been watching the trains.'

'Who was that man I saw leaving the woods just now?'

'Man? What man?'

'I saw a man leaving the woods.'

'I haven't seen anyone. I felt a little better and decided to go for a walk.'

'Annette, we need to talk,' she sighed, taking my hand and leading me out of the clearing. 'You've changed recently, and I want to know why.'

'Changed in what way?' I asked her, clutching the money in my free hand.

'I don't know. You miss college, you seem preoccupied . . . What is it? What's on your mind?'

'I suppose I've been studying a lot, and I have a

pile of homework to do. But there's nothing wrong, mum.'

'If the work is putting pressure on you, do you want me to speak to your teacher?'

'No, no. The work is OK, honestly. It's just that I got behind a little and I have to catch up.'

Crossing the park, I thanked God that she hadn't turned up when the old man had been fucking me over the fallen tree. I should never have gone to the woods, I reflected. I'd suggested that she follow me if she was suspicious, but I'd never imagined she'd come looking for me in the clearing. Another close escape, I thought anxiously as we headed home. God, if she'd turned up when I'd been squatting over the old man's face and sucking spunk out of his cock . . .

'Derek's coming to dinner this evening,' she said as we neared the house.

'Oh, right.'

'You will be there, won't you?'

'I said that I'd meet Diana after college and . . .'

'Annette, you're always going out. You've taken the day off college because you're supposed to be unwell. I really don't think you should go out and meet Diana.'

'I'm feeling better now, mum. Anyway, I'll be back for dinner.'

'Shouldn't you be catching up with your college work? You said that you were behind so . . .'

'I'm leaving college,' I said as she opened the front door.

'I know you are.' Closing the door, she led me into the lounge. 'And then you have university and –'

'No, mum,' I cut in. 'I've been offered a job.'

'What?'

'I've been offered a top job with really good money.'

147

'Annette, you have to go to college and then on to university. If you give up your education and go out to work . . . Is that what's been on your mind recently?'

'Yes, yes, it is. The job is in computers. They're going to train me and . . . The money is excellent, mum.'

'How did you get this job?'

'A friend. Her sister works there and I went to see them. The money is good and the prospects are –'

'Why didn't you tell me about it earlier?'

'I was waiting for confirmation.'

'God knows what your father will say.'

'He'll be pleased, won't he? He's always saying that computers are the way forward. I'll be working for a big company, mum. And I won't be giving up my education because they'll be training me. Rather than learning about history and stuff, which is no good to anyone, I'll be . . .'

'If it's really what you want then, I suppose we can't stop you. Dad will be disappointed, but I'll talk to him about it. He'll be home soon. He's leaving work early to do some paperwork.'

'I know I'm doing the right thing, mum.'

'I hope so, Annette. I hope so.'

Sitting on my bed with sperm oozing into the narrow crotch of my knickers, I wondered why the hell I'd come out with such a fantastic story. One lie would lead to another, I mused, twisting my long blonde hair nervously around my fingers. I'd have to leave the house every day and make out that I was going to work. My parents would ask me about the company, where it was, how I was getting on . . . Lies and more lies. But I was sure that I could make it work.

I'd had a shower and was ready to go to the common to meet my teacher when my dad got home.

I opened my bedroom door and listened as mum told him the news. He was initially angry, but then seemed to calm down a little as mum explained that I'd be given training. Dressed in my miniskirt and a skimpy top, I had to get to the common. But I knew that I'd have to face my dad before leaving the house.

'Sit down, Annette,' he said as I wandered into the lounge. 'Mum's told me about the job.'

'It's really good,' I trilled. 'I can't let an opportunity like this . . .'

'University is an opportunity you can't miss, Annette. What's the salary?'

'Well . . . twenty thousand, to start with.'

'That's pretty good. And you'll get all the training you need?'

'Yes, of course.'

'What is the job, exactly?'

'Computers.'

'Yes, I know that. But what area? Networking, servers –'

'Both,' I cut in. 'Well, servers mainly.'

'That's a lot of money to pay someone of your age. Especially as you have no exams.'

'That's why I don't want to miss out. They're going to give me training and . . . It's what I want, dad.'

'Look, I have a lot of paperwork to do before Derek gets here. We'll talk about it later, OK?'

'OK.'

'I don't like the idea, Annette. But if it's what you want and you've given it serious thought . . .'

'Thanks, dad,' I said, kissing his cheek. 'I'll be back for dinner.'

'Annette, I haven't decided yet. We'll talk later.'

I arrived at the pub in Brighton to find Annette sitting at a corner table scribbling on a notepad. She was making notes for the end of the book, which pleased me because she was obviously still keen. All along, I'd thought that she might have a change of mind and back out. But there was no chance of that happening now. She read the latest chapter and then passed the papers back to me and grinned.

'It's coming on really well,' she said. 'Little Miss Innocent was great with the old man in the woods. Innocence, my trade secret.'

'A fully-fledged prostitute,' I said.

'I'd not planned to become a prostitute. It just sort of happened when I met the old man. He thought that I was a working girl, and I went along with it. That was an amazing encounter because he made the mistake of believing that I was on the game, I made out that I was innocent, and then he coaxed me gently. The whole thing sort of unfolded.'

'And you made a lot of money.'

'God, yes. I was thinking about it the other day. Some girls left school and worked in shops or offices, and some went on to university. And I had sex. I got one hundred and forty pounds from the old man. I mean, where could I earn that sort of money?'

'You said in the book that you had no qualms.'

'That's right, no qualms about sucking off a stranger. At that point, I'd convinced myself that my body was a commodity. My pussy was for bringing me pleasure and money. Sucking off the old man was purely for monetary gain. Having said that, I did enjoy it.'

'Then your mother turned up.'

'That's what started a string of lies. I dreamt up the story about leaving college and getting a job and . . . I suppose it was a stupid thing to do, but my mum went along with it. If she'd turned up earlier, she'd have seen the old man fucking me. I was taking too many risks.'

'You then risked going to the common to meet your teacher.'

'I didn't see that as a risk. Apart from Diana, no one knew about the clearing behind the bushes. As I walked to the common, the only thing on my mind was making more money.'

More Lesbian Sex

Although I was late, my teacher was waiting in the clearing behind the bushes. I'd thought that he'd have given up on me, particularly as I'd not been to college. He was obviously keen to meet me, I mused happily, wondering whether he'd want to fuck me. He looked me up and down appreciatively, his lips furling into a grin as he gazed at my naked legs. Was he picturing my tight little pussy crack? Had he been thinking about me all day? Had he been picturing my hairless pussy lips? Stroking my cheek, he didn't even bother to ask me why I'd not been to college. He was more interested in my young body, I knew, as he brushed my long blonde hair away from my face. Passing me a ten-pound note, he checked his watch.

'I don't have much time,' he sighed. 'I have a meeting at college.'

'We'll leave it, if you want,' I said.

'No, no. Would you just ...' He unzipped his trousers and pulled out his erect cock. 'Would you wank me?'

'All right,' I breathed, wrapping my slender fingers around his solid shaft. This was going to be the easiest ten pounds I'd earned.

'Annette ... I've been thinking about ...'

'About what?'

'I've been thinking about you sucking my cock. Would you suck it?' he asked me sheepishly.

I released his cock and held my hand to my mouth. 'Suck it?' I echoed, stepping back and feigning shock. 'No, I . . .'

'It's something I've been dreaming about. I've been dreaming about you sucking it.'

'Mr Williams, I can't . . . I mean, I've never . . .'

'Please, Annette. You have such a pretty mouth. To feel you sucking me would be –'

'It's not right,' I cut in. 'People don't do that sort of thing, do they?'

'Yes, of course they do. Look, I'll give you another ten pounds.'

'Well . . .' He thrust his hand into his trouser pocket and passed me the money. 'I suppose I could try it,' I finally conceded.

'I'm sure you'll enjoy it.'

'All right,' I sighed, concealing my excitement as best I could.

I knelt before him as he rolled his foreskin back, then took his purple knob into my wet mouth and sucked gently. He let out a low groan and clutched my head as I swept my tongue over the smoothness of his salty plum and probed his small slit. Although I loved cock sucking, I was pleased that he couldn't stay for long as I wanted to get home and make my plans. I had lies to spin, stories to dream up. Sure that I'd already convinced my parents I was doing the right thing, all I had to do was leave college and begin my full-time work as a prostitute. I still didn't like the word, but it didn't bother me.

Wanking my teacher's cock shaft as I gobbled on his beautiful knob, I watched him unbuckle his belt and drop his trousers. I knew that he'd want me to toy with his balls, but I played little Miss Innocent. I was young and inexperienced, a sweet little virgin girl. I didn't know what he wanted me to do. Continuing to wank his cock and suck on his purple knob, I wasn't surprised when he asked me to lick his balls. Slipping his cock out of my mouth, I put on my angelic face and looked up at him with my blue eyes wide.

'Lick them?' I breathed, frowning at him.

'You'll like it,' he said, offering me a smile. 'Girls love doing that.'

'Well . . .'

'Please, Annette. I don't have much time.'

Holding his solid shaft, I moved forward and licked the wrinkled skin of his scrotum. He gasped and trembled as I took one of his balls into my mouth and sucked gently, and I knew that he was pleased with me. The better I was, the more I pleased him, the more money he'd give me. That was the name of the game. Make old men happy, and they'd part with their money. They'd become hooked on me and spend more than they could afford to get their hands on my young body. And I'd earn a fortune.

The fragrance of his pubic hairs filling my nostrils, I felt my clitoris swell and my pussy milk wet the crotch of my tight knickers. Little Miss Innocent, I thought recalling the old man fucking me in the woods. That would be the secret of my success, I mused, as I ran my tongue up and down his twitching cock shaft. I was a sweet little virgin girl displaying an air of angelic innocence. Men would pay dearly to use and abuse me and strip me of my virginity.

Wanking his cock, licking his heaving balls, I knew that he'd soon be pumping out his creamy spunk. Cum-slut: I'd heard the expression somewhere. Annette, the cum-slut. Annette, the innocent virgin girl. Clutching the notes he'd given me as I licked around the rim of his purple knob, I again realised how easy it was to take money from men. Twenty pounds to suck his cock? At this rate, I'd soon be earning more than my dad, and he had a well-paid job. To stay on at college would be madness, I reflected. I'd made the right decision. To go on to university would be a waste of time.

'I'm coming,' my teacher gasped, clutching tufts of my long blonde hair. 'Suck it and swallow my spunk.'

I was going to ask him for more money in return for swallowing his spunk, but thought better of it. I didn't want to push my luck, I thought, taking his glistening knob into my hot mouth. Cupping his heavy balls in my hand, I moved my head back and forth and repeatedly took his ripe plum to the back of my throat. His legs sagging, he let out another low moan as his spunk jetted from his swollen knob and flooded my gobbling mouth.

He must have been in his sexual heaven, I mused, as I allowed my mouth to fill with his salty cream before swallowing hard. I reckoned he must have been thinking that he was the luckiest man on earth. To have one of his young pupils wank his hard cock and suck the spunk from his knob must have been a dream come true. Never in a million years would he have believed that he'd be fucking one of his sweet little girls' mouth and spunking down her throat. Never would I have believed that I'd be earning a fortune from my young body.

'You're beautiful,' he gasped as his sperm-flow stemmed and I slipped his deflating cock out of my mouth. 'You're amazing.'

'Was that all right?' I asked, licking my sperm-glossed lips and looking up with my blue eyes wide. It was all over far too quickly. 'Are you sure it was all right?'

'All right? God, it was incredible.' He zipped his trousers and checked his watch. 'Tomorrow after college?' he asked. He was trembling uncontrollably. 'Will that be all right?'

'Yes, I'll be here,' I replied, rising to my feet.

'I'll have more time tomorrow. I'll strip you naked and . . . I'd better go now.'

Leaving the clearing, he turned and grinned at me before disappearing from view. He was a happy man, I thought, again licking my lips. The taste of sperm lingering on my tongue, I wondered when he'd ask me to allow him to fuck me. The time would surely come when he wanted to sink his hard cock deep into the tight sheath of what he believed to be my virgin pussy. If only he knew that I'd already been fucked by an old man. But he'd never discover the truth. None of my clients would discover that I wasn't the sweet little virgin girl they believed me to be.

I could still taste sperm when I got home and lied to my mum about Diana not turning up. Lies came easily now. Mum told me that Derek was in the lounge and dad had gone back to work to collect some papers. Gazing at her full lips, I wondered whether she'd had her mouth pumped full of spunk. Had my dad fucked her mouth? If she discovered that my college teacher had pumped his spunk down my throat . . . My lies would protect me.

I wasn't going to flash my knickers to Derek, I decided, when mum suggested I go and keep him company while she prepared the dinner. I'd not seen him for some time and really didn't want to have to sit with him, and I certainly wasn't going to show him my wet knickers. He was bound to ask me to meet him in the woods, but I'd decline. I'd like to have kept him on as a client, but he was my dad's boss and I didn't want to play too close too home. He'd want

156

me to meet him and strip naked and . . . The last thing I needed was more blackmail threats, so I was going to have to play this carefully. With mum around, I knew that he wouldn't make a move towards me. I walked into the lounge, smiled at him and sat on the sofa with my thighs pressed tightly together.

'How are you?' he asked as mum went into the kitchen.

'Fine, thanks,' I replied, grabbing a magazine from the coffee table and slipping the money I'd earned between the pages.

'Annette . . .' He looked at the open door and leaned forward. 'Annette, meet me in the woods later, OK?'

'I can't,' I said without raising my eyes from the magazine. 'I have homework to do.'

'And you have a debt to pay,' he persisted. 'You owe me, Annette.'

'I can't,' I repeated, lowering the magazine and staring at him.

But I knew he wasn't going to give up. I went back to reading the magazine, wondering what to do, how to respond. Should I meet him that evening? After all, he was right, I did owe him. But I didn't want to meet him in the woods. What with mum having found me in the clearing by the fence, the last thing I needed was to get caught naked with Derek's cock up my pussy.

'Right,' mum said, popping her head round the door. 'I'm just going up for a shower.'

'OK,' I breathed. 'Is there anything I can do in the kitchen?' I asked her, looking for an escape route.

'No, it's all under control. I won't be long.'

'Annette,' Derek whispered as she climbed the stairs. 'Why have you been avoiding me? What's the matter?'

'I haven't been avoiding you,' I returned.

'I've been to the park several times. Where have you been?'

'I don't spend all my time in the park.'

'Whenever I've come here, you've been out.'

'I'm sorry, but I do have other things to do apart from hang around in case you turn up.'

'We have a chance now,' he said, leaving his chair and standing before me. 'Kneel on the floor and rest your head on the sofa.'

'What?' I gasped. 'Derek . . . my mum's upstairs.'

'We have time,' he continued, kneeling on the floor and unzipping his trousers. 'You owe me a fuck, Annette.'

'No, not here.'

'Now, Annette,' he whispered through gritted teeth. 'When we were last in the woods, I said that once your parents discover what you get up to, you'll be grounded for months on end. I also said that the time had come to stop playing games. Now, what's it to be?'

'All right,' I sighed, kneeling on the floor with my head resting on the sofa cushion. 'But be quick.'

He yanked my knickers down my thighs and stabbed urgently at my wet crack with his bulbous knob. I could hear mum banging about in the bathroom as his knob slipped between my inner lips and drove into the tight sheath of my pussy. I couldn't believe that I was being fucked in the lounge by my dad's boss while my mum was upstairs. I must have been mad, I thought, imagining dad coming back and walking into the lounge. This was so risky that all I could do was hope that he'd spunk me quickly and get it over with.

'Tight little slut,' he gasped, grabbing my hips and fucking me from behind with a vengeance. 'I've been waiting to fuck you.'

'Hurry up,' I whispered, looking over my shoulder. 'My mum will be down in a minute.'

'We have plenty of time,' he returned with a chuckle. 'I'm going to fuck you every day, Annette. I'm going to fuck your tight little college girl cunt every day.'

I buried my face in the sofa cushion, and rocked back and forth as his solid cock repeatedly withdrew and rammed into the hot sheath of my teenage pussy. I'd been fucked twice in one day, by two men. At least John from next door had moved away, so he shouldn't cause me problems. But what the hell was I to do about Derek? How many times would he fuck me before deciding that I'd paid my debt? Blackmailers always come back for more.

His spunk flooded my tight vagina as he rammed his massive cock deep into the squelching sheath of my young body again and again. I heard my dad's car pull up in the drive, mum moving about upstairs . . . This was ridiculous, I thought anxiously as Derek's sperm bubbled from my drenched vagina and streamed down my inner thighs. I'd allowed Diana to masturbate me in my bedroom, and now Derek was fucking me in the lounge. And mum had almost caught me fucking an old man in the woods.

'I'm back,' dad called, opening the front door.

'In here,' I said as Derek yanked his cock out of my sperm-brimming pussy and zipped his trousers. Sitting on the sofa, I prayed that my face wasn't red.

'The papers,' dad said, wandering into the lounge as Derek sat down in the armchair.

'Ah, good,' Derek breathed. 'We'll have to go through the figures and –'

'I'm going to my room,' I cut in, leaving the sofa before the cushion soaked up the spunk filling my knickers.

I grabbed the magazine and bounded up the stairs to my bedroom and closed the door. Another narrow escape, I thought, breathing a sigh of relief as I slipped my wet knickers off. I hid the evidence of my illicit fucking beneath the bed. Brushing my dishevelled hair back with my fingers, I tried to compose myself. I was shaking and my heart was banging hard against my chest. I swore never to take such a crazy risk again. Was the sofa wet? I wondered anxiously, as sperm oozed between the swollen lips of my inflamed vagina.

Flopping on to my bed and opening the magazine, I gazed at the cash and grinned. I was doing very well, but I was playing a dangerous game. Had mum come downstairs and caught me . . . I'd had a narrow escape, been very lucky, and decided not to think about it any more. But I did have to think about my future sexual exploits. I needed somewhere safe to meet my clients. Behind the bushes on the common was fine in the summer months. What would I do in midwinter? Strip naked and get fucked in the snow?

When mum came up and asked me whether I was hungry, I told her I wasn't feeling too good and couldn't face food. The truth was that I didn't want to face Derek. He'd be grinning at me across the table, winking and licking his lips. I'd paid my debt, I decided. He'd fucked me, and that was that. If he wanted more, then he'd have to dig deep into his pocket. I'd told him that I wasn't cheap the first time I'd been in the woods with him. And he'd find out just how expensive my young body was if he wanted more.

I took a shower and washed the spunk from my sex crack and my thighs, then borrowed dad's razor and shaved the stubble from my pussy lips. Little Miss Innocent, I thought, catching my reflection in the bathroom mirror. Sweet little virgin girl. I slipped into a long T-shirt and a pair of clean knickers and lounged on my bed listening to my new stereo system and making my plans. I wouldn't go to college tomorrow, I decided. I had far more exciting and profitable things to do than go to college.

'Hi,' Diana said, entering my room without knocking. 'Your mum said it was OK to come up.'

'Oh, right,' I breathed, eyeing her miniskirt, her slender thighs.

'Why weren't you at college?'

'I wasn't feeling well,' I lied as she sat next to me on the bed. 'It's just a tummy upset.'

'Are you going in tomorrow?'

'No, I don't think so.'

'You should have been there today. I couldn't take my eyes off old Williams,' she said with a giggle. 'I kept imagining him watching you playing with your pussy.'

'I don't want to talk about it,' I muttered.

'Is that why you didn't go to college? Because you couldn't face him?'

'Of course it's not. I felt ill, and I still do.'

'To think that he saw your pussy,' she persisted. 'Wow, he must have . . .'

'Diana, I don't want to talk about it,' I repeated.

'Williams isn't the only one to have seen your pussy,' she murmured mysteriously.

'What do you mean?' I asked her, wondering what the hell she knew about me.

'Exactly what I said. He's not the only one, is he?'

'Have you been following me?' I snapped. 'Have you been spying on me?'

'What's the matter? Why are you angry?'

'I'm not angry.'

'Who else have you been with?'

161

'No one. I just wondered what you meant.'

'I've seen your pussy, Annette. That's what I meant.'

'Oh, yes, of course.'

'You enjoyed it, didn't you? You liked me making you come, didn't you?'

'Diana . . .'

'Look,' she said, lifting her skirt and exposing the crotch of her tight knickers.

'I don't want to look,' I returned, eyeing the damp material. 'I'm not a lesbian.'

I'd never seen another girl's pussy crack, and I found that I couldn't drag my eyes away from the white cotton concealing the most intimate part of her young body. She was deliberately sitting with one foot on the floor and the other on my bed, with her skirt up and her thighs parted, and I knew that she wanted me to touch her there as she talked about masturbation and orgasms. She'd obviously come to my house with one thing in mind, but I wasn't a lesbian. But she was right about one thing. I had enjoyed her intimate caress, her pussy fingering, the beautiful orgasm she'd brought me. Now she wanted me to reciprocate.

'You are funny,' she breathed, her pretty face smiling at me.

'In what way?' I asked her, finally dragging my gaze away from her knickers.

'I know what you want, and you know what I want. But you won't do it.'

'Diana, I'm not a lesbian,' I sighed.

'Neither am I. Just because we . . . What's wrong with playing about with each other?'

'I don't know. I suppose it's just not right.'

'Who says it's not right?'

'Diana . . . It's just not normal, OK?'

'It's perfectly normal. You masturbate, I masturbate, you like coming, I like coming . . . Why not do it to each other?'

I could hear my dad and Derek laughing downstairs. Things seemed normal, but they were far from normal. I'd been fucked in the woods by an old man, I'd sucked spunk from my teacher's cock, Derek had fucked me in the lounge . . . and, now, an overwhelming urge to lick Diana's pussy had gripped me. I was intrigued, I thought, as I gazed at her white knickers. This had nothing to do with lesbian sex, it was simply curiosity.

Saying nothing, she lay back on my bed with her legs wide and her skirt pulled up over her stomach. I could see her sex crack clearly defined by the tight crotch of her knickers as she parted her legs further, and the temptation to reach out and stroke her was irresistible. To part her full lips and examine her inner folds, to slip a finger into her tight sheath and feel the wet heat of her inner flesh, to massage the solid nub of her clitoris . . . I knew that, if I turned away and didn't take the opportunity to experiment sexually with another girl, I'd be left forever wondering.

To my amazement, she slipped her knickers off and lay with her thighs apart. I gazed at the pink petals of her inner lips protruding invitingly from the hairless crack of her pussy, and the gentle rise of her mons, as she parted her legs further. She had a beautiful body, soft, curvaceous, sensual. My finger slipped between her puffy sex lips and deep into her tight pussy with ease. The sheath of her vagina was hot and wet, tight and yet soft. Her outer lips visibly swelled and appeared to open, as if welcoming my finger, as I explored deep inside her vagina. Her clitoris emerging from beneath its pink hood, her juices of arousal flowing from her sex sheath and

163

running over my hand, she arched her back and breathed heavily.

There was more laughter from downstairs. I wondered how Derek could face my dad after fucking his daughter in the lounge. Perhaps he looked upon it as nothing more than a quick fuck, nothing to feel guilty about. I'd been with my teacher behind the bushes, my next door-neighbour, the old man in the woods . . . it was only sex, I reflected. It wasn't a criminal offence. Sex was sex, nothing more, nothing less. My cunt was there to bring me pleasure, and money. Why shouldn't I allow Derek to fuck me over the sofa? My thinking was changing.

Slipping my wet finger out of Diana's tight vagina, I moved up her gaping valley and massaged the erect bulb of her clitoris. Her head lolling from side to side, her young body trembling uncontrollably, she gasped and writhed on my bed. Holding her fleshy outer lips wide apart with my free hand, I peered into the creamy wetness of her open sex hole. I'd never examined myself properly – opening my pussy and using a mirror wasn't easy. But now I was able to peer deep into a girl's vagina. Opening her hole further as I continued to massage her erect clitoris, I imagined a huge cock fucking her there.

My own clitoris was inflating, my pussy-milk flowing into the tight crotch of my knickers, yet I tried to deny my arousal. This was a lesbian sex act, I reminded myself as Diana let out a rush of breath. But I was masturbating another girl purely out of curiosity. This had nothing to do with lesbian sex, did it? Laughter again came from downstairs, but I felt as though I was somehow removed, hiding away in my room, committing a sexual act with another girl in the privacy of my room . . .

'Lick me,' Diana gasped as she writhed on my bed.

A deluge of hot milk flowed from her open vagina. I wondered what she tasted like. I'd sucked knobs and tasted sperm, and I'd tasted my own milk. Should I lick her? Having mouth contact with her body would be like kissing her. Fingering her vagina and massaging her clitoris wasn't intimate contact like locking my mouth to her swollen lips and licking her. She'd not licked me, I reflected, as I leant forward and kissed the gentle rise of her hairless mons. Breathing in her female scent, I trembled as my mouth watered and my arousal soared to frightening heights. Did I want her to lick my crack? Did I want a female tongue delving into my vagina?

My mind in turmoil, my thoughts goaded me. If I didn't lick her, suck and taste her, I'd be left forever wondering. I might never have another opportunity to experiment with another girl. But if I liked it, I'd want more. If I enjoyed the taste of another girl's vaginal milk, I might want more and become a lesbian. Two separate lives, I mused dreamily, massaging Diana's solid clitoris faster as she neared her orgasm. Annette, the innocent little angel. Annette, the bisexual slut.

Peeling her fleshy vaginal pads open with both hands, I pressed my mouth hard against the glistening pink flesh nestling within her wet teenage crack. The taste was very different to sperm. Tangy, slightly bitter and yet sweet with an aphrodisiacal aroma, the flavour of her sex milk drove me wild. Lapping at her open hole, slipping my tongue deep inside her young vagina, I drank her milk and massaged the solid bulb of her clitoris in my sexual frenzy. I was addicted, I knew, as I sucked out her juices of lesbian lust and repeatedly swallowed hard.

Driving two fingers into her tightening sex duct, stretching her puffy lips wide apart with my free hand, I sucked her swollen clitoris into my hot mouth and swept my tongue over its sensitive tip. She moaned softly and clutched my head, her young body squirming on my bed as she announced that she was about to come. Driving two more fingers into her convulsing vagina, sucking hard on her erect clitoris, I lost myself in my lesbian lust as she gripped my head hard and ground her open flesh hard against my mouth.

Her orgasmic juices spewing from her spasming vagina, spraying over my hand as she whimpered and writhed, she let out a cry of pleasure that I thought my parents might hear. I could feel her clitoris pulsating beneath my sweeping tongue, pumping out its waves of orgasm as I sucked and licked and fingered between her twitching thighs. The fragrance of her young body, the taste of her sex crack, the softness, the creamy wetness . . . She was beautiful, and I knew that this was only the beginning of our sexual relationship.

Her climax finally leaving her trembling body, she lay twitching on my bed as I slipped my fingers out of her drenched vagina. Pressing my mouth hard against the pink cone of flesh surrounding her vaginal entrance, I sucked hard and drank her teenage milk. I couldn't stop licking and sucking, kissing and nibbling between her slender thighs. She moaned softly, as if semiconscious, as I worked between the swollen lips of her young pussy. Another deluge of hot cream spewed from her inflamed vagina, and I licked and sucked and lapped it up like a dog.

Biting gently on her puffy outer lips, nibbling her wet sex flesh, I reached up and squeezed the firm mounds of her petite breasts through the thin material of her T-shirt. She wasn't wearing a bra, and I could feel the erect teats of her young breasts pressing against the tight material. Her mounds were hard in youth, well-rounded and beautifully formed. I'd never seen another girl's breasts, another girl's erect nipples. I was learning, discovering.

'God, my cunt,' she breathed shakily as I sucked her ripening clitoris into my hot mouth. 'I need to come. Suck my clit hard and finger my cunt. I need to come again.'

Her sex milk flowed in torrents as I thrust two fingers into the contracting sheath of her vagina. She again gasped and writhed on my bed in the grip of sexual ecstasy. I could hear everyone talking and laughing downstairs, plates rattling in the kitchen, the chink of glasses. The meal was over and they'd soon be settling in the lounge with their drinks. If they knew what I was up to, I thought apprehensively, as I managed to drive all four fingers into Diana's tight vagina . . .

Diana came for the second time with a deluge of orgasmic cream and a wail so loud that I was sure she'd been heard all over the house. Shaking violently, arching her back and gripping my head tightly, she forced my mouth hard against her vaginal flesh and rocked her hips as if fucking me. She was completely lost in the grip of her lesbian orgasm, and I was lost in my sexual frenzy. We writhed on my bed, my mouth locked between her pussy lips, her milk flooding my face, as I sustained her pleasure with my sweeping tongue and thrusting fingers.

Twisting and pushing my fingers deeper into her rhythmically contracting vagina, I thought that my fist was going to sink into her young body. Her outer lips stretched to capacity, her clitoris forced out from beneath its pink bonnet, I licked and sucked on her pleasure bud as she gasped that she was coming again. In the grip of a multiple orgasm, she let out a wail of pleasure. My parents would hear her, I was sure, as my fist was sucked into the hot cavern of her vagina. Her outer labia stretched tautly around my wrist. I could believe that her teenage pussy had swallowed my hand. Her eyes rolling, her head lolling from side to side, she was obviously enjoying the abuse of her young vagina.

'No more,' she finally managed to gasp. 'Annette . . . God, no more.'

'Shush,' I whispered loudly as she cried out again. 'Diana, shut up.'

'God, that was . . . Take your hand out. That was amazing.'

'Keep your voice down,' I ordered, slipping my fist out of her vagina with a loud sucking sound. 'If my mum comes up and . . .'

'It's OK now,' she breathed, propping herself up on her elbows. 'That was fantastic. God, look at my cunt lips. Did you get your whole hand up me?'

'Yes, I did,' I replied as she sat upright. Showing her my creamed hand, I giggled. 'That's been right inside you,' I said, clenching my fist.

'Bloody hell. I'm not that big, surely? I can't believe it.'

'Neither can I, but it's true.'

'Are you all right in there?' my mother called through the door.

'Yes, we're fine,' I replied as Diana leapt off the bed

'I thought you were in pain,' she said, opening the door and gazing at me.

'It's OK, mum. We were just messing about.'

'Your face is red, Diana. I hope you're not going down with whatever Annette has got.'

'No, no. I'm hot, that's all.'

'Right. I'll leave you to it, then.'

She closed the door and went downstairs. Diana burst out giggling. It wasn't funny. Had my mum come in and caught us entwined in lesbian lust, God knows what she'd have said. But I had more important things to think about than my mother. What the hell had I done? I wasn't a bloody lesbian, and yet . . . and yet I couldn't deny the immense pleasure I'd derived from licking and fingering Diana's pussy. Lost in confusion, I didn't know what to do as Diana lifted my T-shirt up and slipped her hand down the front of my knickers.

'No,' I breathed as her finger slipped between the puffy lips of my pussy. 'Diana, I . . .'

'Let me make you come,' she whispered huskily.

'No, I can't,' I whimpered futilely. I was becoming weak with arousal. 'Diana, I . . .'

'You know you want to come, so lie on the bed and relax.'

'Just quickly, then,' I conceded.

Lying on my bed, I allowed Diana to pull my knickers down and slip them off my feet before parting my legs wide. I wanted to come, I needed to come, but not with another girl. I'd enjoyed her masturbating me before, and I'd loved fingering and licking her to orgasm, so what was the problem? I had to come to another decision, I knew, as she settled on the bed between my legs and kissed the fleshy cushions of my pussy lips. I had to stop fighting and decide what it was I wanted.

Her fingers slid deep into my wet vagina and her tongue swept over the sensitive tip of my erect clitoris. I knew that I couldn't stop her now. The decision had been made for me. I was bisexual, and I could no longer deny it. A bisexual slut? Since I'd discovered the power of flashing my knickers, I'd changed beyond belief. This was my life now. As

Diana stretched my pussy lips wide apart and sucked my solid clitoris into her hot mouth, I knew that I didn't have to make any more decisions.

Pulling my T-shirt up and exposing the firm mounds of my petite breasts, I toyed with my elongated nipples to add to my incredible pleasure. Desperate to come, I opened my legs to the extreme and gave my body completely to Diana. The squelching of my sex milk resounding around my bedroom, the sucking and slurping of Diana's mouth heightening my pleasure, I arched my back and gasped as my orgasm exploded within the pulsating bulb of my clitoris.

Again and again, my young body rocked with powerful tremors of sex as Diana licked and sucked and fingered my pussy. Sustaining my multiple orgasm with her licking and sucking, she was driving me into a sexual frenzy. I pulled and twisted my nipples, blowing my mind away with pleasure as my climax peaked and shook my writhing body to the core. My sex milk spewed from my inflamed vagina and splattered my inner thighs as she repeatedly rammed her fingers deep into my contracting love hole.

Oblivious to my surroundings, lost in my lesbian-induced orgasm, I imagined licking and sucking Diana's clitoris as she licked and sucked mine. Sixty-nine, both entwined in lesbian lust, both sucking out each other's orgasms. The ultimate sexual experience? I mused, as another gush of milk spewed from my fingered vagina. This was another step in my journey of sexual discovery, another step towards complete and utter sexual gratification.

My pleasure finally melting, I lay quivering uncontrollably on my bed as Diana slipped her fingers out of the fiery sheath of my drenched pussy and sat upright. Dirty thoughts filtered into my mind as I lay there recovering from my massive orgasm. I imagined a man thrusting his huge cock into my tight cunt as I sucked on Diana's orgasming clitoris. Pictures of a solid cock fucking my cunt and another pumping spunk into my mouth loomed in my mind. I could see myself licking the wet shaft of a cock as it slipped in and out of Diana's teenage cunt. Where were these thoughts coming from?

'I want to do sixty-nine with you,' I whispered. Her pretty face was coming into focus as my orgasm subsided.

'So do I,' she said, licking her pussy-wet lips. 'Both naked, licking and sucking and . . .'

'You'll have to come for a sleep-over. That way, we'll have all night to love each other.'

Leaning over me, she sucked my nipples in turn. 'You're beautiful,' she whispered. 'I want to lick you all over.'

'We will, but not now.'

'I'd better go,' she said as laughter emanated from downstairs. 'I'll see you at college, yes?'

'I don't think I'll go in tomorrow. I'll see how I feel.'

'OK, I'll see myself out. Thanks for . . . well, you know.'

'Yes, thanks. It was . . . God, it was amazing.'

Once she'd gone, I slipped beneath the warmth of my quilt and relaxed after my incredible orgasm. I could feel my pussy-milk oozing between the wings of my inner lips and trickling over my thigh as I closed my eyes and drifted in and out of sleep. It had been another exciting and profitable day, I mused dreamily. What would tomorrow bring? More orgasms, more lesbian sex, more fucking and spunking . . .

Annette and I walked along Brighton sea front and found a small café. It was a hot summer day, and Annette looked stunning in a short white dress. Over coffee, we talked about the chapter I'd just completed. She read the chapter and was very pleased, but she obviously had something on her mind. I asked her about her feeling when she'd been in the lounge with Derek knowing that her mother was upstairs.

'To be honest, when Derek fucked me in the lounge, I found the mixture of danger and excitement extremely stimulating. When my dad came back, he'd been so close to catching me in the act but ... as I said, the danger, the prospect of getting caught, was enthralling. I suppose it was the thought of dad catching me, and realising that his sweet little daughter had grown up.'

'You then went all the way with Diana.'

'God, yes. That was something I'll never forget. At the time, it seemed so natural. We'd been friends forever and it was like a natural extension of our friendship. The first time, when she'd masturbated me, I was really confused about the whole thing. But when we played with each other and both came, it was amazing. As I said, it seemed natural.'

'You thought of yourself as Annette, the bisexual slut. Didn't that worry you?'

'I'd got to the stage where I'd done so much that nothing really worried me. I just thought that sex was sex. It didn't matter whether it was with men or Diana. I loved sex.'

'Earlier that day, you met your teacher on the common.'

'The thing with my teacher was strange. It wasn't like being with the other men. I suppose he'd always been in a position of authority and, to an extent, he still was. Although I was in control, he was still my teacher. Again, I played the innocent virgin girl and he gave me money. He was happy, and so was I.'

'You'd arranged to meet the three men in the woods the following evening. How did you feel about that?'

'I got to the park early and . . .'

Sinking Lower

I leant against the fence and watched the trains go by. Three men, I mused uneasily. Three men, three cocks ... another new sexual experience. Was this what I wanted? Being with one man was fine, but to have three men ... I wondered whether I was having a change of mind, as I imagined three cocks fucking and spunking my tight cunt in turn. But the thought of the money quelled my anxiety. It would only take an hour or so, and then I'd have more cash than ever before.

What if they forced me to do things I didn't want to do? I was being silly, I realised. What could they force me to do? They'd fuck me and slip their knobs into my mouth and pump sperm down my throat. I didn't have a problem with that, so I had no need to worry. My concern was my mother. What if she turned up and caught me with one cock fucking my cunt and another spunking in my mouth? She'd see that I'd shaved my pubic hair off. She'd ask me why I'd shaved and she'd probably realise that I masturbated ... but that would be the least of her worries.

'I said she'd turn up,' the old man said triumphantly as he walked into the clearing, followed by his equally elderly friends.

'Bloody hell,' one of them muttered, dumping a carrier bag on the ground. He was old and bald like a granddad. 'You're a little beauty.'

'Are you ready, then?' the old man asked me.

'Yes, I suppose so,' I replied. 'What do you want me to do?'

'Everything,' the third man quipped. His hair was snow-white, his face tanned. 'Absolutely everything.'

As each man passed me a wad of notes and looked me up and down approvingly, I knew that I was doing the right thing. I'd told mum that I was going to college that evening to a drama rehearsal. I'd said that we were doing a play about a group of schoolgirls, which gave me an excuse to wear my old school uniform. I'd learned many things, not least that old men loved girls in school uniform. Why was that? What was it about schoolgirls that turned old men on? Young, fresh, curvaceous, firm, tight . . . This was their lucky day.

Stuffing the cash into my blouse pocket, I listened to the crude comments passing between the men. *A dirty schoolgirl slut, a tight hairless cunt, a fuckable little mouth, a tight arse, puffy nipples and pussy lips* . . . I didn't know what to expect as they ordered me to strip naked. I knew that I'd be fucked by three hard cocks, but I had no idea just how far they'd want me to go. Did it matter? They'd paid me a fortune, so did it matter what they wanted in return?

Slipping my blouse off my shoulders, exposing the firm mounds of my teenage breasts, my ripe nipples, I watched the men as they watched me. They licked their lips and grinned. This was an exciting game, I thought, as I released my skirt and allowed it to fall down my legs and crumple around my ankles. Exciting and profitable. Running my hands over my young breasts, I wondered whether their cocks were hard. Did old men wank?

Kicking my skirt to one side, I took my shoes and socks off and stood before my appreciative audience in my white knickers. They were my special knickers, the ones with the narrow crotch, and the men obviously loved the sight of my hairless outer lips bulging either side of the tight material. My clitoris stirring, my pussy milk flowing, I hoped that they'd push their tongues into my vagina and lick me. How many times would I come? They'd want me to whimper and writhe during my orgasms. I knew exactly what to do to please them. Annette the slut had experience.

Twisting my long blonde hair nervously around my fingers, I bit my lip and tried to look sweet and innocent as my clients moved closer and examined the erect teats of my young breasts. A hand slipped down the back of my knickers and fingers explored my anal crease. Another hand squeezed my breasts, and fingers pressed into the material of my knickers, probing to contain my swollen pussy lips. More hands wandered over my semi-naked body, but they didn't pull my knickers down. As they tweaked my erect nipples and stroked my breasts, I reckoned that they were saving the best bit until last.

They talked about me, my young body, as if I wasn't there. That's when I realised that I was nothing more than an object they'd paid for. They weren't interested in me as a person, they'd simply bought me to play with. Their only interest was my teenage body and, once they'd finished with me, they'd discard me. But that didn't worry me at all. All I wanted was their money, and all they wanted was my body. Fair exchange.

One of the men knelt before me and pressed his face into the swell of my wet knickers. Another knelt behind me, his nose pushed into my anal crevice through the tight material of my knickers. I could hear him breathing, sniffing the perfume of my bottom-hole, as the other man sniffed the scent of my pussy. My knickers wetting with my juices of arousal, I closed my eyes as the last man sucked on each nipple in turn. I'd never known such heavenly sensations, and I wondered who was deriving more pleasure – my clients, or me? Quivering, I breathed heavily as the three men sniffed and licked and sucked the wet material of my knickers. There was something that old men liked about my knickers. That was how my games had started, wearing my short skirt, parting my slender thighs and flashing my knickers . . . I'd come a long way since that fateful day in the lounge.

Although I'd sold my body to the old men and I belonged to them for an hour or so, I still felt that I was in control. I was the boss, they were my customers. They had money and I had what they wanted. It was a simple business arrangement. This was also my first real job as a prostitute, the first time I'd taken decent money in return for sex, and I was enjoying every minute of it. They were gentle with me, not pushing me too far too soon. They were old and kindly, like granddads. Granddads looked after little girls, didn't they? I was sure that this was going to be easy money.

The man kneeling before me finally yanked my knickers down to my ankles and ran his tongue up and down my hairless crack. I could feel his hot breath against my skin, his saliva running down my inner thighs, as he licked and slurped between my swollen vaginal lips. As the man behind me parted my firm buttocks and licked the sensitive brown tissue surrounding my anal hole, I felt my womb contract. Two tongues licking my sex holes, my nipples each

177

sucked into a hot mouth, I stepped out of my knickers and parted my feet wide. I'd found my sexual heaven.

My clitoris was becoming painfully erect beneath the man's sweeping tongue. I let out a gasp as another tongue entered the tight duct of my rectum. The third man slipped my erect nipple out of his mouth and unbuckled his belt, and I knew that my first fucking was imminent. Lowering his trousers, he grinned as I eyed the huge shaft of his solid cock, the purple globe of his swollen knob. His heavy balls swinging beneath his shaft, his cock twitching expectantly, he grabbed the carrier bag and ordered his friends to stand up.

I didn't know what was happening as they pulled lengths of rope from the carrier bag. Mumbling to each other, they tied ropes around each of my legs, just above the knee, and instructed me to kneel on the ground. Taking my position on all fours, I again wondered what they were planning as one man parted my knees wide and the others pulled on the ropes and secured the ends to nearby trees. Why tie me up like that? I wondered in my naivety. I would have knelt with my knees wide apart, so there was no need for the ropes.

Hearing movements behind me, the unzipping of trousers and murmurings, I assumed that they were trying to decide who should fuck me first. I thought it odd when one of them lay on the ground and positioned himself beneath me. Why not kneel behind me and fuck me? His swollen knob stabbing between the gaping lips of my pussy, he finally drove his solid cock deep into my tight cunt. I could feel my pussy lips stretched tautly around the base of his shaft, his knob pressing against my cervix, and I waited in anticipation for the fucking to begin.

I finally realised what was going on when fingers stretched my naked buttocks wide apart and another knob pressed against the well-salivated ring of my anus. Grimacing, I didn't dare protest as the huge plum slipped into the tight sheath of my rectum and began its illicit journey to the hot depths of my bowels. My holes stretched open to the extreme, I thought I was going to split open as the gasping men rocked their hips and double-fucked me. My pelvis inflating and deflating as their cocks glided in and out of my sex ducts, I stared wide-eyed at the third man's huge cock as he knelt before me and lifted my head by my hair. Three holes, three cocks, I thought anxiously, as he ordered me to suck his knob. I'd not expected this, but the notion excited me.

My tethered body rocking back and forth with the three-way fucking, I imagined my mother turning up and staring in horror at the lewd scene. Did this debauched behaviour run in the family? I wondered, trying to picture my mother getting fucked by three dirty old men. What had she been like when she was in her teens? Had men fucked her mouth and her arse? The man beneath me pulled and twisted my erect nipples, adding pain to my pleasure as I listened to the sound of flesh meeting flesh.

'Filthy little slut,' he breathed, his fingernails biting into the sensitive flesh of my firm breasts.

'She's the dirtiest little slut I've ever fucked,' the man shafting my arse said with a chuckle.

Their crude remarks were punctuated by gasps of pleasure. I closed my eyes and tried not to listen to them. *Slut, whore, tight-cunted little tart, cum-slut, anal slag . . .* I could easily endure this, I was sure, as I thought of the money I'd earned. Once they'd pumped me full of their spunk, it would all be over and I could go home and have a shower. I'd thought that I'd have to spend an hour with them but, at this rate, I reckoned that they'd be finished with me within fifteen minutes.

My vaginal sheath tightening, my rectum becoming inflamed, I hoped that they'd soon pump out their spunk to lubricate the pistoning of my holes. Crude comments again disturbing the still summer air in the woods as I sucked on the man's ballooning knob, I moaned through my nose as he clutched my head and almost rammed his cock-head down my throat. Nearly choking on the solid cock as the man behind me slapped each naked buttock in turn, I realised how much I was enjoying the crude attention. I'd been paid for this, I reminded myself, as another hard slap landed on my stinging buttock. My young body was theirs to do with as they wished. Besides, I rather liked the crude treatment.

At last, my mouth flooded with spunk. Repeatedly sucking and swallowing, I drank from the throbbing knob as my inflamed vagina filled with sperm and my burning rectal sheath was lubricated with male cream. I couldn't believe what a filthy whore I'd become. From a truly innocent college girl to a debased slut in such a short space of time . . . I wondered how much lower I'd sink in the mire of depraved sex. But I was leading two separate live, I reflected, as the men fucked my three holes and filled my young body with spunk. No one would ever discover my darker side.

Sucking the remnants of spunk from the knob bloating my mouth, I hung my head and breathed heavily as all three male organs left my trembling body. The man slid out from beneath me and I rested my head on the soft grass, imagining the sight of my gaping holes as spunk streamed down my inner thighs. I was exhausted, but I'd played my part in the crude sex games. I'd earned my money, all I had to do now was go home and take a shower and rest after my incredible ordeal.

Hearing movements behind me, I assumed that the men were dressing before releasing me. Again picturing my gaping bum-hole oozing with spunk, I was happy to think that I'd experienced anal sex at last. The men talked about fucking my cunt and my arse, and I felt dirty as never before. Saying that I was a tight-arsed little whore, a cum-guzzling slut, they were obviously happy with my young body. The old man I'd met originally lifted my head and grinned at me, and I thought he was going to praise me – until someone parted my naked buttocks to the extreme.

'We're going to swap places now,' he said. 'We'll all move on to the next hole and then the next until we've each fucked your cunt, your arse and your mouth.'

'But, I thought . . .' I began. 'I thought you'd finished?'

'Finished? We've hardly started,' he returned with a chortle. 'We want more than one fuck each for our money.'

I was sure that I couldn't endure three fuckings in each hole, but there was no point in protesting. *We want more than one fuck each for our money.* They'd paid me well, and I could quite understand that they wanted their money's worth. It was only fucking and spunking, I reflected. My mouth, my tight little cunt and my arsehole . . . that's what they were for, fucking and spunking. And making money, of course. While the other girls at college were studying for exams and spending their pocket money in town each Saturday, I was earning a fortune, and enjoying myself immensely. I'd definitely done the right thing.

A man positioning himself beneath me, another opening my anal hole with his fingers, I opened my mouth obediently as the last man offered his bulbous knob to my mouth. I could taste a cocktail of spunk and my sex juices as I sucked on his purple knob. Creamy, savoury, aphrodisiacal. Running my tongue over his sperm-slit, sinking my teeth gently into his solid shaft, I was surprised that he could manage another erection. The men were old, but they were certainly fit, I thought as two cocks drove deep into the inflamed holes between my spunk-splattered thighs. It was a shame that David hadn't been more interested in my young body, my three accommodating holes.

My body rocking back and forth with the three-way fucking, I again wondered whether my mother had been with more than one man at once. I then thought of my neighbours, the women who lived in my street. There was a young woman over the road with full red lips, and I wondered whether she'd ever had a cock fucking her mouth and spunk bathing her tongue. Had she had her arse fucked and spunked? Did she shave her pussy hairs and masturbate? Although I was naive, I was sure that I wasn't the only girl in the world who'd had all three holes fucked by three men at once.

My mouth flooded with fresh spunk, and my vagina and rectum were filled with creamy male lubricant. I gulped down the third man's sperm. All three men groaned, and the squelching sounds of sex resounded throughout the trees as the spunk flowed into my trembling body. my clitoris massaged by the rock-hard shaft pistoning my vagina, I finally reached my own mind-blowing climax. Wave after wave of orgasm crashed through my tethered body, my eyes rolled, my heart banged hard against my chest and the heavenly sensations blew my mind away on a wind of lust and touched my soul.

Lost in a world of orgasmic ecstasy, drifting on clouds of lust, I was unconscious of my surroundings. In a dream-like state, I thought I heard voices calling my name. Had I passed out? I could no longer feel

182

the ropes around my knees, the grass beneath my hands. Only the tremors of orgasm filled my senses as I seemed to leave my naked body and float high above the woods. Had I died?

Finally coming back to earth, aware of distant male voices, I lay crumpled on the ground with sperm oozing from my shaking body. Never had I experienced an orgasm of such strength and duration, never had I known the pleasure derivable from my naked flesh. I could feel spunk bubbling from my inflamed anus, trickling from the gaping entrance to my burning vagina. Used and abused in return for cash, I really was a fully-fledged prostitute.

Coming to my senses, I raised my naked body on my hands and opened my eyes. The three men were kneeling before me, their solid cocks in their hands, their purple knobs only inches from my mouth. Was I dreaming? I wondered as they ordered me to suck them. How many times could they spunk? My eyes rolling, my breathing deep and heavy, I parted my sperm-glossed lips and almost choked as the three purple plums drove into my mouth. The men wanking their solid shafts, my tongue snaking over the silky-smooth surfaces of their knobs, I didn't think that I'd be able to endure much more. My young body awash with sperm, I prayed for the men to come quickly and put an end to my beautiful ordeal.

Gobbling and slurping, licking and sucking, I did my best to ensure that they got their money's worth as they gasped and shuddered. The arrangement was for me to meet them once a week in the woods. I had my college teacher and other men to satisfy, but they weren't as demanding as the old men and I knew that I'd have plenty of time to recover between each gruelling sex session. Paid a small fortune to be fucked senseless every week by three dirty old men?

Easy money, I thought, as the knobs swelled within my mouth.

The men losing themselves in their fantasies, I listened to their crude comments as they neared their orgasms. *Filthy little schoolgirl slut, hairless cunt crack, tight-arsed whore, fuckable blonde nymph, cunt-wet school knickers* ... As they signalled the imminent coming of their spunk, I knew they'd become regular clients. This was our first sex session, and I was in no doubt that I'd pleased them, sexually gratified them. They'd be back for more and more crude sex, and they'd part with their cash in return.

The three knobs throbbing, pumping fresh sperm into my gobbling mouth, I couldn't swallow fast enough and the cream overflowed and ran down my chin. I could feel my cunt lips opening as my clitoris again inflated and called for attention. A blend of sperm and vaginal milk streaming down my inner thighs, I half-hoped the old men would be able to fuck me again. What had I become? I mused, as I drank from the three orgasming knobs. Annette, the filthy whore.

One of the cocks slipped out of my mouth and I sucked on the remaining two as the man wanked his shaft and splattered my face with his spunk. As the creamy liquid rained over my nose and cheeks, drenching my hair and squirting into my eyes, I knew that I must have looked like a real cum-slut. I *was* a real cum-slut. A girl at college had used the term, and I'd been so innocent that I didn't know what she was talking about. When I'd discovered the meaning, I'd shuddered with disgust, but now ... now, I was a true cum-slut. I loved spunk, the taste, the feel of the cream flooding my cunt and filling my arse. To think that I was being paid to drink spunk was amazing. Annette, the filthy little spunk-guzzling cum-slut.

The men finally slipped their knobs out of my spunk-drenched mouth, their dripping cocks deflating before my sperm-glazed eyes. I poked my tongue out and lapped up the cream from around my lips and chin. I didn't know how long I'd been in the woods, and I was losing count of the times my holes had been fucked and spunked. But I was sure that the crude sex was over as the old men clambered to their feet and moved behind my tethered body. My stomach awash with spunk, my bowels flooded with male cream, my cunt drenched in the orgasmic milk, my face and hair dripping with sperm . . . I was going to have to clean myself up before going home.

I could hardly believe it when one of the men positioned himself beneath my aching body and drove his erect cock deep into the sheath of my fiery cunt. Reckoning that they were on some sort of erection pills as a solid knob pressed hard against the brown ring of my anus, I realised that I might be fucked a dozen times or more before being released and allowed to stagger home. I could feel the two cocks deep within my sex ducts, the hard shafts pressing together through the thin membrane dividing my cunt and my arse. This had to be the last time, I thought, as they began withdrawing their cocks and rammed into me in unison. As much as I craved the beautiful abuse of my young body, I couldn't take any more.

'God,' I cried as the cock slipped out of my burning rectum and tried to gain entry to my already bloated vagina.

'A double cunt fucking,' someone said with a chuckle from behind me. 'Two cocks fucking your sweet little cunt.'

'God, I can't take it,' I whimpered as the male shaft forced its way alongside the first cock and drove slowly into my cunt.

'Of course you can. You're a slut, and sluts love a double cunt fucking.'

'Yes. I want my cunt fucked,' I breathed. 'Double-fuck my cunt.'

My vaginal canal stretched to capacity as the two knobs pressed hard against my ripe cervix, I rested my head on the ground and dug my fingernails into the soft grass. I would split open, I was sure, as the men rocked their hips and began their fucking motions. I'd split in two, tear open and ... Laughter resounded through the woods as my bladder drained and hot urine squirted from between my hairless cunt lips and splashed my inner thighs. I knew that I'd reached the bottom of the pit of degradation. To piss myself in front of the men was humiliating beyond belief, but I couldn't halt the gushing flow of urine. Laughter again filled my ears as the splashing of piss became louder. I couldn't believe the depths to which I'd sunk – nor how much I was enjoying the crudest sex imaginable.

'Piss-slut,' someone said. 'She's pissed herself.'

'Drink it,' another rejoined. 'Drink it from her cunt.'

Trying not to listen to their coarse comments as my young body rocked back and forth with the double shafting of my aching vagina, I imagined my mother walking into the clearing and witnessing my debased behaviour with three old granddads. I was a teenage girl, slim and curvaceous and attractive with long blonde hair and ... I was a piss-slut, a dirty little cum-slut. What the hell would my mother think? She'd disown me, that was for sure. Two cocks fucking my cunt, piss gushing from my pee-hole, my hair matted with spunk, sperm oozing from my gaping anus, my face dripping with male orgasmic cream ... She'd throw me out of the house and never speak to me again.

'Do you like pissing yourself when you're being fucked?' the bald man asked me, kneeling before me.

'No,' I gasped, my vaginal canal seemingly stretching open further.

'Come on, you love it. I'll bet you're a right little water sports slut.'

'I can't take any more,' I whimpered as spunk gushed into my vagina. 'I do love it, but I can't –'

'You've got to earn your money,' he cut in. 'We can't let you go until you've been fucked good and proper.'

As he lifted my head, I gazed at his semi-erect cock and thought that he'd order me to suck his knob. Holding his shaft by the base, retracting his foreskin fully, he held my head up and chuckled. He ordered me to open my mouth as I stared at his purple knob, and I was sure that I was in for another throat spunking. Little did he know that I was enjoying the game as much as he was. How much sperm could a man produce? He chuckled again, and I squeezed my eyes shut and pursed my lips as hot liquid jetted from his slit and squirted over my face. My arousal running higher than ever, I opened my mouth and tasted the beautiful liquid. I was a real piss-slut.

'More,' I spluttered as my mouth filled.

'You want more piss?'

'Yes, more. Give me more.'

My cunt overflowing with spunk, urine soaking my hair and running down my neck, I wondered how I was going to explain the state I was in when I got home. The men murmured their crude words again, and I wondered what my mother would think. *Cunt, double cunt fucking, cunt spunking* . . . words that were once vulgar to me were now words of beautifully crude sex. Cunt, fuck, spunk, cum-slut, piss-slut . . . words that now came all too easily to me. Words that described the filthy whore I'd become.

The flow of urine stemming, the spent cocks slipping out of my gaping vagina, I was exhausted and hoped that my beautiful ordeal had at last come to an end. Shaking uncontrollably, my naked body dripping in urine and sperm, I rested my head on the soft grass as the men moved about behind me, chuckling and whispering to each other. Breathing a sigh of relief as the ropes were released, I closed my eyes and rolled over on to my back. Brushing my wet hair away from my flushed face, I felt pleased with myself. I'd earned my money, and now it was over.

Hot liquid rained down over my breasts and stomach. I opened my eyes and stared as the three men drained their bladders. Laughing uncontrollably as they drenched me, they aimed at my pussy and my petite breasts. I rolled on to my side, but the hot shower was inescapable. If my mother could see me now, if Diana knew what a slut I was . . . But I didn't want to escape the golden rain. What the hell had I become? I wondered as the rain finally ceased. What sort of teenage girl was I? A common prostitute.

The men dressed hurriedly and said that they'd meet me next week in the clearing. That was it, I thought. They'd had what they'd wanted from me, for the time being. Alone on the ground, soaked and used and abused, I rested for some time before managing to haul my naked body up. Swaying on my sagging legs as spunk gushed from my gaping sex holes and streamed down my inner thighs, I grabbed my school blouse. The money was still in the pocket. They'd kept their part of the bargain, and I'd certainly kept mine.

Emerging from the woods, I sat on the bench by the pond and gazed at the ducks. I'd changed, I thought, breathing in the fragrance of sperm and urine as I brushed my wet hair away from my face.

188

When I'd first started my games, taking presents in return for stripping naked and allowing men to finger my pussy, I'd never thought that I'd end up like this. Tied up with rope and pissed on, my every hole fucked and spunked . . .

What had I expected prostitution to be like? I wondered. In my naivety, I'd thought that the three men would take turns to fuck me. I realised that they'd finger and lick me, and fuck me. But I'd never dreamt that I'd have one cock fucking my arse and another fucking my teenage vagina, let alone two cocks forced deep into my tight cunt. Cunt, a dreadful word. Fuck, cunt . . . The words of a prostitute. I'd been a sweet little college girl working hard to go on to university. And now? Now, only a few weeks later, I was a common slut of a prostitute taking money in return for allowing three granddads to fuck me senseless and piss on my naked body. Do granddads look after little girls? Do they fuck?

In only a few weeks, I'd changed beyond all recognition. I used to sit by the pond wondering, dreaming, thinking. Now I was sitting there with the taste of spunk lingering on my tongue, spunk oozing from my arsehole and my cunt, my blonde hair dripping with piss. And several hundred pounds in my blouse pocket. The things I'd done were very bad, I knew. But the bad girl, Annette the slut, wasn't the real me. That was my other life, my separate life, my secret life. I was Little Miss Innocent, wasn't I?

Two rock-hard cocks forced up my teenage cunt. I couldn't get the beautiful thought out of my mind. Was that normal? It was if I wanted it to be. What was abnormal? Who said that only one cock should fuck one cunt at any one time? Who made the bloody rules, anyway? God? I'd never been to church. Although my mother had wanted me to go to Sunday school and church, I'd never been. Why should I? Besides, from what I'd read and heard, vicars and priests were bloody perverts.

Finally heading home, I wondered what to say to my mother, how to explain why my hair was dripping wet. My bum-hole was very sore, my vagina ached and my knickers were soaked with sperm. I'd dash upstairs and take a shower before mum caught me, I decided as I reached my house. It was a shame that it hadn't been raining, I thought as I opened the front door. Perhaps I could say that I'd been swimming.

'What on earth has happened to you?' my mother asked, emerging from the lounge and staring at my wet hair. 'Annette, what . . .'

'We had a water fight at college,' I lied.

'I thought you were supposed to be rehearsing?'

'Yes, we were. I . . . I'd better go and have a shower.'

'Are you all right? You look flushed and tired.'

'I'm fine, mum. I'll have a shower and then . . .'

'Your dad's in the shower. Come into the lounge and say hello to Derek.'

'No, I . . . I'd better get out of these clothes,' I stammered as the phone rang.

'I'll take that in the dining room. You go and say hello to Derek.'

Wandering into the lounge, I gazed at Derek and smiled. He looked me up and down, his eyes widening as he focused on my naked thighs. Licking his lips and grinning, he obviously liked my school uniform. He'd want me to kneel on the floor with my head on the sofa cushion and my wet knickers pulled down. But with mum in the dining room I was safe. As he beckoned me with his finger, I decided to tease him. Standing by his chair, I felt powerful, in control. Why was I teasing him? I wondered as hr slipped his hand up my skirt. I couldn't help it. I knew what he was thinking, I knew what he wanted, and I couldn't help teasing him.

'Your knickers are soaked,' he whispered. 'What have you been up to?'

'That's my business,' I replied softly as he pulled my knickers aside and drove a finger deep into my sperm-drenched vagina.

'God, you're wet. Have you been with a boy?'

'You could say that.'

'You've been fucked, haven't you?' he persisted, slipping a second finger into my tightening vagina.

'Maybe.'

'Dirty little slut,' he whispered with a chuckle. 'You're a dirty girl, Annette. Do you know what you do to me?'

'I make your cock stiff,' I replied impishly, cocking my head to one side. 'You'd like to fuck me, wouldn't you?'

'God, yes. If it wasn't for your parents –'

'I'm going upstairs,' I interrupted. His fingers slipped out of my pussy as I stepped back. 'You'd like to fuck my bum, wouldn't you?'

'Is that what you've been ... Have you had anal sex before?'

'Maybe.'

'You're as bad as your mother,' he said, grinning at me.

'What do you mean by that?'

'Why do you think I'm always round here?'

'You haven't ... My mum wouldn't ...'

'Wouldn't she?'

'You're lying.'

'I have no need to lie, Annette. I used a little ploy, and it worked very well.'

'I'm not listening to your lies,' I returned.

'I told her that I'd fucked you.'

'Now you're being ridiculous. If you told her what we'd done, she'd . . .'

'She'd want to put a stop to it, wouldn't she?'

'She'd go mad.'

'She did go mad. I told her that I wouldn't fuck you again if she allowed me to fuck her instead.'

'My mum and dad are happy together. There's no way she'd want you. And if you told her about us, the things we've done, she'd go mad at me.'

'OK, believe what you want.'

I left the lounge, and went up to my bedroom and locked the door. Derek was lying, he had to be. My mum wouldn't have sex with him, would she? She'd always been so prim and proper, and strict with me. She had morals, I reflected. Unlike me, she had morals and she was decent. I was a prostitute, a dirty, filthy little slut. My mum was a decent, refined lady. And Derek was a lying bastard.

Hiding my money beneath the bed, I lay on top of my quilt and gazed up at the ceiling. Thoughts haunted me, images of Derek's cock fucking my mum's pussy loomed in my mind. Derek was a bastard, and there was no way I'd let him anywhere near me again. He'd ended our relationship with his crazy lies. He could have fucked me again, but not now. I'd strike him off my list of clients.

It was lashing with rain when Annette and I dived into a coffee shop. We'd always talked about the past, so I asked her about the present. Where was she working? Where was she living? Grinning triumphantly, she said that she'd reveal all at the end of the book.

'Let's get back to the past,' she said as the waitress brought our coffee over.

'OK. So, you'd been with three old men in the woods, and then Derek told you that he'd been with your mother. How did you feel?'

'I felt that things were a complete mess,' Annette sighed. 'I was a complete mess, and I decided to end my games. The things that Derek had said to me about my mum . . . I felt awful and, that night in my bed, I decided that my life as a prostitute had come to an end. It was easy money, good money, but I didn't want the complications.'

'Did you stick to that decision?'

'Yes, I did. I left college and got a job in an office. It was boring and the money was terrible. My parents thought that I was working with computers, which made matters worse because I had to keep lying to them. I couldn't say that I'd got a badly-paid office job because they'd have gone on about university and stuff. After six months at the office, I was really fed up. I was broke, bored and totally pissed off.'

'Did you have any relationships during that time?'

'I had a few, but then I met a man who I thought was special. His name was Barry, and he was kind and caring. He also earned good money, which was a plus. After my exploits, I felt that I'd sort of grown up and was ready for a proper relationship. Barry had a nice flat and, as I was desperate to leave home, I moved in with him. He knew nothing about my past, of course.'

'Did that work out?'

'I was really happy for the first few months. Barry was doing well, so I left the office job and became a sort of full-time housewife. But there was something missing in my life.'

'Sex?'

'Sex with Barry was great. Nothing like I'd been used to, but it was great. But there was something missing that I couldn't put my finger on. I was happy, I had no money worries ... I discovered what was missing one morning when Barry's father came round. Barry was out and ...'

My New Life

Barry's father, Rob, was in his sixties, not bad looking, and I knew that he'd make a good father-in-law. Marriage? I pondered. I was happy enough living with Barry, but did I want to walk down the aisle with him? I'd always got on well with Rob. He was good company and fun to be with and, when he came round to the flat one morning to drop a book off for Barry, I made him a cup of coffee and we sat in the lounge chatting.

I was sitting opposite him on the sofa when, for no apparent reason, I recalled my knicker-flashing days. I didn't know what was happening in my mind but I was wearing a short skirt and the temptation to part my thighs was overwhelming. I'd had no intention of returning to my old habits, especially in front of Barry's father, but I couldn't help myself as I parted my legs just enough for him to spy my knickers. I'd not wanted this, I thought anxiously. I'd left those days far behind me but . . . As we chatted, he gazed up my skirt, and all the old feelings flooded back to me. The excitement, the danger, the arousal . . .

My stomach somersaulted, my clitoris swelled and my sex milk flowed into the tight crotch of my knickers. I'd not had those incredible feelings for so long, and I realised just how much I'd missed flashing my knickers. I could feel my nipples becoming erect and acutely sensitive, my clitoris transmitting little ripples of pleasure throughout my pelvis. My hands trembling, I tried to press my thighs together and control myself, but I didn't have the willpower.

When I'd moved in with Barry, I'd vowed to myself to be faithful to him. He knew nothing about my sordid past and, as far as I was concerned, it was history. I'd left my days of crude sex and prostitution behind and had become a decent young lady, loyal and loving, and I wanted to stay that way. But, showing my knickers off to Rob, knowing what he was thinking, imagining his cock stiffening . . . my arousal went through the roof. The monster had risen once again.

Repeatedly telling myself that this was only a harmless game and it wouldn't lead anywhere, I parted my thighs a little further. Well practised in the fine art of knicker-flashing, I came across, once again, as Little Miss Innocent. As we talked, I moved about on the sofa and he couldn't take his eyes off my knickers. I was only teasing him, having a little fun, but I realised that I could never give up my games. Nodding and smiling at him as he chatted, I wasn't really listening. My thoughts centred between my slender thighs, the triangular patch of white material swelling to contain my full sex lips. I felt as horny and dirty as I used to when flashing to old men in the park, and I was loving it.

But I knew that this was wrong and, again, I tried to control myself. This was Barry's father, I repeatedly reminded myself. He was an old man and . . . was that the attraction? A balding man in his sixties, desperate to have sex with a young girl . . . a glimpse of a young girl's knickers, images of puffy lips and tight sex cracks . . . I knew the dirty thoughts that older men harboured. I knew what they wanted.

'You're an attractive girl, Annette,' he said, smiling at me.

'Thank you,' I replied. This was just like the old days.

'Barry's a lucky man.'

'I'm the lucky one, Rob. I was going nowhere before I met Barry.'

'Oh? I thought that you were doing quite well? Barry said that you . . .'

'Barry doesn't know about my past,' I deliberately blurted out.

'Your past? Tell me about it.'

'No, no . . . it's history and I try not to think about it.'

'Come on, Annette. You can tell me.'

'Well . . . I was a naughty girl.'

'That sounds interesting.' He leant forward in the armchair. 'How naughty were you? What did you get up to?'

'I'd had a very sheltered life. I'd never mixed or made friends easily and . . . and when I discovered sex, I went for it in a big way.'

'You had a lot of boyfriends?'

'Yes, no, I mean . . . I couldn't mix with boys of my own age. For some reason, I just didn't get on with them.'

'But you said that you went for sex in a big way?'

'I used to go with older men,' I confessed.

'Older men?'

'I'd rather not discuss it, Rob. I've never talked about it before.'

'Annette, I . . . I've always been fond of you. You're an extremely attractive girl and . . .'

'And what?'

My thighs parted, I reclined on the sofa and brushed my long blonde hair away from my face. My womb contracted, my clitoris pulsated gently beneath its little pink bonnet, and more memories came flooding back to me. This was wrong, I was treading a dangerous path, but I couldn't close my legs. As Rob stared at my knickers, I knew that I should stop the game. Dangerous games, I mused as my outer lips swelled and my juices of desire flowed from my tightening vagina. I should stop the game before it ended in tears, as it inevitably would. But the monster had risen, and had taken control of my female desires.

'And what?' I repeated. 'What were you going to say?'

'I don't know,' he sighed.

'Barry earns good money,' I said, coming up with an idea.

'What? Oh, yes, yes he does. He's doing very well.'

'He doesn't want me to go out to work. Which is OK, but . . . I wish that I could earn some money. I don't like having to ask him for cash.'

'No, I suppose you don't. What sort of job would you like?'

'Something part-time would suit me. Barry's adamant that he doesn't want me to work, so I'd have to earn money on the side.'

'That wouldn't be easy, Annette. He'd soon discover that you're going out to work.'

'Yes, but if I worked from home . . . a couple of hours here and there would be great. Just to bring in some cash so that I'd be a little more independent.'

'What sort of work could you do from home?'

'You tell me.'

'Perhaps I could help you out?' he said mysteriously.

'Help me out? How?'

'Well, you could work for me now and then.'

I frowned at him. 'Work for you?' I breathed innocently. 'But you're retired.'

'Well . . .' He rubbed his chin pensively. 'I just thought . . .'

'Tell me what's on your mind, Rob. What sort of work are you offering me?'

'I'd like to see more of you, Annette. I'll pay you to spend some time with me.'

'We're spending time together now.' I giggled and, keeping my thighs apart, I perched my buttocks on the edge of the sofa. 'Don't be silly, Rob. You don't have to pay me for a coffee and a chat.'

'No, I mean . . . I want us to spend some time together, and be a little closer.'

'Closer? Rob, are you saying that . . . You can't really mean that you . . .'

'I'm sorry. I . . . I got it wrong. Let's forget about it, OK?'

'Hang on, I'm not sure what it is that we're supposed to be forgetting about. You said that you wanted to see more of me.'

'Look, I made a mistake. When you talked about older men, I thought . . . I don't know what I thought.'

'I like you very much, Rob. We've always got on really well together, but . . .'

'Just forget what I said, OK?'

'Rob, if you're suggesting that we . . . Would it help to talk about it?'

'It's just that I'm always thinking about my younger years, my youth. I think about the young girls I used to know and . . . I miss those days terribly,' he sighed. 'I see girls in the street and . . . I imagine their young bodies.'

'Is that what you meant when you said that you wanted to see more of me?'

'Well, yes.'

'I can't believe this,' I gasped, holding my hand to my mouth. 'You mean that you want me to take my clothes off?'

'No . . . Look, just forget about it.'

'Rob, what did you mean?'

'Annette, you're my son's girlfriend. You may even become his wife one day.'

'Tell me what you meant, Rob.'

'All right, all right,' he sighed. 'I'd like to see you in your underwear.'

'My underwear . . . But . . .'

'Now let's forget about it. Let's talk about something else.'

'Rob, if that's what you want . . . if that's all you want . . . I don't mind you looking at me.'

'Really?'

'I do understand that men fantasise. If it will refresh your memory, I don't mind at all. It's not as if I'll be naked, is it? I'm not going to be embarrassed by showing you my knickers and bra. I mean, it's no different to wearing a bikini.'

I rose to my feet, slipped my blouse over my shoulders and tossed it on to the sofa. He watched me closely as I dropped my skirt and stepped out of the garment. Standing before him in my knickers and bra, I knew that I could never give up my old games. I was proud of my young body, my curves and mounds, and I'd missed stripping naked and allowing old men to gaze at me. A pang of excitement coursing through me as he cast his eyes over my curvaceous body, I reckoned that he'd soon be asking to see more of me. How far did he think I'd be willing to go? I mused as my clitoris swelled. More to the point, how much would he pay me?

'You're beautiful,' he breathed. 'God, you're beautiful.'

'There,' I said, smiling at him and doing a turn before him. 'Now you've seen a girl in her underwear.'

'Annette ... when you said that you went with older men, did you mean that you had sex with them?'

'Yes, I did,' I confessed, hanging my head. 'It was stupid of me, but ... they took an interest in me. They bought me presents and took a real interest in me. Looking back, I know that it was wrong. But I was young and naive.'

'You're still young, and you're beautiful.'

'What did you mean when you said that I could work for you?'

'To be honest, I meant that I'd pay you to strip naked.'

'What?' I gasped in disbelief. 'Rob, you can't be serious?'

'I am serious, Annette. As you know, I'm not short of money. When you said about doing part-time work from home ...'

'For God's sake, Rob. I'm not a prostitute.'

'No, no ... I didn't mean that. I don't know what I meant. I thought I'd help you out by giving you some cash.'

'Cash in return for ... I can't believe this.'

'It sounds terrible, doesn't it? I wish I hadn't said anything.'

'I do need some cash, but ... I can't take my clothes off.'

'I shouldn't have said anything, Annette. You're so young and attractive and ... I suppose I just wanted to bring back memories from my youth.'

'I know how you must feel, but ... God, I feel sorry for you now. Look, if I strip naked, it'll be our secret.'

'Yes, of course.'

Biting my lip, I shook my head negatively. 'I really don't think I should do it, Rob.'

'Fifty pounds?'

'Fifty? Rob, I'm not a prostitute.'

'Think of the money as a separate thing. Think of it as a gift.'

'You're Barry's dad, for God's sake.' I paused and offered him a slight smile. 'I suppose . . . If you only want to look at me . . .'

'I only want to look, I promise.'

'Well, all right. I'll do it, just this once.'

'Will you, really?'

'Yes, if you only want to look.'

I reached behind my back, unhooked my bra and peeled the cups away from my petite breasts. Rob's eyes widened as he focused on the ripe teats of my nipples, and I reckoned that he'd become a regular client. There was no point in fighting the monster within me, I knew, as I dropped my bra on to the sofa. I'd led two separate lives for so long, and then done my best to deny that the other Annette existed . . . If I pulled my knickers down and displayed my sex crack to Barry's father, I knew that I'd go further. This could destroy my relationship with Barry. If he discovered the shocking truth about his so-called loyal and loving partner . . . if his mother discovered the way her husband had behaved . . . I could destroy the whole family. But I was weak with arousal, hooked on the thrill of the game. Once a slut, always a slut.

Easing the front of my knickers down, very slowly, revealing the top of my sex crack, I again felt my womb contract as he gazed longingly at my young body. Even though I'd stopped my games when I'd moved in with Barry, I'd carried on shaving my pubic hair. Barry liked it that way, and so did I. He loved licking and tonguing my hairless cunt. Was that what his father wanted to do? Pulling my knickers down my thighs, I knew that Rob also liked my shaved pussy as his eyes lit up. If that didn't remind him of the girls he'd known in his youth, nothing would, I thought.

'Annette . . .,' he breathed softly as I released my knickers and allowed them to fall down my naked legs. 'You look so, so young and fresh and . . . you're an angel.'

'Hardly,' I said, walking over to his chair and standing with my feet slightly parted. 'Well, have I refreshed your memory?'

'God, yes. It's been so long. It's been so bloody long.'

'I don't think it's a good idea, teasing you like this. I'd better get dressed.'

'No, please . . . not yet. Just allow me to look for a while longer.'

'All right, but I don't think this is a good idea.'

'Your stomach is so smooth and flat, your pussy lips are beautifully formed and . . . A girlfriend of mine used to shave. We were both in our teens and she loved me licking her. I'd spend hours licking her crack and –'

'That's enough, Rob,' I cut in.

'I'm sorry, it's just that it's been so long since I've seen a naked young girl. Would you allow me to touch you?'

'No, Rob. God, I should never have agreed to this.'

'I only want to stroke your lips, Annette. Allow me to stroke you, and then I'll go.'

'You promised me that you only wanted to look.'

'I know, I'm sorry.'

'All right,' I conceded, my stomach somersaulting. 'Touch me there, if you want to.'

203

Reaching out, he ran his fingertip over the fleshy pads of my outer lips and up and down my moistening sex crack. I tried not to quiver, tried to conceal my arousal, as my vaginal milk flowed and my clitoris emerged from beneath its hide. This was just like the old days, I thought, my nipples rising proud from the darkening discs of my areolae. The only difference was that I didn't have to worry about my mother discovering my debauched behaviour.

'Rob, that's enough,' I said softly as his fingertip slipped into my crack. I wanted to order him to open my cunt lips and suck my clitoris to orgasm, 'Please, Rob . . .'

'All right,' he breathed, reclining in the chair. 'Thank you for allowing me to touch you.'

Why wasn't he asking for more? I wondered despondently. 'I'd better get dressed,' I sighed.

'And I'd better go home.'

'I . . . I feel all quivery now,' I murmured. Why the hell hadn't he wanted more? 'God, I'm trembling all over.'

'You'll be hot and ready for Barry when he gets home,' he said with a chuckle.

'I don't think I can wait that long,' I sighed. Little Miss Innocent was going to have to take a back seat. 'You've really turned me on, Rob.'

'I'm sorry, I should never have . . .' Getting up from the armchair, he smiled at me. 'Maybe it wasn't such a good idea. I'll leave you to get dressed and . . .'

'You don't have to rush off. Why not stay and have another coffee?'

'This is all rather awkward. All right, you get dressed and I'll make the coffee.'

'For God's sake, Rob. You've turned me on, and I need to come.'

'But, I thought . . .'

'I don't care what you thought,' I returned, sitting on the sofa with my legs wide open. 'Think of that teenage girl who shaved, and remind yourself of those days by licking my cunt.'

Wasting no time, he knelt between my feet and gazed longingly at the hairless lips of my teenage pussy. Reclining, I moved forward on the sofa until my buttocks were over the edge of the cushion. Offering him my open cunt, I felt wicked as he leant forward and ran his wet tongue up and down my opening sex crack. What were his thoughts? I wondered as he lapped at my vaginal entrance. Tonguing my vagina, sucking out my hot sex milk . . . Was he imagining his son's cock there, fucking and spunking me? God, I was a cheating, lying little slut.

Barry had an older brother and an ageing uncle. Would they like to lick me? I mused dreamily as Rob's tongue entered the hot depths of my milk-drenched vagina. Would they drive their solid cocks deep into my tight cunt and cheat on their wives? Parting my swollen outer labia, opening my sex valley to the extreme, Rob repeatedly swept his wet tongue over the sensitive tip of my erect clitoris. Was he thinking of his wife? I wondered as a quiver ran through my contracting womb and my sex milk flowed in torrents. Did he lick her cunt? Did he fuck her mouth and spunk down her throat? She ironed his shirts and cooked lovely meals and kept the house pristine. She was Rob's twee little wife, and I was his dirty little slut on the side.

Gazing at the light shining on Rob's balding head, I again recalled my days in the woods. I should have fucked more old men, I reflected. I should have pleased dozens of ageing men – and taken their money. Happy days, dangerous days. I'd given up my life of prostitution and tried to become a decent young lady, but I should have known that I'd never succeed in a long-term relationship. I was nineteen years old with long blonde hair and a curvaceous body. Firm breasts with elongated nipples, hairless pussy lips and a tight little cunt ... I had what men wanted, and I knew that I could never remain faithful to one man.

As Rob licked and sucked on my erect clitoris, I looked around the lounge at the things Barry and I had bought to build our home together. The new coffee table, the pictures on the walls, ornaments and bits and pieces ... but I felt no guilt. The photo I'd taken of Barry seemed to return my gaze from the mantelpiece. His dark eyes watched as his father licked my cunt, but I felt no guilt. Sitting on the sofa with my legs wide open and Rob licking my cunt, I felt somehow removed from my relationship with Barry. Two separate lives, I mused as my clitoris began to pulsate. Annette, Barry's loyal and loving partner. Annette, the filthy whore.

'Do you lick your wife's cunt?' I asked Rob as my orgasm neared.

'No,' he replied as he slurped and sucked between my puffy lips.

'Does she suck your cock?'

'No, she ... Let's not talk about her.'

'How often do you fuck her?' I persisted.

'I don't,' he returned. 'We don't have sex.'

'It's just as well that you have me, then,' I said with a giggle. 'I'm ready to come now. Finger my wet cunt and suck my clit and I'll come for you.'

My crude words exciting me, I let out a rush of breath as he thrust two fingers deep into the contracting sheath of my teenage vagina. Kneading the firm mounds of my petite breasts, I pulled and twisted my erect nipples to add to my incredible pleasure as he sucked and mouthed expertly on my solid clitoris. His cock would be straining the zip of his trousers, I thought dreamily. His balls would be full, his cock desperate to fuck and spunk my cunt. Words of sex, I reflected. Fuck, cunt ... crude words of crude and illicit sex.

Whimpering and writhing on the sofa, I let out a cry of pleasure as my orgasm exploded within my clitoris and shook me to the core. Wrapping my legs around Rob's back, clutching his head and grinding my open sex flesh hard against his face, I felt my orgasmic milk pump out. I'd missed the use and abuse of my naked body. Teasing old men with my knickers, allowing them to gaze at my shaved pussy and finally agreeing to them fucking me ... I'd missed Annette the dirty little slut. But she was back, with a vengeance.

Before my climax had faded, Rob slipped his fingers out of my hot sex sheath and parted my legs wide. I grinned as he pulled out his hard cock and drove the entire length of his veined shaft deep into my contracting vagina. This was what I'd wanted, I thought happily, as his bulbous knob pressed hard against my ripe cervix. I could feel his heavy balls against the firm cheeks of my naked buttocks, my outer lips stretched tautly around the root of his beautiful cock. His eyes glazed and he began fucking motions, letting out gasps with each thrust of his huge cock. He was happy, I mused, as his swinging balls battered my bum cheeks. He was happy in his illicit fucking, in his adultery.

Listening to the squelching of my pussy milk as Rob fucked me, I imagined Barry walking in and witnessing our crude coupling. He wouldn't be home until the evening, so I was safe enough. But he might notice the stains of sex on the sofa. He might want sex and ask me why my pussy lips were red and sore. I needed a flat of my own. I needed my own space and privacy. Did I want to end my relationship with Barry? I wasn't sure what I wanted.

Rob announced that he was about to come.

'My arse,' I breathed shakily. 'Fuck my arse.'

'What?' Rob said, frowning at me in disbelief.

'Fuck my arse,' I repeated. 'Just do it, Rob.'

Slipping out of my burning vaginal duct, he pressed his wet knob hard against my anal ring as I lifted my legs high in the air. His knob drove past my anal sphincter muscles, stretching me open to capacity as it began its journey along my rectum to the hot depths of my bowels. The brown tissue of my anus taut around the root of his rock-hard cock as he impaled me fully, I wondered what he must have thought of me. A dirty, cheating, two-timing little tart? And what was he? An adulterous bastard? It didn't matter what we thought of each other. We were fucking, anal fucking, and enjoying our forbidden coupling.

Rob grimaced and gasped and increased his thrusting rhythm as his cock swelled, and I knew that he was about to lubricate the inflamed sheath of my tight rectum with his warm cream. It seemed strange to think that Barry's father was arse-fucking me on the sofa we'd bought only two weeks previously. Barry wanted our flat to be the marital home, wedded bliss. I wanted the flat to be my place of work. The feel of an old man's spunk flooding my rectum brought back more memories. I realised I had to get out of the relationship with Barry. It wasn't fair to cheat on him like this, especially with his father. All I wanted to do was get out and live my life.

Rob's sperm gushed into my bowels and oozed from my inflamed anus. Groping between my swollen pussy lips, he drove two fingers deep into my neglected vaginal cavern. My sex holes full, I was again reminded of my escapades in the wood. Three cocks ramming into my holes, fucking me, spunking me . . . the thought drove me into a sexual frenzy. I felt wicked in the extreme as Rob managed to force half his hand into my contracting sex sheath.

Again, I looked at the photograph of Barry on the mantelpiece. I tried to drag my gaze away from his smiling face, close my eyes and push all thoughts of him from my mind. But my wickedness gripped me and the notion of him watching me fucking his father sent my arousal soaring. Perhaps I wanted him to discover the truth. Perhaps I wanted him to discover what sort of person I was. There'd be rows, heart-break, destruction. Was that what I wanted? I knew that I couldn't lead two separate lives while I was living with Barry. It was one thing fucking old men in the woods, but I couldn't invite a string of clients to what was to be the marital home.

Rob finally halted his anal shafting, his deflating knob embedded deep within my hot bowels as he slumped over my naked body and breathed heavily in the aftermath of his illicit fucking. He'd done it, I'd done it. He'd arse-fucked his daughter-in-law to be, I'd cheated on Barry . . . Would I ever become a loyal and faithful wife? I mused as Rob withdrew his flaccid cock. To have and to hold, to honour and obey, let no man put asunder.

'Annette . . .,' Rob began as he zipped his trousers and stood before me. 'Annette, I . . . I don't know what to say.'

'You were going to give me some money,' I reminded him.

'Oh, er . . . yes, of course.' He opened his wallet and he passed me the cash. 'You will stay with Barry, won't you?' he breathed softly. 'I mean, what we did won't affect your relationship with Barry, will it?'

'What you mean is, will I always be here as your bit on the side?' I replied.

'No, I . . . well, that did cross my mind. Obviously, I'd like to see you again.'

'You'd like to fuck me again?'

'Well, yes.'

Spreading the ten-pound notes in my hand, I frowned. 'Fifty,' I sighed.

'Is that all right?'

'I suppose so. I was hoping to buy some new clothes, but not to worry.'

'I could give you a little more,' he said, again opening his wallet.

'Another fifty would be great,' I trilled, smiling at him.

'Another fifty? Er . . . although I'm not short of money, I can't afford to give you cash every time I see you.'

'I understand that, Rob. And you must understand that I won't be able to give you what you want every time I see you.'

'So, what you're saying is . . .'

'What I'm saying is, if I have to get a part-time job, I won't always be here for you.'

He bit his lip as he passed me the notes. 'I can't give you one hundred pounds every time I come round,' he sighed.

'Aren't I worth it?' I asked him, cocking my head to one side and parting my thighs.

'Yes, but . . . I didn't mean that.'

'So that I don't have to get a job, so that I'm always here for you, give me one hundred each week and you can come round whenever you like.'

I rose from the sofa as he contemplated my offer, grabbed my clothes and began dressing. Barry's father now knew that I was a prostitute, but I was sure he was only too happy with our illicit arrangement. He had plenty of money, I had a beautiful young body, so we were both happy. But I wasn't just doing it for the money. It was the excitement, the sexual gratification, the danger, and the power I had over older men. The thrill was knowing what older men were thinking when they glimpsed my tight knickers, and I knew that I could never stop flashing.

'Until today, until just now, I didn't know you at all,' Rob said as I saw him to the front door.

'And I didn't know you,' I returned. 'Doesn't it bother you to think that you're sharing my body with your son?'

'Yes, of course it bothers me. There again . . . what Barry doesn't know can't hurt him, can it?'

'That's true.'

'Annette, are there other men?'

'You're the only one, Rob. Would it bother you if I did have other men?'

'No, it's just that . . .'

'Just that you'd like to keep it in the family?'

'I don't know. I'll ring you, OK?'

'Yes, that's fine.'

'Thanks, Annette.'

'Thank you, Rob. I'll see you soon.'

After cleaning the sperm from the sofa cushion, I had a shower and used hair-removing cream on my pussy and slipped into my special narrow-crotched knickers. My arousal reached frightening heights as I dressed in a loose-fitting blouse and miniskirt, and I felt sexually alive, wicked in the extreme. I wanted to go to the park and sit on the bench by the pond. The summer had gone and the leaves had been stripped from the trees, but I wanted to flash my knickers and excite old men and lure them into the woods and take their money. I wanted to get fucked in the snow.

I was about to leave the flat when Ian, a friend of Barry's, called round. He was in his late forties and not bad looking. I'd met his wife on a couple of occasions and had thought her rather stuck up, but Ian seemed to be happy enough with her. He'd come round to borrow one of Barry's DVDs, but I thought that it might be an idea to give him something else. My pussy lips swelling, my clitoris emerging from beneath its pink hood, I invited him into the lounge.

'Any wedding plans yet?' he asked, sitting in the armchair as I made myself comfortable on the sofa.

'Not yet,' I replied, parting my thighs a little. 'I'm in no rush to get married.'

He lowered his gaze to my knickers. 'You're young,' he said, his eyes widening. 'You've got plenty of time.'

'I don't think I'm ready for a monogamous relationship just yet. Don't get me wrong, I'm not playing the field. It's just that I'm not ready to settle down.'

'You're an attractive girl, Annette. I'm sure you could have any man you wanted.'

'How's your marriage, Ian? I don't mean to pry, it's just that . . . I suppose so many couples split up these days that I wonder whether it's worth getting married.'

'My marriage is OK. Julia isn't as much fun as she used to be. But I suppose things change over the years.'

'Fun? What do you mean?'

'Oh, I don't know. We used to go out and have a laugh, have a good time. Now, all she's interested in is having a new kitchen, replacing the three-piece suite and . . . She's very materialistic.'

'She's not at all like me, then. I love going out, enjoying life and having fun.'

'She's also a prude, which doesn't help,' he confessed. 'Sorry, I shouldn't be discussing my sex life with you.'

'No, no, that's all right. To be honest, I think that's what frightens me about marriage. The flame of passion inevitably burns low, and then years of nothingness follow.'

I parted my thighs further as he talked about his prudish wife and his nonexistent sex life. My hairless pussy lips were bulging out either side of the narrow crotch of my tight knickers, and I knew that sight met his eyes. I also knew his male thoughts. My sex milk flowing, my nipples erect beneath the silky material of my blouse, I wondered whether to play Little Miss Innocent or tell him that I was a slut and I wanted sex. Little Miss Innocent hadn't done very well with Rob, and I didn't think she'd stand a chance with Ian. An idea coming to mind, I concealed a grin.

'Is it hot in here or is it me?' I sighed, holding my hand to my head.

'I think it must be you,' he replied. 'Are you OK?'

'I feel a little faint. I haven't eaten today, which is probably why. God, I think I'm going to faint.'

Flopping back on to the sofa, I lay with my legs wide apart and my eyes closed. Ian again asked me whether I was all right as he left his chair and knelt between my feet. Saying nothing, I lolled my head to one side. I could feel the crotch of my knickers buried within my sex crack, and I wondered whether he'd touch me there. Could he resist? I opened my eyes just enough to gaze at him through my lashes. He was staring at my pussy lips, his eyes sparkling and, no doubt, his cock stiffening.

This was a game I'd not played before, and I felt quite pleased with my idea. Little Miss Innocent didn't come into it, and neither did Barry's loyal and

213

loving partner. The trouble was that Ian had no idea how long I'd be out for. He could hardly pull my knickers off and fuck me, but I hoped that he would stroke me or perhaps lick the fleshy lips of my pussy. Feeling despondent as he leaped to his feet and left the room, I wondered what he was up to. When he returned and placed a glass of water on the coffee table, I reckoned I'd chosen the wrong man. I was about to open my eyes when he again knelt between my feet.

The feel of his fingertip running over the puffy lips of my pussy sent quivers through my womb, I knew that Ian couldn't resist me. What man could deny himself the pleasure of my young body? This was taking my knicker-flashing to the extreme, and I knew that I'd be playing my fainting game again. The next time Ian came round, I'd have to mention that I sometimes pass out for fifteen minutes or more. That would give him plenty of time to do as he wished with me, with my sweet cunt. This was another new and exciting game.

He pulled my knickers to one side, parted my swollen sex lips and slipped a finger deep into the wetness of my hot vagina. I could hear him breathing deeply as he explored the creamy walls of my tightening sex sheath, and I wondered just how far he'd go. I also wondered whether he realised that I was feigning unconsciousness. To lie there with my legs wide apart and my hairless pussy lips bulging out either side of my knickers was rather obvious, wasn't it? Maybe not.

His wet tongue sweeping over the exposed tip of my erect clitoris, he drove a second finger deep into my yearning cunt. He was a normal man, I reflected happily, as my juices of desire flowed and my clitoris responded beneath his lapping tongue. I wanted to come, I needed an orgasm, but . . . was it possible for a girl to have an orgasm when she'd fainted? The way Ian was licking and sucking my solid clitoris, I knew that I'd have no choice but to climax.

'You're beautiful,' he murmured, massaging the inner flesh of my sex-drenched vagina. 'God, you're beautiful. I've always fancied you. I've always imagined fucking you.'

His crude words heightening my arousal, I wanted to thrust my hips forward and grind my open cunt flesh hard against his face. But I daren't move or whimper if I was to keep up the farce. He slipped his fingers out of my contracting vagina and stretched my outer lips wide apart. Pressing on the pink flesh surrounding my clitoris, forcing out the entire length of my sex bud, he repeatedly swept his tongue over the sensitive tip. I could hold back no longer as he sucked my clitoris into his hot mouth. Trying not to whimper, trying to remain still as I felt the beginnings of my orgasm building deep within my young womb, I held my breath.

A deluge of sex milk spewed from my gaping vaginal entrance as my orgasm erupted within my pulsating clitoris. I quivered and whimpered softly in the grip of my incredible coming. Waves of pure sexual ecstasy crashing through my young body, I dug my fingernails into the sofa cushion and stifled my gasps of pleasure. The thought that Barry's father had arse-fucked me on the sofa only an hour earlier drove me into a sexual frenzy. I wondered how many more men would use and abuse me while Barry was at work.

Finally coming down from my climax, I shuddered as Ian slipped his fingers out of my inflamed vagina and sucked the last of my pleasure from my deflating clitoris. Moving down my valley and locking his lips to the wet flesh surrounding my sex hole, he sucked out my hot milk. I could hear him gulping, swallowing hard, drinking from my trembling body, as my breathing slowed. Recovering from my amazing orgasm, I relaxed as he sat back on his heels and gazed at my gaping sex. Would he be a regular visitor? Would he pay me for sex?

Finally he adjusted my knickers, slipped the crotch back into my dripping crack, stood up and took the glass of water from the coffee table. He moved to the lounge door and hovered there, and I knew that was my cue to return to consciousness. Opening my eyes, I looked about me and feigned disorientation. He waited for a few seconds before walking into the room with the glass of water and smiling at me.

'Are you all right?' he asked me.

'Yes, I think so,' I replied, sitting upright. 'I'm sorry about that. Was I out for long?'

'Only about twenty seconds. Just time enough for me to get you a glass of water.'

Sipping the water, I looked up at him. 'I am sorry, Ian,' I sighed. 'I'm prone to fainting. Sometimes I'm out for fifteen minutes or more.'

'Don't worry about it, Annette. Look, I'd better be going. I'll call round again when I'm passing, if that's OK?'

'Yes, yes, of course. I'm usually here.'

'Are you sure you're going to be all right?'

'Yes, don't worry.'

'OK, I'll see you soon.'

I felt no guilt as I heard the front door close. I was Little Miss Innocent, but it was another kind of innocence this time. And it had worked extremely well. Barry would be home from work at around six, as usual, and he'd ask me whether I'd had a good day. I'd had a very good day. I'd been fucked by his father and licked to orgasm by his friend. Pouring myself a large vodka and orange, I wondered what tomorrow would bring. More crude arse-fucking, more cunt-licking, more spunk, more orgasms . . . Back to the good old days.

Annette sat opposite me in the bistro enjoying spaghetti bolognaise as we talked about the book. I said that we were coming to the end of her story, and she laughed.

'I haven't given you the last chapter yet,' she said. 'So you don't know how, or even whether, it ends.'

'You go off into the sunset with the man you love?' I proffered.

'I might go off into the Greek sunset and get laid on a sandy beach,' she returned with a giggle. 'Seriously, there were no sunsets. At that stage, living with Barry in the flat with his constant talk of wedding bells, I knew that I had to come to a decision. On reflection, I always had to make decisions. But this was a big one. I either stayed with Barry and did my best to conform to married life and monogamy or I went off on my own and did my own thing. I knew that I could earn more than enough money to live comfortably. But I still didn't know what I really wanted. If I stayed with Barry, I'd cheat on him several times a day. If I got a flat of my own . . . It was selfish, I realise that now. But I wanted the best of both worlds.'

'So you left the flat?'

'After a huge row with Barry, yes. He kept on and on about marriage and I just couldn't take any more. I was fucking his father more or less every day and Ian called round now and then . . . I couldn't marry him. I couldn't spend a lifetime lying to him. When he was at work one morning, I packed my bags and left.'

'You went back to your parents?'

'No, that wouldn't have worked out. I had a thousand pounds put by, so I rented a room above a shop in town. It wasn't too bad, but nothing like I'd been used to. I didn't want to become a full-time prostitute, but I did want to earn proper money, decent money. I sat on the bed flicking through the local paper one evening and I came across an advert for a drama teacher at a private college. The money was crap, but the job came with a small cottage in the college grounds. That would give me a regular salary and somewhere to live and . . . well, work from home now and then to boost my income.'

'But you had no experience or qualifications.'

'No, but I did have knicker-flashing experience. I'd always got what I'd wanted by flashing my knickers. So I reckoned that I might be able to use my skills and get the job. It was a long shot, of course. It was a posh college and, for all I knew, the Dean might have been some old fart who went strictly by the book. But I decided to go for it. Lying my head off on the phone, I got an appointment for an interview. The college was on the outskirts of town. When I got there, I was ushered through a musty old corridor to the Dean's study.'

Moving On In Life

'Miss Declan to see you, sir,' the elderly man said as he ushered me into the Dean's study.

The Dean looked up from his desk and frowned. 'Not what I'd expected,' he murmured, staring hard at me. 'All right, Johnson, that will do.' The man left the room and closed the door. 'So, Miss Declan . . . sit down, sit down.'

'Thank you,' I said, sitting opposite him at the huge desk.

'You're rather young, aren't you?'

'There was no age specified in the advert,' I returned with as much confidence as I could muster. 'I hope I haven't wasted my time.'

'I'm a busy man, Miss Declan. It's my time I'm concerned about. I have six people to interview today. One of them will be working here full-time as from Monday of next week. You, Miss Declan, are the first. This is a boys' college, and I'm looking for a male drama teacher.'

'There was no gender specified in the advert,' I said. 'And the man I spoke to on the phone didn't seem to have a problem with my sex.'

'That was Johnson, he's a fool.'

'Then why give the job of arranging interviews to a fool?'

He placed his elbows on the desk, rested his chin on his clasped hands and frowned at me. 'Got all the answers, haven't you?' he said.

'No, it's just that, had I been given the job of arranging interviews, I'd have done it properly.'

'Would you, now? Do you think that you'd fit in at a boys' college?'

'I wouldn't be here if I didn't. I'll be honest with you, Dean.' Leaving my chair, I walked around the room and displayed my long legs. 'I don't have a great deal of experience, but I'm good at what I do. If it's a drama teacher you need, then look no further.'

'You're a confident young lady, I'll give you that. But you'll need more than confidence. I'm sorry, Miss Declan, but I am unable to offer you the job.'

'I'm not sure that I'd have taken it had you offered it to me.'

'Oh? Why's that?'

'I teach drama, Dean,' I said, perching my buttocks on the edge of his desk and parting my thighs a little. 'I'm looking for a rewarding and challenging position.'

'The position is rewarding and most challenging, I can assure you.'

'I'm also looking for excitement, Dean.'

'Excitement?' he echoed, eyeing my naked thighs. 'This is an independent college for boys, Miss Declan. You'll find no excitement here.'

'I'm talking about the excitement of writing plays and directing stage productions. The excitement of rehearsals and . . . You're quite right, Dean. There is no excitement to be found here. I'm just sorry that I've wasted my time.'

'I've always found you drama lot to be peculiar,' he said with a chuckle.

'And I've always found Deans to be peculiar,' I returned, parting my thighs further.

'Perhaps we're both peculiar in our own ways.' He gazed at the triangular patch of my knickers and grinned. 'I like you,' he said, raising his head and smiling at me.

'And I'm sure that I could get to like you, in time.'

'People don't get to like me, Miss Declan. They're frightened of me. The boys are terrified of me, and poor old Johnson quakes when I speak to him. Frightening people, especially the boys, is part of a Dean's job.' He paused and again focused on my knickers. 'Why don't I frighten you?' he asked me pensively.

'I have experience of older men, Dean. I know what older men think, I know what they want. And I don't find that frightening.'

'You're a pretty little thing, Miss Declan. I'm not sure that I could have you running around college in that short skirt.'

'Are you suggesting that I take it off, Dean?' I quipped with a giggle.

He placed his hand on my knee and winked at me. 'I'm going to take you on,' he said. 'Be here at eight-thirty sharp on Monday morning.'

'I haven't decided whether to accept the position yet, Dean. I'll need to know the salary and look over the living accommodation before making a decision.'

'You're supposed to be grateful,' he sighed. 'You drama lot certainly are peculiar. However, the starting salary is sixteen thousand rising to twenty-three after a period of –'

'If the accommodation suits me, I'll start on twenty-three,' I cut in. 'I'm worth more than that, but I'll accept twenty-three.'

'Will you, now? The rent on the cottage is –'

'According to the advert, according to Johnson, the cottage goes with the job.'

'You drive a hard bargain, Miss Declan. The cottage wouldn't normally be rented to a member of staff. It's just that it's empty and the damp will set in unless it's occupied. However, the salary and the rent on the cottage aren't down to me.'

'You have no influence, Dean?' I asked incredulously.

'Influence has nothing to do with it. The directors of the college . . .'

'I'm sure that you're given some leeway, Dean,' I said, parting my thighs even further. 'I mean, if we're to get to know each other, if we're to become friends . . .'

'It's not my policy to become friendly with the staff, Miss Declan. Although, in your case, I'm sure that we'll get on admirably. Do you think we'll get on admirably, if you see what I mean?'

'Definitely, Dean.'

'You're a cunning little minx, aren't you?'

'I do my best, Dean.'

'All right, twenty-three and the cottage thrown into the bargain. But you'll be on probation for three months.'

'I'm sure that I'll be able to win you over within three days, Dean.'

'I have a feeling that you may be right there. I'll get Johnson to show you the cottage. Oh, there is just one thing. Do try to come across as frightened of me when others are around.'

'I'll come across as terrified, Dean.'

'Good. Well, that's settled, then.'

As he pressed a button on the intercom and summoned Johnson to show me around the cottage, I slid off his desk and adjusted my skirt. I could hardly believe that I'd got the job as Johnson appeared and ushered me out of the study. What was it about me that had swayed the Dean? Was it the sight of my tight knickers hugging my full pussy lips? Or had my confidence impressed him? My knickers had been the influencing factor, I decided. No man could resist an opportunity to get inside my tight knickers.

The cottage was small but cosy. There was one bedroom and the furniture in the lounge had seen better days, but I knew that I'd be happy there. Johnson said nothing as he showed me round and finally passed me the keys, and I was sure that he didn't approve of me. He looked me up and down several times and frowned, but I wasn't bothered about him. I had the Dean on my side, that was all that mattered. And it wouldn't be long before I was entertaining a few of the little rich boys and boosting my income.

I couldn't wait to leave the rented room I'd come to hate, so I moved into the cottage straightaway. One advantage was that Barry had no idea where I was working or living, and I swore to keep it that way. My parents had no idea where I was, either. I'd have to tell them at some stage, but not yet. At last, I had a home and a place to work from – and I was free of Barry. This was the beginning of my new life, I mused as I settled in that evening. How I was going to teach drama, I had no idea. But I was determined to make a success of my teaching career. And my illicit business, I thought happily as the doorbell rang.

'Yes?' I breathed, finding a fresh-faced boy standing on the step.

'I'm Gibson,' he said, lowering his eyes to my partially open blouse, the cleavage of my firm breasts. 'I've come to put you right on a few things.'

'Put me right?' I echoed. 'What do you mean?'

'I suppose you're just out of teacher training college and this is your first job?'

'You suppose wrong, but go on.'

'The other boys and I ... we don't take any nonsense. You keep in with us, play your cards right, and you'll keep your job.'

'Is that a threat, Gibson?'

'It's just a little friendly advice.'

'Then let me give you some friendly advice.' I invited him in, closed the door and led him through the hall to the lounge. '*I* don't take any nonsense,' I stated firmly, making myself comfortable on the sofa. 'You've got things back to front, Gibson. It's not a case of my keeping my job unless I play my cards right. The reality of the situation is, you'll find yourself leaving the college unless *you* play *your* cards right. Do I make myself clear?'

He eyed my knickers as I parted my thighs. 'I ... What I mean is ... we could make things difficult for you,' he stammered.

'Why would you want to do that?'

'Well, because ...'

'Because you're a silly boy? I must warn you that I've had experience of power struggles. Who's going to be in control, who's going to call the shots ... I have more experience than you could ever imagine. Just bear in mind that I could make things extremely difficult for you, Gibson.'

'We don't like newcomers,' he muttered as I parted my thighs a little further. 'We have our ways, and we don't like change.'

'I have my ways, Gibson. And I can assure you that I don't plan to change anything.'

'Good, as long as you know where you stand.'

'I know exactly where I stand. Draw the curtain,

please. It's getting dark and we don't want people looking in, do we?'

Reclining on the sofa and pulling my skirt up just enough to ensure that he had a good view of my knickers, I knew that I was going to have to start off on the right foot. If I allowed Gibson and his friends to take control on day one, I'd never be able to exert any authority. Drawing the curtains, he turned and lowered his eyes to the tight crotch of my knickers. Flashing my knickers had always got me what I'd wanted. No doubt Gibson had his male thoughts, and I saw no reason why he shouldn't succumb to my sluttish charms.

'There's a bottle of wine in the fridge,' I said as he stared at my knickers. 'Pour me a glass, please.'

'I haven't come here to run around after you,' he returned.

'Pour me a glass of wine, and then we'll have a talk about your problems,' I instructed him.

As he went to the kitchen, I thought how good he looked in his blazer, white shirt and college tie. He looked smart, and he obviously thought he was smart. He must have been eighteen, and no doubt thought he was a man. But he was up against Annette the slut. I doubted that a mere boy stood the slightest chance of winning against the likes of me. I'd learned a lot since my first knicker-flashing episode. I was older, wiser, and had more experience than ever. Gibson returned and, as he placed a glass of wine on the coffee table, asked me if I knew who his father was.

'He's high up in government,' he enlightened me before I'd had a chance to say anything.

'Good for him,' I returned.

'He has influence, so you'd better . . .'

'I'm not interested in your family, Gibson. I don't

know your father, and I have no interest in what he does for a living.'

'All I'm saying is . . .' Unable to take his eyes off my knickers, he adjusted the crotch of his trousers. 'What I mean is –'

'Come and sit next to me, Gibson,' I interrupted, patting the sofa cushion. 'Let's talk this over, shall we?'

'I'd rather stand,' he returned.

'In that case, stand here, in front of me.'

'The other boys and I have had a chat,' he began, standing before me. 'We just want you to know that . . .' His words tailing off, he stared wide-eyed as I tugged his zip down.

'Carry on,' I said, smiling at him as I groped inside his trousers.

'We . . . I . . . What are you doing?'

'I have special ways to deal with naughty boys,' I breathed, hauling out his flaccid penis. 'I don't take any nonsense, Gibson. You look after me, and I'll look after you.'

Saying nothing as I released his belt and tugged his trousers down to his knees, he gazed in disbelief as I cupped his young balls in my palm and ran my free hand up and down the length of his stiffening cock. This had been the last thing he'd expected, I mused as he breathed heavily. And the last thing I'd expected was to be threatened by a pupil. But I knew that it wouldn't take teaching skills to tame the boys. I had no teaching experience, but I had sexual experience.

'You have a lovely cock, Gibson,' I murmured. 'Tell me, do you wank?'

'No, I . . .'

'All boys enjoy wanking, Gibson. Are you a virgin?'

'No, well, I . . .'

'As I said, I don't take any nonsense. If you and your friends make my time at the college pleasurable, I'll certainly make your time pleasurable. Do you understand?'

'Yes.'

'Yes, Miss Declan.'

'Yes, Miss Declan.'

'Good. So, why were you chosen to come here? Are you the leader of a gang?'

'Sort of, Miss Declan. It's called The Coffee Club.'

'I'm thinking about starting a club, Gibson. Would you like to be the first member?'

'Yes, Miss Declan.'

'It's called The After Hours Club. There's only one problem. Virgin boys will not be accepted.'

'But I'm not a virgin.'

'And neither will liars, Gibson. But I'm sure that we can change things to make you eligible to join. Take your clothes off, and we'll get to know each other a little better.'

Wasting no time, he slipped his trousers and shorts off. Almost ripping his shirt off, he stood before me with his youthful cock standing to attention. Tickling his rolling balls with my fingernails, I watched the solid shaft of his teenage cock twitch expectantly. He'd be able to shoot his spunk two or three times, I mused, running my fingertip up and down his veined shaft. Retracting his fleshy foreskin and exposing his glistening knob, I knew that he'd be able to manage several orgasms before leaving my cottage.

Leaning forward, I sucked his ripe plum into my wet mouth and ran my tongue over its silky-smooth surface. He gasped and shuddered as I took his swollen knob to the back of my throat and sank my teeth gently into his rock-hard shaft, and I knew that

I'd gained control of him. There'd be no more threats, I thought happily, savouring the salty taste of his teenage cock. Breathing in the scent of his black curls, moving my head back and holding his knob between my succulent lips, I wanked his shaft to the accompaniment of his gasps of pleasure.

His fresh spunk gushed from his throbbing knob and bathed my tongue. He swayed on his sagging legs and let out a moan of pleasure as I wanked his shaft faster. My mouth filling with his orgasmic cream, I thought it a shame that he couldn't have held back, as I'd have liked to enjoy his cock for a while longer. He was young and obviously had no control, but this was only his first spunking. Before I'd finished with him, he'd have pumped out at least three loads of sperm. Before I'd finished with him, he'd have lost his virginity and have discovered manhood.

Swallowing hard, I licked his knob and gobbled and sucked until he crumpled as if in agony and finally collapsed on the floor. What would he tell his friends? I pondered as he lay gasping and writhing at my feet. The big man, the leader of the gang, had been defeated by a mere girl. No doubt a second boy would be sent to put me right on a few things. But I'd soon bring the rest of the gang to their knees. Flashing my knickers, I'd soon control the naughty boys.

Ordering Gibson to kneel between my feet, I thought what a good-looking lad he was. He'd also have money, I mused, parting my thighs and pulling my short skirt up over my stomach as he took his position. As he gazed longingly at the tight crotch of my knickers, I wondered how many twists and turns my life would take. From college girl to college teacher, I thought happily. This was far better than university. Who needed qualifications?

'Press your face against my knickers and breathe in my scent,' I ordered Gibson. He was fairly muscular, his skin tanned, his cock again solid and ready for another spunking. He was also under my command. I'd have no trouble from the boys, I knew, as he sniffed the crotch of my knickers. 'Lick my knickers,' I said, leaning back and parting my thighs to the extreme. 'Lick them and suck them. Bite my pussy lips gently through the material. If you make me nice and wet, I'll allow you to pull my knickers down.'

Eagerly complying with my crude request, he nibbled the fleshy lips of my pussy through the wet cotton of my knickers. My clitoris swelling, my juices of desire flowing from my tightening vagina, I clutched tufts of his black hair and gasped and writhed on the sofa as my arousal soared. I was back in business. I had my own home, a well-paid job and a never-ending supply of little rich boys to attend to my female needs and boost my income. What more could I ask for?

I allowed Gibson to suck and lick my knickers for a while before ordering him to remove the garment. His eyes lighting up as he pulled the wet cotton away from my hairless crack, he tugged my knickers down and pulled them off my feet. Gazing wide-eyed at the swollen lips of my pussy, my opening sex crack, he leant forward and instinctively ran his tongue up and down my valley of desire. I watched him licking between my puffy lips, his mouth slurping, his tongue lapping up my cream. He must have been in desperate need to shoot his spunk, I mused in my wickedness. But I wasn't going to allow him to lose his virginity yet.

'Does it taste nice?' I asked him.

'Yes, Miss Declan,' he replied, his dark eyes catching mine as he looked up.

'Is your cock stiff, Gibson?'

'It's very stiff, Miss Declan.'

'Good boy. Now, I want you to pull my pussy lips wide apart and push your tongue deep into my wet cunt.'

Surprise was reflected in the dark pools of his eyes. He'd probably never heard such language from a girl before. And he'd certainly never had a girl ask him to push his tongue into her wet cunt. He stared appreciatively at my gaping sex crack, licking his lips as he scrutinised the most private part of my young body. He then complied eagerly with my demand, his tongue entering the hot sheath of my cunt and lapping up my flowing sex cream. He was the first member of my illicit club, I thought, as his nose rubbed against the sensitive tip of my erect clitoris. He was the first of many members, hopefully.

Again following my instructions, he pressed on the pink flesh surrounding my erect clitoris and eased out its full length. After gazing in awe at my swollen sex button, he leant forward, sucked it into his mouth and repeatedly swept his tongue over its sensitive tip. He was young and inexperienced, and I was used to older men, but he worked expertly on my clitoris. I was going to reach my orgasm quickly, I knew, as I felt my womb contract and my vaginal milk flow. The thought of a virgin college boy licking and sucking between my puffy outer lips sent my arousal through the roof. I was about to enjoy a much-needed massive orgasm.

'Finger my cunt,' I gasped, gripping the sofa cushion and arching my back. 'I'm coming, I'm coming . . . Force your hand up my cunt.'

'My hand?' he murmured.

'Just do it, Gibson. Fuck my cunt with your fist.'

He managed to push half his hand into the cream-drenched cavern of my vagina, stretching my muscles to capacity as he sucked and slurped my solid clitoris. My orgasm built and suddenly erupted within the pulsating head of my clitoris. I cried out as my young body shook violently. I could feel my vagina rhythmically contracting, gripping his hand as he flexed his fingers and massaged my inner flesh. My mind blown away as my orgasm heightened, I whimpered and writhed on the sofa as my young pupil expertly sustained my incredible pleasure. He was good, for a first-timer, and I hoped that his friends were as adept at satisfying my desires.

I'd teach the boys the fine art of attending to a girl's needs, I mused dreamily. I'd teach them how to pleasure me and bring me multiple orgasms. I had a nice home, money, and a never-ending supply of fresh teenage cocks. Had I found my niche in life at long last? I wondered, as the squelching sounds of crude sex resounded around the lounge. Far removed from Barry and my parents, no longer having to sneak off to the woods or the common, I was free to live my life the way I wanted.

My climax finally receding, I ordered Gibson to pull his hand out of the inflamed cavern of my abused vagina and suck out my orgasmic milk. He complied, locking his lips to the wet flesh surrounding my sex hole and drinking from my young body. I could hear him sucking, slurping, gulping down my milk. I'd feed all my pupils, I decided, squeezing my vaginal muscles and forcing out another deluge of sex cream. I'd have all my boys drinking from my cunt every day. This was the beginning of a new and exciting era.

'That's enough, Gibson,' I breathed. 'Is your cock stiff?'

'Yes, Miss Declan,' he replied, looking up at my flushed face and licking his pussy-wet lips.

'Good. Are you ready to fuck me and lose your virginity?'

'Yes, Miss Declan.'

'OK, ease your cock into my cunt. Take your time and slip it gently into my wet cunt.'

Holding his rock-hard penis by the root, he pushed his purple knob between the dripping wings of my inner lips. Leaning forward, I watched his virgin cock sink slowly into the hot sheath of my wet cunt. He would have pictured this during his teenage wanking sessions, I thought, as the sheer girth of his cock shaft stretched me wide open. He'd have imagined driving his cock deep into a girl's hot cunt and fucking her. Driving his penis fully home, his knob pressing against my cervix, he no longer had to imagine. He was no longer a virgin boy. This was the first of many young cocks to fuck me, I mused happily, as he withdrew his shaft and rammed into me. How many boys were at the college? There must have been six hundred or more. A never-ending supply of hard cocks and fresh sperm.

Unfortunately, he shot his spunk before I'd had a chance to enjoy the illicit shafting and reach my own orgasm. Repeatedly ramming into my tight vagina, he fucked me with a frenzied urgency and obviously had no concern for my sexual gratification. But he was young and discovering new things. I'd have to teach him how to fuck a girl properly, I reflected. Slowly, in and out, quickening to a gentle pace, orgasms building ... He had a lot to learn. But he had the best teacher.

His balls swinging, battering the naked cheeks of my firm buttocks, he held my hips and threw his head back as his sperm flooded my vaginal cavern. He'd found manhood, I mused, as he gasped and grunted with every thrust of his solid cock. His virginity gone for ever, he was the first member of my After Hours Club. He continued to fuck me until his cock deflated and finally slipped out of my spunk-brimming vagina. Sitting back on his heels, his face beaming triumphantly, he watched his male cream oozing from the gaping hole of my inflamed sex sheath.

'Good boy,' I said approvingly. 'That wasn't bad for your first time.'

'Thank you, Miss Declan,' he replied, his gaze transfixed on my sperm-oozing sex hole.

'How much money do you have with you?'

'Money? Er . . . well, I . . .'

'You'll need to pay the club fees, Gibson.'

He reached for his blazer and pulled out his wallet. 'How much, Miss Declan?' he asked me.

'Twenty pounds a week.'

'Twenty?'

'It's not a lot to pay for what you'll get in return, Gibson.'

'No, I suppose not,' he murmured, passing me the cash.

'How many boys are in your club?'

'There are fifteen of us, Miss Declan. Fifteen sort of committee members, and then about sixty ordinary members.'

'Sixty? How interesting. I want you to send the other fourteen boys to see me. One at a time, of course. Once I've dealt with the committee members, I'll move on to the ordinary members. Oh, and tell them to bring the fees with them.'

'Yes, Miss Declan. Shall I get dressed now?'

'Yes, Gibson. Get dressed and go back to the college.'

Shortly after Gibson had left, the doorbell rang. I'd washed my pussy and cleaned myself up in readiness for the next boy but, when I opened the door, I found the Dean hovering on the step. Hoping that he'd not seen Gibson leaving my cottage, I invited him in and led him through to the lounge. Sitting in the armchair, he looked me up and down, eyeing my long legs, my naked thighs, as I asked him whether he'd like a cup of coffee.

'No, thanks,' he said. 'I have a meeting to attend, so I can't stay. Johnson said that you were moving in so I thought I'd see how you were getting on.'

'I don't have many belongings,' I began, sitting on the sofa. 'I mean, I do but . . . I decided not to bring all of my things as the cottage is fairly small.'

'But it suits your needs?'

'Oh, yes, Dean. It suits my needs perfectly.'

'Good, good. A word of warning, Miss Declan. The cottage is out of bounds to the boys. As you're an attractive young lady, I'm sure that one or two of the boys will try –'

'Don't worry, Dean,' I cut in. 'I shall ensure that the rule is adhered to.'

'I'm pleased to hear it. You, er . . . you won't mind if I visit you now and then?'

'I'd be delighted, Dean. Do you live in with your wife?'

'I have living quarters in the college, yes. I'm not married, Miss Declan.'

'Oh, I see.'

'You know why I offered you the job, don't you?'

'Well, because I . . .'

'Not because of your qualifications. I'm in need of a little . . . How shall I put it?'

'Company, Dean?' I proffered, smiling at him as I parted my thighs.

'Yes, yes, company. The life of a Dean is a lonely life, Miss Declan. The college has to come first. I have no time for a wife. Having said that, there are things, needs, male needs . . .'

'I know exactly what you mean, Dean.'

'Do you?'

234

'Oh, yes. And I'm sure that we'll get on very well together.'

'I was wondering ...' His words tailing off, he stared at the triangular patch of my white knickers as I parted my thighs a little more. 'What I mean is ... I won't beat about the bush, Miss Declan.'

'Why don't you come and stand over here, Dean? Stand in front of me and I'll ... I'll get to know you a little better.'

Saying nothing, he left his chair and stood before me with expectation reflected in his dark eyes. This was what I'd been hoping for, I thought, as I tugged his zip down. Pleasing the Dean would get me through my probation period and secure my job. Hauling out his erect penis, I retracted his foreskin and rubbed my thumb over the glistening surface of his swollen knob. Another old man to pleasure, I reflected, reckoning that he was in his sixties. I wouldn't charge him, of course. He'd given me the job, and I was indebted to him for that.

I don't know why, but I'd imagined that he'd have a small cock. It was, in fact, the largest I'd ever seen. His knob was huge, like a purple balloon, and his shaft was thick and extremely hard. Wanking him, watching his foreskin rolling back and forth over his bulbous knob, I again thought of the incredible power of flashing my knickers. I'd landed myself the position of drama teacher at a private college for boys simply by parting my thighs and showing off the tight crotch of my knickers. And now I was securing my job by wanking the Dean.

'It's been a long time, Miss Declan,' he breathed shakily. 'I'm most grateful to you.'

'The pleasure is mine, Dean,' I replied. 'And I can assure you that you'll not have to wait again, now that I'm living here.'

The last thing I wanted was the Dean turning up when I was dealing with one of the boys. I'd made mistakes in the past and wanted to get things right this time. I was going to have to make plans, give the Dean times when he could call. I was used to planning and lying, and I was sure that I'd have no problems. My only real concern was that the other teachers might discover my illicit business. I doubted that the boys would go blabbing about their visits to my cottage, but they might be seen arriving or leaving. They'd have to use the back door, I decided, as I contemplated sucking the Dean's ballooning knob.

'You're an angel, Miss Declan,' the Dean gasped as his cock swelled.

'I don't know about that,' I returned with a giggle.

'I'm nearly there, Miss Declan. Keep going, I'm . . . I'm nearly there.'

'Would you like me to suck your cock, Dean?'

'Yes, yes. Suck it.'

Leaning forward, I engulfed his purple knob within my hot mouth and sucked gently. He gasped again, his body trembling as his knob throbbed against my tongue. He was big, I again thought, as I savoured the taste of his salt. His huge knob stuffing my mouth, my lips stretched tautly around the rim, I knew that this would be the first of many mouth fuckings. This was all so easy, I reflected, as his spunk jetted over my tongue and filled my cheeks. He clutched my head as his body crumpled and his spunk flowed, and I reckoned that he'd think me the best drama teacher he'd ever had.

'Swallow,' he breathed. 'Swallow it.'

I had no intention of wasting fresh cream, I thought, as I swallowed hard. This was the second helping of spunk I'd had, and I'd only just moved into the cottage. Wanking the Dean's hard shaft, drinking from his orgasming knob, I wondered how much spunk I'd be swallowing each week. I'd have the boys fill my mouth and my cunt with their teenage sperm. I'd have to introduce them to anal sex, of course. I wondered whether the Dean would like to sink his massive cock deep into my rectum and flood my bowels with his spunk. One thing was for sure. I was going to have more than enough sex, and earn some decent money. I was going to enjoy my time at the college.

'No more,' the Dean gasped, his dripping cock sliding out of my mouth as he staggered back. 'That was . . . that was wonderful.'

'I did my best, Dean,' I said, licking my sperm-glossed lips.

'You're perfect, Miss Declan. I can see that we're going to get on very well together.'

'Indeed we will, Dean. Indeed we will.'

He zipped his trousers and checked his watch. 'I'd better get to the meeting,' he sighed. 'Come to my study in the morning, Miss Declan. I have some papers for you to sign. Your contract of employment and some other bits and pieces.'

'I'll be there, Dean. By the way, how often will you be visiting me?'

'Oh, I should think two or three times each week.'

'When I see you tomorrow, we'll set times for your visits. Just to make sure that I'm here when you need me, you understand.'

'Of course. Right, well . . . until the morning, Miss Declan.'

I saw him out, then returned to the lounge and punched the air with my fist. I was over the moon, elated, and decided to pour myself a very large vodka to celebrate my new way of life. The taste of sperm lingering on my tongue, I slipped my hand down the front of my knickers and massaged the solid bulb of my clitoris. I needed sex, I mused dreamily. I needed a good fucking, I needed several massive orgasms. But with several hundred boys at my disposal, I had no need to masturbate. Knocking back my drink, I could hardly wait for the morning to come. More sex, more spunk . . . I'd found my niche in life, at long last.

'Only one chapter to go,' Annette said as we walked into a small pub just off The Lanes in Brighton.

'Are you still working at the college?' I asked her.

'You'll have to read the last chapter,' she replied. We ordered our drinks and sat at a table. 'I was only nineteen when I started at the college. I'm twenty-two now and . . . well, you'll have to read the last chapter.'

'How did you get on with teaching drama?'

'I knew nothing about drama and I had no interest in the subject. But with the help of the boys I muddled through. We even put on a college play, and it went down very well with the parents.'

'I have to ask you this,' I said. 'How many boys did you . . . I mean, did you count the number of boys you entertained at the cottage?'

'No, I didn't. But I must have had well over a hundred. The Dean came to see me three times each week, so he was happy, and there was always a queue of boys waiting to see me. Luckily, none of the other teachers were suspicious. In fact, I got on very well with them.'

'So how long did you last at the college?'

'I'd been there for a year and, as far as I was aware, things were fine. I'll never forget that Monday morning when I was summoned to the Dean's study.

I knew that something was wrong when I knocked on the door. And I was right. The directors of the college, governors or whatever, were waiting for me. In front of the row of chairs they were sitting on was a solitary chair. The Dean looked awkward as he invited me to sit down, and I reckoned that my short-lived career was over. The old farts frowned at me as I sat before them. There were eight or ten of them, and they must have had a collective age of seven hundred years. Luckily, I was wearing a knee-length skirt, so I didn't look too sluttish. They started firing questions at me and all I wanted to do was get out of that study. I saw no point in their asking me questions. It was obvious that they were going to sack me, so why not just get on with it? Then the announcement came . . .'

An Incredible Development

The row of old men stared hard at me as I sat before them. Although I'd done fairly well at the college in the year I'd been there, I couldn't blame them for sacking me. I had no qualifications, knew nothing about drama, I was only twenty years old ... I felt nervous as they began questioning me about my teaching. Did I enjoy it? What were my long-term plans? I answered as best I could, but I didn't hold out much hope for my future. I didn't know what to do to save myself from being sacked, but I thought it best not to flash my kickers.

'We bear bad news, Miss Declan,' one of them said, his grey moustache twitching. 'The Dean, Mr Russell, began his life at this college as a pupil. He has served the college well over the decades. However, we have recently learned that ...'

'I know what this is about,' I sighed. 'Look, there's no need to ...'

'You know?' he breathed, his beady eyes frowning at me.

'I've said nothing,' the Dean chipped in from his chair at the end of the row. 'I've not mentioned this to anyone.'

'How do you know, Miss Declan?' another ageing man asked me. 'Who told you that the Dean is resigning?'

'Resigning? Oh, I thought . . . I'm sorry, I thought you were talking about something else.'

'We're talking about the Dean resigning, Miss Declan,' the man with the twitching moustache echoed. 'His replacement will be announced later today. In the meantime, we need to ask you a few questions. You've only been at the college, for a year, and you've done very well. The Dean informs us that you're liked by the boys but, at the same time, you have authority over them. That's a fine quality, Miss Declan. You're punctual, your skills and management qualities have been exemplary, you've got on well with the parents . . . We're extremely pleased with the effort you've put in over the last year and the results you've achieved. However, there is one matter that concerns us.'

'And that is?' I dared to ask, fearing the worst.

'What are . . . I should say, what were your long-term plans?'

'Well, to stay on at the college.'

'You had no aspirations?'

'I . . . I had hoped to stay on as drama teacher. I don't know what else . . .'

'I'll come straight to the point, Miss Declan. Your age is against you.'

'Oh, right.'

'When Mr Russell took you on a year ago, we were against giving you the position. However, he talked us into giving you a chance. If fact, Mr Russell was extremely persuasive. We were against the idea because of your age and your gender. This is an all-boys college, and the notion of a female teacher went wholly against the grain. The notion of a nineteen-year-old female teacher was, to put it bluntly, ludicrous. However, we were proved to be wrong. You're intelligent, trustworthy, reliable, you have an air of authority . . . We've all witnessed your authority over the boys on various occasions. Even the most unruly boys are completely under your control. I have no idea how you do it, Miss Declan. It's quite amazing. I'd go as far as to say that you have greater authority over the boys than Mr Russell. Er . . . With all due respect to Mr Russell. As I said, Miss Declan, we were proved to be wrong. Now, after much deliberation, we've come to a decision. A decision which, I have to say, was extremely difficult to reach.'

'Tell me the worst,' I said, forcing a smile.

'Would you consider accepting the post of Dean?'

'What?' I gasped, holding my hand to my mouth. 'Dean? I mean . . .'

'Yes, Miss Declan.'

'I . . . I don't know what to say. I mean, I'm young and . . . What if I'm no good? No, I don't mean that. What I mean is . . .'

'If we thought for a moment that you'd be no good, as you put it, we wouldn't be offering you the position. With all due respect to Mr Russell, the college needs new blood, fresh and innovative ideas. You probably think us a bunch of old fuddy-duddies, and you're right. Times are changing, Miss Declan. And the college should change with the times. I think that's all we have to say at this stage so, please, give it some thought.'

'Yes, yes, I will. Thank you.'

'We'll meet here at two o'clock when you will, hopefully, inform us of your decision.'

As the Dean opened the door and ushered me out of the study, I felt my knees weaken. I couldn't believe it. Dean? I'd expected the sack, not promotion to Dean. I walked along the corridor in a dream-like state, left the Victorian building and headed for my cottage. In the kitchen, I eyed the bottle of vodka on

242

the table. I needed a drink to calm myself, but it was far too early. My hands were trembling as I made myself some coffee, and I felt my confidence drain. I imagined myself sitting behind the Dean's huge desk. I couldn't do it, I thought anxiously. Dean of a private college for boys? I'd fail miserably, I was sure.

Sitting on the sofa in the lounge, I sipped my coffee and reflected on my first knicker-flashing experience with Derek. What had started out as a silly game had moulded my life. I'd come a long way since that fateful day in my parents' lounge. Threatened by John, my neighbour, allowing the old men in the woods to do as they wished with my young body, sucking my teacher's cock and swallowing his spunk, and then moving in with Barry and allowing his father to fuck me . . . Annette the slut was to become Miss Declan the Dean. And I had my knickers to thank for that.

Finishing my coffee and getting up from the sofa as a knock sounded on the back door, I knew that I'd have to accept the position of Dean. My job at the college was secure, but I couldn't go on teaching drama for the rest of my days. Besides, I couldn't risk an outsider moving into the Dean's study and taking control. What would my salary be? I wondered. Would I keep the cottage, or have to move into the Dean's living quarters? Opening the back door to find Gibson and several other boys hovering on the step, I thought it best not to mention my news before the formal announcement had been made.

'Don't you have lessons?' I asked Gibson, checking my watch as he led his flock into the kitchen.

'We skipped lessons to come and congratulate you, Dean,' he said, grinning at me.

'How on earth . . .,' I began, following the boys into the lounge. 'Who told you?'

'We bugged the Dean's study,' he said. 'We like to know what's going on, so we bugged the study a year ago.'

'Good God,' I sighed. 'That's illegal.'

'No, it's not. Anyway, we have a present for you.' He passed me a thin bamboo cane and grinned. 'You'll need this for the first-year boys,' he said with a chuckle.

'Thank you, thank you all very much. I should use the cane on you for bugging the study, Gibson.'

'We thought we'd use it on you, Miss Declan. We thought we'd use it on you as a sort of initiation into your new job as Dean.'

I didn't put up a struggle as the boys unbuttoned my blouse and yanked my skirt down to my ankles. After my time in the Dean's study, I was in need of several damned good orgasms. I'd never been happier, and I decided to allow to the boys to do whatever they wished to my young body by way of a celebration. I wanted to celebrate my femininity, my new post as Dean, and my deviousness. Annette, the wanton slut. Annette, Little Miss Innocent. Annette, the Dean.

Having stripped me naked, the boys ordered me to stand behind the armchair. My clitoris swelling, my juices of desire flowing, I did as I was told and leant over the back of the chair until my head rested on the seat cushion. My feet wide apart, the hairless lips of my pussy were bulging between my naked thighs, my open crack inviting the boys to fuck me. My stomach churning, my womb contracting, I felt alive with sex. I'd reached the stage where I craved crude sex, longed to have my body used and abused for sexual gratification, and I hoped that the boys would commit the most degrading and depraved acts imaginable. There were eight of them, paid-up members of my club, and

I had no doubt that they wanted to get their money's worth.

I'd never been caned before, and I let out a yelp as the first swipe of the thin bamboo across my tensed buttocks jolted my naked body. Again the cane landed on the firm flesh of my naked buttocks. This was a new and exciting experience, but I didn't think that I could take it as the cane swished through the air and the stinging pain permeated the burning cheeks of my bottom. I tried to stand upright to halt the gruelling thrashing, but two boys pinned me down and the merciless initiation continued. My juices of arousal streaming down my inner thighs as my buttocks numbed, I discovered that the enforced thrashing was driving me into a sexual frenzy. Again and again, the cane lashed my tensed buttocks, the loud cracks resounding around the room as my vaginal milk spewed from my sex hole and splattered my inner thighs.

Fingers entered the contracting sheath of my cunt and hands massaged the firm mounds of my petite breasts. I knew that I was going to reach a massive orgasm as the gruelling thrashing continued. Hands ran over my naked body, massaging, caressing, groping between my parted thighs. I again realised that I could never have remained faithful to Barry. This was my life, I reflected as the cane repeatedly swished through the air and landed across the numb flesh of my naked buttocks. I could never remain faithful to any man, no matter what he offered me. I really had discovered my niche in life. I was Annette, the sluttish Dean.

The thrashing finally stopped and I felt a solid knob stabbing at the crack of my sex-dripping pussy. I'd enjoyed the cane, but what I really needed was a damned good fucking. The boy drove into me, his solid cock opening my vagina wide as he impaled me completely on his beautiful organ, and I gasped and writhed with pleasure. Two other boys were still holding my arms and pinning me down, more hands groped my breasts, fingers twisted and pulled on my erect nipples and another finger drove deep into the tight duct of my rectum . . . I felt dizzy with crude sex. Used and abused, I recalled the old men in the woods, their cocks pissing all over my naked body. Annette, the filthy dirty whore.

The finger slipped out of my anus, my buttocks were yanked wide apart, and I knew that I was in for an arse-fucking. I'd initiated the boys in the crude art of anal sex and they'd often flooded my hot bowels with their spunk. Now, after the thrashing of my young life, I was to have fresh spunk pumped deep into my bowels again. The cock slipped out of my hot vagina and drove into my rectum with such force that I thought I'd split open. Most of the boys had large cocks, but I knew that this massive specimen belonged to Harrison. He was by far the biggest, and there was no mistaking his magnificent organ as he began his anal fucking.

My young body jolting with the crude shafting, I wondered whether the boys were queuing up to pump my bowels full of spunk. Eight hard cocks taking turns to fuck my arse? I'd lost count of the times I'd enjoyed an arse-fucking, but I knew that I could take eight cocks in a row. My mouth, my vagina, my rectum . . . I'd been used to having every hole fucked and spunked time and time again. Eight cocks would be no problem at all.

Harrison came quickly, his knob swelling and pumping his spunk into my bowels as I quivered uncontrollably and gasped over the back of the armchair. I could feel his cream lubricating my anal canal as his solid cock repeatedly drove deep into the core of my young body. The sensations were heavenly, and I could hardly wait for the next stiff cock to fuck me there. The boy's spunk gushing, his balls pummelling my shaved pussy lips, he continued his illicit fucking to the accompaniment of chuckles from his audience. This was what I craved, I ruminated, as spunk trickled down my inner thighs. I was hooked on the obscene use and abuse of my young body.

His sperm-flow finally ceasing, he slowed his fucking rhythm and finally stilled his deflating member with his knob embedded deep within my creamed bowels. As soon as he'd withdrawn his cock, another boy had impaled me on his solid organ and the second anal fucking commenced. My feet yanked further apart, my vaginal lips gaping, I breathed heavily as fingers slipped into my drenched pussy and massaged my inner flesh. My tits kneaded, my nipples pulled and twisted, I opened my mouth wide as my head was pulled up by my blonde hair and a swollen knob hovered before my wide eyes.

Taking the boy's erect cock into my mouth and sucking on his ballooning knob as the anal shafting continued, I savoured the taste of his salt and breathed in the scent of his teenage pubes. He gasped, holding my head tight as he rocked his hips and fucked my mouth in time with the solid cock fucking my tight bum. Fingers were driving deeper into my vagina, and I quivered as my cavern stretched open to accommodate a fist. My mind swimming with images of crude sexual acts, my womb contracting, I knew that I'd soon be in the grip of another powerful orgasm.

The days of playing little Miss Innocent were gone, I mused, as my bowels flooded with a second deluge of spunk. Playing the innocent little girl in the park, inadvertently showing the tight crotch of my knickers, making out that I was a naive virgin ... they were early days of sexual discovery, days of learning. I had no need for such ploys now. The boys knew that I was a slut, and they treated me so. I was also earning good money, two hundred pounds each week from the members of my After Hours Club. And every year a fresh bunch of boys reached their eighteenth birthdays, and would no doubt join my club.

Apart from earning money and enjoying sexual gratification, I looked upon my role as preparing the young men for their journey out into world. Before they left the college and went on to university, they would have experienced just about every sexual act imaginable. There'd be no fumbling up girls' skirts, no blind groping between their thighs ... My boys would know exactly what to do, exactly how to please a girl. Not that all girls would be pleased to have their bottom-holes shafted and spunked. Girls should be taught the fine art of knicker-flashing, I reflected, as my clitoris swelled and my juices of arousal flowed over the fist embedded deep within my vagina.

My inflamed rectum again flooding with fresh spunk, I gobbled and sucked on the cock fucking my mouth as a deluge of creamy sperm bathed my tongue. Swallowing my prize, I felt dizzy in my arousal, drunk on crude sex. The squelching of my spunk-bubbling rectum filling the room as the boy shafted me in his sexual frenzy, I sucked out the last of the cream issuing from the knob crammed into my mouth. How much sperm had I swallowed since I'd started at the college? How much spunk had been pumped into the depths of my bowels?

Before the next boy in the queue rammed his solid cock deep into my inflamed anal canal, I was to endure another thrashing. The cane swished through the air, landing squarely across my burning buttocks. I almost choked as a fresh cock drove into my hot mouth. Sucking and gobbling on the ripe plum, desperate for another deluge of male cream to flood my mouth, I grimaced and squeezed my eyes shut as the cane repeatedly swiped my bum cheeks. Five, six, seven . . . Losing count of the lashes, I knew that I'd reached the bottom of the pit of depravity as a gush of hot urine flooded the fist embedded deep within my hot cunt.

The boys cheered and clapped as the golden liquid rained over the floor and one of them said that I was the best Dean ever. The thrashing halted and another solid knob glided along my anal tube to my cream-flooded bowels. I quivered as my clitoris exploded in orgasm. I was going to be the best Dean ever, I decided. This was an opportunity that I wanted to seize and, with the help of my boys, I aimed to do well in my new position. Annette, the Dean.

My inflamed anal duct brimming with sperm, I was relieved as the last boy drove his erect cock deep into my bum and began his shafting motions. Panting for breath as my tethered body rocked back and forth, I was pleased to think that I'd managed to take eight teenage cocks up my bum. A new record, I reflected, as the boy gasped and my rectum again flooded with male lubricant. Could I take ten or twelve consecutive anal fuckings? Annette, the anal slut.

The boys finally left the cottage and I lay on the sofa exhausted in the aftermath of my multiple anal shaftings. Sperm was oozing from the inflamed eye of my anus, trickling from the gaping entrance to my hot vagina, dribbling down my chin . . . The boys had well and truly fucked me senseless. My naked buttocks stinging like hell, I thought about using the cane on the boys. As Dean of the college, it was my duty to administer punishment to the naughty boys. I was going to enjoy my new job, and earn a small fortune. Running my fingers through the mess of my hair, I realised that I'd never been happier.

I'd moved into the Dean's study and was settling into my new job very well. I'd discovered that the role of Dean was more or less a status symbol for the college. There was no real work to do, apart from being there to talk to the parents and sorting out the odd dispute between the staff. The salary was amazing, and I had plenty of time to myself for my other activities. I'd stayed on in the cottage rather than move into the college because I had more privacy there. Things couldn't have been better, until the front door bell rang one morning.

I'd expected to find the retired Dean standing on the step. The boys used the backdoor, so I knew that they weren't calling for a session of crude sex. The Dean probably wanted hand relief, I mused happily as I opened the door. My heart racing, my stomach sinking, I stared hard at Derek. He was grinning triumphantly, his dark eyes looking my curvaceous young body up and down as if he was expecting to have sex with me.

'What are you doing here?' I asked him.

'Paying you a little visit, Annette,' he replied, walking past me into the hall.

'Derek, I . . .' I closed the front door and followed him into the lounge. 'Derek, how did you find me?'

'It's not too difficult to track down a prostitute,' he returned. 'Your parents have been worried about you.'

'I write to them regularly. They don't know where I work, but they do know that I'm all right. What do you want?'

'A blowjob would be nice.'

'I don't do that any more. And, for your information, I'm not a prostitute.'

'Once a slut, always a slut. You've done well for yourself, Annette. Dean of a private college for boys? You've done very well. Now, I have a proposition for you.'

'I'm not interested, Derek. Whatever it is, I'm not interested.'

'I want us to get back together again. I could call round here to see you two or three times each week and –'

'I said, I'm not interested,' I interrupted angrily. 'I've moved on, and I don't want . . .'

'I know Mr Russell, the retired Dean. Our firm has done some work for the college – that's how I discovered that you were here. Russell happened to mention that he'd retired. When he said that a girl had taken his place, a Miss Declan . . . You've done very well, Annette. I wouldn't want to have to spoil things for you.'

'You like resorting to blackmail, don't you? Well, it won't work this time.'

'Oh, but it will. Do you think that the board of governors will be happy to think that they have a prostitute as Dean of their college? Now, why don't you strip naked for me? We'll have some sexy fun, Annette. It'll be just like the old days.'

I didn't know what to do as he stared at me. The Dean would back me up if Derek started blabbing about my past, but the old men on the board wouldn't want a possible scandal on their hands. Derek was a bastard, I mused as he grinned at me. My knicker-flashing, my experience . . . Nothing would get me out of this, I was sure. If I did as he asked and stripped naked, I'd forever be in his clutches. If I told him to leave . . .

'Come on, Annette,' he sighed impatiently. 'Let's have some fun.'

'What sort of work has your firm done for the college?' I asked him.

'Architectural planning, things like that. There's more work coming up, a nice contract. Your dad won't be involved, this one will be to my credit. I'm hoping to become a director of the company and ... Let's not talk about that. Take your clothes off, Annette.'

'All right,' I conceded. 'You win, Derek.'

'I thought you'd see sense,' he said, beaming.

'Just let me go over to the college and cancel a meeting, and then I'll do anything you want.'

'I'll be ready and waiting.'

Leaving the cottage, I headed for the college. This was a long shot, I mused as I reached my study. I sat down at my desk and summoned Johnson on the intercom, sure that he'd be able to help me. We'd got on quite well since he'd accepted that I was the Dean. In fact, I think he rather liked me. When he arrived I asked him about the contract for the work to be done on the college. He said that the contract didn't involve us as the governors dealt with that sort of thing, but he did fill me in on some details. I gave him his instructions and finally returned to the cottage to find Derek sitting in the armchair with his trousers bulging and his face grinning.

'I've waited long enough,' he breathed. 'I want you to strip naked, Annette.'

'I had to cancel the meeting,' I sighed, unbuttoning my blouse. 'Aren't you going to take your clothes off?'

'Of course,' he replied, leaping up from the armchair and removing his jacket.

Once we were both naked, I suggested that Derek lean over the back of the armchair. He was too excited to ask me what I was up to as I went into the kitchen and grabbed a reel of nylon string. When I returned I saw that his naked buttocks were perfectly positioned. As I talked about sucking his cock and fingering his bum, I ran the string round and round the chair and trussed him up like a chicken.

'You're nice and hard,' I said, reaching between his thighs and wanking his cock.

'I'm always hard when I'm with you, Annette. This will be just like old times, won't it?'

'Yes, Derek, just like old times.'

Grabbing my bamboo cane, I swiped his naked buttocks as hard as I could. He cried out, protesting and struggling to free himself as I brought the cane down for the second time. I was enjoying this, I thought excitedly, repeatedly swiping his reddening buttocks with the thin bamboo. He threatened me, swore to have me sacked and said that I'd be disgraced and I'd never find work again. Giving him a dozen or so lashes, I halted the gruelling punishment as his mobile phone rang.

'You'd better answer it,' I said, taking the phone from his jacket pocket and holding it to his ear. 'It might be important.'

'Mr Burrows?' he breathed shakily. 'Yes, yes, I'm ... We might lose the contract? I don't understand. No, I haven't been to the college. Well, I did call in to ... the Dean? I've been sexually harassing the Dean? No, no, I ... yes, Mr Burrows. I'll be with you in five minutes.'

'Everything all right?' I asked, switching the phone off.

'What the hell have you done?' he growled. 'That was my boss and he said –'

'I've had to cancel the contract,' I cut in. 'Sorry about that, Derek.'

'You can't cancel ... Burrows said that I'd been sexually harassing the Dean and ...'

'That's true, isn't it? Now, where were we? Ah, yes, the cane.'

'Annette, let me go. I have to get back to the office and sort this out.'

'All in good time, Derek. All in good time.'

'Burrows has threatened me with the sack, for God's sake. If I don't get back within five minutes ...'

'You'll be looking for a new job?'

Bringing the cane down across his burning buttocks, I let out a wicked giggle. I had power, I mused happily, as he cried out and begged for forgiveness. I had power over all men. It was ironic to think that I'd inadvertently flashed my knickers to Derek in my parents' lounge on that fateful day. I had him to thank for my success. And now I was punishing him. Repeatedly caning his red-raw buttocks, I decided to phone the company and suggest that someone else deal with the contract. Burrows might suggest that my dad sort the contract out. Now that would be poetic justice.

Finally dropping the cane, I knelt behind Derek and pulled his cock out from between his thighs. Retracting his foreskin and sucking his knob, I decided to see how many times he could fill my mouth with spunk. He complained as I tongued his sperm slit and kneaded his heavy balls. He had to get back to the office, he had to put things right with Burrows ... He then offered me money if I let him go. I didn't need money, and I was in no hurry. After all, I had the rest of the day to amuse myself.

Although Derek was anxious about his job, far from relaxed, he managed to pump my mouth full of spunk. I gobbled and repeatedly swallowed his jetting cream as he gasped and writhed and pulled against his bonds. He had a beautiful cock, I mused, as I sucked out the last of his sperm. It was a shame that he wasn't a nicer person. We might have got on well, had he not resorted to blackmail. But that was his way, and he wasn't going to change.

Unfortunately, he couldn't manage another orgasm. Going on about his boss, he begged me to free him. But I couldn't. This was part of his punishment for crossing my path, for trying to get me sacked. I had to teach him a lesson, a lesson that he wouldn't forget. He'd once said that he'd fucked my mother, and that had really got to me. My mother was a refined lady, and there was no way she'd go with another man. This was Derek's punishment, and there was no way I was going to allow him his freedom for several hours.

I spent the afternoon in my study going through papers and doing Dean-type things. There were several phone calls, but one was most interesting. It was from Mr Burrows. He apologised profusely for Derek's behaviour and assured me that he'd put another man on the job. When I suggested that Mr Declan might be suitable, he asked me whether he was a relation of mine. I enlightened him and he immediately praised my father, saying that he was a top man and he'd be replacing Derek. How ironic, I thought. Derek gets the sack and my dad gets his job, and it was all my doing. Derek had said three years previously that my dad would get promotion if I stripped naked and allowed him to have sex with me. If it hadn't been for Derek, I'd probably have been working in a boring office environment and my dad would still be trying to get promotion. Thanks, Derek.

The End?

* * *

Annette was over the moon to think that her book had been completed. Over a celebratory meal in a small restaurant, I asked her whether she was still Dean of the college.

'Three years,' she said. 'I've been Dean for three wonderful years, and I've loved every minute of it.'

'So, where to from here?' I asked her. 'Will you stay on at the college? What are your plans?'

'I haven't spent any of the money I've earned since starting at the college. I eat with the staff in the dining room, I have no bills . . . I've saved more than enough money to buy a flat, but I'm happy in my little cottage. My plans? I don't really know. I suppose I'll stay on at the college until . . . until I'm rumbled and sacked? I don't think that will happen. The After Hours Club is a tight ship. The boys don't go blabbing because, obviously, they want things to carry on as they are. But, apart from the club, I've done wonders for the college. Exam results are up, discipline is excellent . . . I've not only fitted into the role of Dean, but I'm bloody good at it. Even the old fuddy-duddies are pleased.'

'Do you think they know what you get up to?'

'No, I don't. Well, maybe they've had their suspicions. Anyway, why should they worry? I'm doing a good job, and that's all they're bothered about.'

'You've come a long way in the four years since you inadvertently exposed your knickers to Derek in the lounge. On reflection, would you change anything?'

'No, I don't think so. I made a few mistakes but . . . I look at it this way. My dad is due to become a director of the company, and I'm Dean of a private college for boys. And it was all my doing. Pretty good, huh?'

nexus

The leading publisher of fetish and adult fiction

TELL US WHAT YOU THINK!

Readers' ideas and opinions matter to us so please take a few
minutes to fill in the questionnaire below.

1. Sex: Are you male ☐ female ☐ a couple ☐?

2. Age: Under 21 ☐ 21–30 ☐ 31–40 ☐ 41–50 ☐ 51–60 ☐ over 60 ☐

3. Where do you buy your Nexus books from?

☐ A chain book shop. If so, which one(s)?

_____

☐ An independent book shop. If so, which one(s)?

_____

☐ A used book shop/charity shop
☐ Online book store. If so, which one(s)?

_____

4. How did you find out about Nexus books?

☐ Browsing in a book shop
☐ A review in a magazine
☐ Online
☐ Recommendation
☐ Other _____

5. In terms of settings, which do you prefer? (Tick as many as you like.)

☐ Down to earth and as realistic as possible
☐ Historical settings. If so, which period do you prefer?

_____

☐ Fantasy settings – barbarian worlds
☐ Completely escapist/surreal fantasy
☐ Institutional or secret academy

☐ Futuristic/sci fi
☐ Escapist but still believable
☐ Any settings you dislike?

_____

☐ Where would you like to see an adult novel set?

_____

6. In terms of storylines, would you prefer:

☐ Simple stories that concentrate on adult interests?
☐ More plot and character-driven stories with less explicit adult activity?
☐ We value your ideas, so give us your opinion of this book:

_____

_____

_____

7. In terms of your adult interests, what do you like to read about? (Tick as many as you like.)

☐ Traditional corporal punishment (CP)
☐ Modern corporal punishment
☐ Spanking
☐ Restraint/bondage
☐ Rope bondage
☐ Latex/rubber
☐ Leather
☐ Female domination and male submission
☐ Female domination and female submission
☐ Male domination and female submission
☐ Willing captivity
☐ Uniforms
☐ Lingerie/underwear/hosiery/footwear (boots and high heels)
☐ Sex rituals
☐ Vanilla sex
☐ Swinging
☐ Cross-dressing/TV
☐ Enforced feminisation

☐ Others – tell us what you don't see enough of in adult fiction:

_____
_____
_____

8. Would you prefer books with a more specialised approach to your interests, i.e. a novel specifically about uniforms? If so, which subject(s) would you like to read a Nexus novel about?

_____
_____
_____

9. Would you like to read true stories in Nexus books? For instance, the true story of a submissive woman, or a male slave? Tell us which true revelations you would most like to read about:

_____
_____
_____

10. What do you like best about Nexus books?

_____
_____

11. What do you like least about Nexus books?

_____
_____

12. Which are your favourite titles?

_____
_____

13. Who are your favourite authors?

_____
_____

14. Which covers do you prefer? Those featuring:
(Tick as many as you like.)

- ☐ Fetish outfits
- ☐ More nudity
- ☐ Two models
- ☐ Unusual models or settings
- ☐ Classic erotic photography
- ☐ More contemporary images and poses
- ☐ A blank/non-erotic cover
- ☐ What would your ideal cover look like?

_____

15. Describe your ideal Nexus novel in the space provided:

_____

_____

_____

_____

16. Which celebrity would feature in one of your Nexus-style fantasies? We'll post the best suggestions on our website – anonymously!

_____

THANKS FOR YOUR TIME

Now simply write the title of this book in the space below and cut out the questionnaire pages. Post to: Nexus, Marketing Dept., Thames Wharf Studios, Rainville Rd, London W6 9HA

Book title: _____

NEXUS NEW BOOKS

To be published in August 2007

SWEET AS SIN
Felix Baron

Trixie, a widow, was petite, curvaceous, wealthy and sexually adventurous. Rolf, a widower, was tall, good-looking, even wealthier than Trixie and had been celibate for far too long. His son and Trixie's daughter made a handsome couple. Both relationships seemed to have been made in heaven, except that Rolf lusted after the daughter as much as he did the mother. Penny, he discovered, only looked pure. Beneath her innocent exterior, she was ten times as kinky as her mother. Penny was sweet, all right – *as sweet as sin*.

£6.99   ISBN 978 0 352 34134 1

A TALENT FOR SURRENDER
Madeline Bastinado

Jo Lennox is a woman with a secret. By day she is headmistress of an exclusive private school: by night, a sexual adventurer who loves to dominate and humiliate men. Dan Elliot is a documentary film-maker who uses his looks and charm to persuade his subjects to expose their secrets. When their paths cross, Dan realises how much he has to learn about his own nature and his hidden desires. He becomes her willing pupil, eager to obey and hungry for experience. And Jo assumes the role of his teacher and guide, providing punishment, pleasure and the perverse by initiating him into a world of darkness and extreme submission.

£6.99   ISBN 978 0 352 34135 8

If you would like more information about Nexus titles, please visit our website at www.nexus-books.com, or send a large stamped addressed envelope to:
  Nexus, Thames Wharf Studios,
  Rainville Road, London W6 9HA

NEXUS BOOKLIST

Information is correct at time of printing. To avoid disappointment, check availability before ordering. Go to www.nexus-books.com.

All books are priced at £6.99 unless another price is given.

NEXUS

☐ ABANDONED ALICE	Adriana Arden	ISBN 978 0 352 33969 0
☐ ALICE IN CHAINS	Adriana Arden	ISBN 978 0 352 33908 9
☐ AQUA DOMINATION	William Doughty	ISBN 978 0 352 34020 7
☐ THE ART OF CORRECTION	Tara Black	ISBN 978 0 352 33895 2
☐ THE ART OF SURRENDER	Madeline Bastinado	ISBN 978 0 352 34013 9
☐ BEASTLY BEHAVIOUR	Aishling Morgan	ISBN 978 0 352 34095 5
☐ BEHIND THE CURTAIN	Primula Bond	ISBN 978 0 352 34111 2
☐ BELINDA BARES UP	Yolanda Celbridge	ISBN 978 0 352 33926 3
☐ BENCH-MARKS	Tara Black	ISBN 978 0 352 33797 9
☐ BIDDING TO SIN	Rosita Varón	ISBN 978 0 352 34063 4
☐ BINDING PROMISES	G.C. Scott	ISBN 978 0 352 34014 6
☐ THE BOOK OF PUNISHMENT	Cat Scarlett	ISBN 978 0 352 33975 1
☐ BRUSH STROKES	Penny Birch	ISBN 978 0 352 34072 6
☐ CALLED TO THE WILD	Angel Blake	ISBN 978 0 352 34067 2
☐ CAPTIVES OF CHEYNER CLOSE	Adriana Arden	ISBN 978 0 352 34028 3
☐ CARNAL POSSESSION	Yvonne Strickland	ISBN 978 0 352 34062 7
☐ CITY MAID	Amelia Evangeline	ISBN 978 0 352 34096 2
☐ COLLEGE GIRLS	Cat Scarlett	ISBN 978 0 352 33942 3
☐ COMPANY OF SLAVES	Christina Shelly	ISBN 978 0 352 33887 7

NEXUS CLASSIC

------ ✂ ---------------------------

Please send me the books I have ticked above.

Name ....

Address ....

....

....

.... Post code ....

Send to: **Virgin Books Cash Sales, Thames Wharf Studios, Rainville Road, London W6 9HA**

US customers: for prices and details of how to order books for delivery by mail, call 888-330-8477.

Please enclose a cheque or postal order, made payable to **Nexus Books Ltd**, to the value of the books you have ordered plus postage and packing costs as follows:
    UK and BFPO – £1.00 for the first book, 50p for each subsequent book.
    Overseas (including Republic of Ireland) – £2.00 for the first book, £1.00 for each subsequent book.

If you would prefer to pay by VISA, ACCESS/MASTERCARD, AMEX, DINERS CLUB or SWITCH, please write your card number and expiry date here:

....

Please allow up to 28 days for delivery.

Signature ....

Our privacy policy

We will not disclose information you supply us to any other parties. We will not disclose any information which identifies you personally to any person without your express consent.

From time to time we may send out information about Nexus books and special offers. Please tick here if you do *not* wish to receive Nexus information. ☐

------ ✂ ---------------------------